THE BUTCHER OF TANGIER

GORDON WALLIS

This book is dedicated to the memory of two friends,
Richard Eatwell & Richard 'Dick' Collins.

Table of Contents

Chapter One: North Coast Of Morocco. 34 km West of Tangier. Present Day. 1

Chapter Two: London, Present Day. 19

Chapter Three: Recovery 23

Chapter Four: Marrakesh. 27

Chapter Five: Options. 36

Chapter Six: Professor Tremblay. 41

Chapter Seven: Samuel. 44

Chapter Eight: The Dig Site. 48

Chapter Nine: Samuel. 56

Chapter Ten: The Caves. 59

Chapter Eleven: Samuel. 74

Chapter Twelve: Green. 77

Chapter Thirteen: Samuel. 83

Chapter Fourteen: Green. 85

Chapter Fifteen: The Road To Freedom. 89

Chapter Sixteen: The Storage Facility. 94

Chapter Seventeen: Pierre Lumumba. 109

Chapter Eighteen: Darko Zukman. 111

Chapter Nineteen: Pierre Lumumba. 116

Chapter Twenty: Anomaly. 118

Chapter Twenty One: Pierre Lumumba. 122

Chapter Twenty Two: Feeler Gauge. 124

Chapter Twenty Three: Pierre Lumumba. 126

Chapter Twenty Four: Plans. 129

Chapter Twenty Five: Pierre Lumumba. 132

Chapter Twenty-Six: Green. 135

Chapter Twenty Seven: Preoperative. 143

Chapter Twenty-Eight: Revisit. 146

Chapter Twenty Nine: Midazolam. 154

Chapter Thirty: Preparation. 155

Chapter Thirty-One: Panic. 158

Chapter Thirty-Two: Aerials. 161

Chapter Thirty-Three: Samuel. 166

Chapter Thirty-Four: Discovery. 168

Chapter Thirty-Five: Awakenings. 173

Chapter Thirty-Six: Dinner Date. 175

Chapter Thirty-Seven: Samuel. 180

Chapter Thirty-Eight: Unlawful Entry. 182

Chapter Thirty-Nine: Awakenings, Part 2. 187

Chapter Forty: Secrets Underground. 190

Chapter Forty-One: Pierre Lumumba. 197

Chapter Forty-Two: Rat in a Drain Pipe. 200

Chapter Forty-Three: Pierre Lumumba. 204

Chapter Forty-Four: Surrender. 207

Chapter Forty Five: Pierre Lumumba. 210

Chapter Forty-Six: Interrogation. 213

Chapter Forty-Seven: Pierre Lumumba. 219

Chapter Forty-Eight: Incarceration. 222

Chapter Forty-Nine: Pierre Lumumba. 226
Chapter Fifty: Green. 230
Chapter Fifty-One: Darko Zukman. 234
Chapter Fifty-Two: Green. 237
Chapter Fifty-Three: Pierre Lumumba. 239
Chapter Fifty-Four: Breakout, Part One. 241
Chapter Fifty-Five: Pierre Lumumba. 253
Chapter Fifty-Six: Breakout, Part Two. 255
Chapter Fifty-Seven: Pierre. 263
Chapter Fifty-Eight: Plans. 265
Chapter Fifty-Nine: Tangier. 273
Chapter Sixty: Complications. 279
Chapter Sixty-One: Mercy Mission. 283
Chapter Sixty-Two: Fisherman's Blues. 290
Chapter Sixty-Three: Amsterdam, One Week Later. 296
Chapter Sixty Four: Darko Zukman. 303
Chapter Sixty-Five: London. Two Months Later. 314
Dear Reader. 317

Chapter One: North Coast Of Morocco. 34 km West of Tangier. Present Day.

Thirty-five year-old Samuel Kisimba was bone-weary. It had been almost 7 hours since he had lifted his six-year-old daughter, Lucia, into the back of the steel sided panel van in the dusty industrial area on the outskirts of the ancient city of Marrakesh. A former refrigerated vehicle, the 7-tonne lorry had spent much of its working life transporting loads of frozen meat to every corner of the sparsely populated North African country of Morocco. It had been 3 years previous when the cooling system of the heavy vehicle had finally packed up, and the wealthy owner had converted it to carry a very different kind of cargo. The stacked shelving from the sides and the meat hooks that had hung from the insulated ceiling had been removed, and a series of tiny air holes drilled along the base and upper levels of the load bay. But this pitiful ventilation had been woeful during the seemingly never-ending journey North through the desert to the port city of Tangier. The single electric bulb that hung in the interior of the load bay had flickered on and off due to a loose wire and the majority of the journey had been spent in total darkness. By the time they had reached the city of Rabat, the heat on the inside had reached alarming levels and when the light illuminated due to a bump in the road, it revealed the fear on the faces of the 18 other hopeful souls that were crammed into the small, cramped space.

Thankfully the heat had begun to subside by the time the truck had passed the city of Casablanca and the cool evening air began to filter through. Seated on the hard steel floor next to Samuel and his young daughter was a fellow Congolese national by the name of Elizabeth Nkulu. A nurse by trade, she had fled her home town in the Kasai region in the centre of the central African country. Her reason for leaving was the same as Samuel's. The conflict and deadly fighting between the military and various other splintered ethnic militias had become unbearable. It had resulted in the violent murder of Samuel's wife, the mother of Lucia. Like many others, Samuel Kisimba, a teacher by profession, had fled the Congo and had spent the past year travelling North through Africa by any means possible.

The treacherous journey had seen him and his young daughter walking, sometimes for months on end, through The Central African Republic and Chad before finally securing onward passage through Libya on trains and desert buses.

Young Lucia had been terrified at first when they had climbed into the truck with the others. The darkness had scared her since their arrest off the coast of Sabratha in Libya 3 months beforehand. Their journey across the Mediterranean ocean to Italy had been cut short by the Libyan police and coastguard and they had been transported to a detention centre in the capital, Tripoli, where they had been detained for 6 weeks. Samuel had lost a good amount of his life savings to the people smugglers who had offered him safe passage and had it not been for young Lucia, he might have found himself being sold in one of Tripoli's notorious modern slave markets.

Thankfully they had managed to escape and had made the equally dangerous journey West through Algeria and finally into Morocco. It had been there that Samuel and Lucia had met the Congolese nurse, Elizabeth Nkulu. A strong but kindly woman, her reasons for wanting to make a new life in Europe were the same as

Samuel's. Their home country was in complete turmoil and they knew full well that neither had any future there. As qualified professionals, they had both managed to build up some modest savings although these had been rapidly depleted during their respective journeys. It had been Elizabeth who had told Samuel of the route to Southern Spain from Tangier. Many others had made the crossing successfully using the same method, and as far as she had heard there had never been any problems. All that was needed was to make it to the city of Marrakesh to book and pay for the passage. From there it would be only a matter of days before the phone call to meet the vehicle to make the journey North to Tangier to the boat. The short, 30 km sea journey would take place in the dead of night where they would be dropped on a deserted beach and finally, they would be in Europe. Samuel looked down at the sleeping figure of his daughter, Lucia, who lay with her head on his lap. Elizabeth Nkulu, who was seated next to him, smiled and passed him the water bottle she had been keeping in her bag nearby.

"Thank God it's cooling down now." she said in her native Luba-Kasai dialect.

"Yes..." said Samuel as he took the bottle and drank from it "At one stage I was worried we would all suffocate"

"It will not be long now and we will be on our way across the sea..." said Elizabeth over the drone of the engine.

"Yes..." said Samuel "God willing, tonight we shall finally be free."

Samuel and Elizabeth sat in silence for the next 5 minutes as the truck drove on through the night. Occasionally the overhead light would flicker and illuminate the frightened faces of the others.

"Are you afraid of the ocean, Samuel?" asked Elizabeth.

"No..." he replied, "But I worry for my daughter."

"Of course..." said Elizabeth looking down at the sleeping child "That is natural, but for me, all alone, there will only be one of two possible outcomes."

"What are those possible outcomes?" asked Samuel.

"Death..." came the reply "Either death or a new life."

Samuel Kisimba blinked silently in the humid darkness as his fears grew. Although he had tried to shield his daughter from the horrors of the final months in their home country and the subsequent journey, he knew that this had all had a profound effect on her. He leant his head back on the steel wall of the vehicle, closed his eyes, and whispered a silent prayer.

It was four hours later that the truck finally turned off the remote tarred coastal road and began its descent down the rocky escarpment towards the abandoned stretch of coastline below.

The exhausted occupants of the truck were jolted awake and thrown from side to side in the darkness as the vehicle lurched over the rocky surface of the mountain track. Eventually, the terrain evened out and the engine revved as the truck crossed the thick sand on its way to the drop off point.

Suddenly the engine stopped and all was silent. It was five minutes later when the voices came. There were at least three men, all talking in Arabic, near the side of the vehicle. Samuel Kisimba recognized two of the voices as being that of the driver and his assistant, Uday. The driver was laughing and Samuel recalled the same man's belly wobbling as he had joked while loading the occupants of the truck that morning at the warehouse back in Marrakesh. It was 2 minutes later when the large steel doors of the truck were unlocked and swung open noisily.

Instantly there was a rush of fresh, salty, sea air and the occupants gasped as they breathed it in. The 3 men who had been talking outside were standing at the rear of the truck. All of them held powerful flashlights which they shone into the load bay of the vehicle, temporarily blinding the occupants.

"Daddy, where are we?" asked young Lucia sleepily.

"Hush, child.." whispered Samuel "I think we have arrived."

"Everybody out!" shouted Uday in English "We are now at the pick-up point!"

Slowly and silently the occupants of the truck got to their feet and began climbing out onto the sand. Samuel Kisimba's bones ached from being seated for so many hours but he stood up, took Lucia by the hand, and followed Elizabeth to the rear of the vehicle.

"Hurry up!" shouted Uday impatiently as he shone his flashlight into Samuel's eyes.

It was only then that Samuel saw the Belgian Fabrique Nationale automatic rifle in the man's right hand. Although he held it at his side in a non-threatening manner, the very fact that it was there served as a grim reminder that the journey they were about to attempt was perilous and potentially deadly.

Samuel jumped from the back of the vehicle onto the fine sand below. He quickly turned and lifted Lucia down before retrieving the large canvas bag that held his meagre worldly possessions.

"Follow the others..." shouted Uday "Quickly!"

The night was cool and dark and the stars were blocked by a thick layer of swirling mist that rolled in from the sea. Although Samuel could hear the waves crashing into the shoreline nearby, he could not see them due to the heavy rolling fog that surrounded them. Samuel lifted his bag in his right hand and pulled young Lucia towards him with his left. Twenty metres ahead of where the vehicle had parked, a temporary lamp post had been erected in the sand.

A small petrol generator powered a single all-weather bulb that cast a pale yellow glow over the small group of hopeful migrants now seated on the damp sand beneath. Lucia clung to her father's jacket nervously as they made their way across to join their friend Elizabeth who was seated on the sand with the others. The wide eyes of the eighteen hopeful souls were testimony to every one of their respective journeys. Journeys that had collectively come to this point and time on a barren and deserted stretch of beach on the North Coast of Morocco.

The group sat in silence for the next five minutes as the three men laughed and joked near the truck behind them. Eventually, the portly driver and his tall wiry assistant arrived and stood in front of the group. The driver had pulled a large canvas bag across the sand from which he began to remove flimsy-looking life jackets. He tossed one to each of the migrants who silently strapped them to their shoulders and around their waists. Samuel assisted Lucia with hers and immediately noticed the life jackets were thin, tatty, and of poor quality. In his mind, he wondered if they would actually keep the young girl afloat let alone a fully grown adult. It was when all 20 migrants had donned their life jackets that the tall wiry man with the gun, Uday, stepped forward to speak. In the yellow glow of the overhead lamp, Samuel could see the man had a hard face. His cheeks were hollow, his lips thin and set in a permanent and cruel smirk. The man's eyes were deep-set, dark and close to each other giving him the look of a weasel.

He wore faded camouflage longs with a khaki short-sleeved shirt that revealed powerful, sun-bronzed arms, and he held the heavy automatic weapon in his right hand as if it was a toy. The loose curls of his jet black hair blew in the sea breeze as he stared fiercely at the group of people seated in front of him.

"Tonight you will all be crossing into Spain!" he shouted in English with a strong Arabic accent. "Although the journey is short, it can be extremely dangerous. For your safety, I would implore you to do exactly as I say. Am I understood?"

The expectant crowd grunted and nodded in understanding.

"What did he say, Daddy?" whispered Lucia.

"Hush, child..." said Samuel. "This is the man who will take us across the sea. We must do as he says..."

Uday continued.

"The boat will be arriving within an hour," he said. "All of you must remain sitting here and be ready to follow me when I call you. Understood?"

Once again the crowd nodded and mumbled in agreement. The man spoke a few words in Arabic to the driver then both broke into a burst of spontaneous laughter as Uday pulled a half-smoked cigar from his top pocket. He lit it with a disposable lighter and walked off into the mist with the cigar clamped between his teeth and machine gun in hand. Samuel Kisimba watched the man as he disappeared into the darkness. Something deep inside him warned him he was not to be trusted. Had it been his cruel grin or perhaps his dark, close-set eyes? He could not put his finger on it but deep in his consciousness, alarm bells were ringing. Everyone seated on that dark, barren piece of coastline had paid a cash fee of USD $2000.00 to be there.

This was the crossing fee for the journey into Spain. Samuel Kisimba did the maths in his mind. The small group of migrants had paid the organizers a total of US $40000.00 on that night alone.

It was clearly an extremely profitable business. At that moment, the face of Uday came back into his mind; there was something about his smile or perhaps it was in his eyes. Samuel shook his head to rid himself of the negative thoughts and looked down at his side where Lucia sat wide-eyed and awake. Her face was full of excitement but there was also a measure of fear. He glanced at his friend, Elizabeth, who was sitting on the sand next to him.

They had been through a great deal of pain and hardship to get to this point in their lives. *Think positive.* He told himself. *We are here now, and this will soon be over. Finally, we will be free.*

It was exactly 45 minutes later that they all heard the powerful outboard motors of the approaching boat crashing through the waves. Suddenly there was frantic shouting in Arabic from the men who had been waiting near the truck behind them. Soon after, Uday emerged from the thick mist at the shore. The stub of the cigar was still clamped between his teeth and he held the machine gun at his side.

"Everybody up. Now!" he bellowed at the seated group.

They all complied immediately, with a tangible air of excitement.

"You will follow me down to the waiting boat and wait in line as I board you one by one" he shouted "Is that clear?"

Suddenly the group of waiting passengers were bathed in the beam of a powerful spotlight from behind. The driver of the truck had produced it from the cab and was walking towards them.

"Right!" shouted Uday "Follow me, please!"

The group made their way through the mist towards the shoreline 40 metres ahead. Soon they saw the long, modern, semi-rigid boat that was to take them across the ocean to Spain. Its driver stood at the steering console having driven the deep 'V' hull up onto the sand.

The constant waves rushed and hissed around the inflatable sides of the fibreglass gunwales. Samuel Kisimba breathed a sigh of relief as he eyed the craft. He had heard many of the horror stories of migrants drowning at sea due to the shoddy and condemned vessels used by the people smugglers. *No.* He thought. *This is a good and modern craft. It looks like it would carry thirty people easily. On this boat, we will be safe. Thank God.* With his confidence buoyed, Samuel hugged Lucia closer to his side and spoke.

"See, my girl..." he said "This is a good and safe boat. Soon we will be in Spain with our friend Elizabeth and we will start our new life."

Still clinging to his jacket, Lucia looked up at him with wide eyes and nodded with a nervous smile.

"All will be well, Daddy," she said. "Like you always say..."

At that moment a powerful gust of wind began blowing in across the sea from the North. It blew the thick mist in driving gusts, obscuring the boat and lifting the beach sand so that it stung the exposed flesh of the group as they waited. Samuel Kisimba expected the freak gusts to pass quickly but they kept blowing. This seemed to agitate the driver of the boat who began shouting in Arabic at the truck driver and his assistants standing on the shore. Gesticulating wildly with his arms, the boat driver pointed at the group of migrants as they stood waiting to board the vessel. It was clear to Samuel that they were arguing about the rapidly deteriorating weather. The heated conversation continued for another minute until it was decided that the crossing would go ahead as planned. By then the waves had picked up and were rushing in, soaking the feet of the waiting passengers. Uday turned to the crowd from where he had been standing at the bow of the boat and shouted at the passengers over the now howling gale.

"Attention!" he called out with a grin. "We will now board the boat in single file. Step forward in an orderly fashion and I will help you aboard..."

Blinking the sand from his eyes, Samuel Kisimba watched as the first of the passengers stepped forward to be boarded. By the time the first of them reached the side of the long boat, the waves were frothing and foaming around their knees. With the machine gun still held in his left hand, Uday lifted and pushed the passengers aboard over the inflatable gunwale at the side of the boat. The intensity of the wind increased as Samuel, Lucia, and Elizabeth approached. Now there was a constant howling in their ears and great droplets of salty seawater blew into their faces as they approached the waterline. Hugging Lucia closer to his side, Samuel lifted his gaze to look at the boat driver.

He stood in position at the rigid steering console near the front centre of the boat and pulled the hood of his jacket around his face in an effort to stay dry. But it was the look on the face of the boat driver that alarmed Samuel. He had seen it a thousand times before in recent years. There was no mistaking this common human emotion. The man was afraid. Clearly, the intensity of the approaching storm had rattled him and the heated conversation had been about whether or not to attempt the journey.

But it had been Uday who had won the argument and he continued to shove the passengers aboard with the stub of the cigar clamped between his teeth and a sly grin on his face.

Samuel pulled the hood of Lucia's blue anorak over her head and tightened it with the drawstrings. *At least now she won't be frightened by the sound of the wind.* With his left hand, he gently shielded her face from the blowing sand as they stepped into the water and approached the boat. Elizabeth was first to board. Uday tossed her bag into the boat and easily lifted her heavy frame onto the gunwale before roughly shoving her aboard. It was clear to Samuel that the man was surprisingly strong. The sun-bronzed skin of his arms rippled with muscle as he did so. The howling wind and driving spray seemed to have little effect on the man as he worked with the permanent cruel grin fixed on his face. Samuel lifted his daughter to keep her legs dry as they approached the boat. Uday quickly grabbed her around the waist and shoved her over the gunwale into the arms of Elizabeth who was blinking from the salt spray. Lucia cried out in fear as he did so.

"She is just a child..." said Samuel firmly as he tossed his canvas bag to Elizabeth. "There is no need to be rough."

"Shut up you fucking baboon!" shouted Uday "Get on the boat now!"

Samuel Kisimba was a big man. Certainly as tall as the man who had just insulted him. Both stared each other in the eyes for a brief moment until Samuel dropped his gaze in surrender and climbed onto the gunwale. *Now is not the time for arguments. He told himself. Lucia is already afraid.* The wind continued to build in intensity as the three men pushed the long boat out into the waves. Samuel pulled Lucia closer to where he sat and shielded her eyes from the stinging spray. He glanced at Elizabeth who sat on his left. Her face was wet with seawater and she sat with her eyes closed, repeatedly kissing the St. Christopher pendant that hung from her neck.

The atmosphere on the boat had changed from hopeful expectation to one of fear as the waves grew in size and rocked the boat violently. The driver began shouting at the men on the shore in Arabic, obviously urging them to reconsider their choice. This protestation was met with fierce opposition by Uday, who deftly leapt over the gunwale and took his position near the driver at the wheel. He turned briefly to cast his eyes over the seated passengers and Samuel Kisimba once again saw the cruel smirk illuminated by the glow of the powerful spotlight. He shouted once again at the driver who quickly turned the key on the fibreglass steering console. The powerful motors at the rear of the boat roared into life as the driver engaged reverse gear. All around was a confusing cacophony of howling wind and the revving of the engines as they fought the powerful waves that crashed and frothed over the transom at the rear of the boat. Within a minute the driver changed to forward gear and the boat lurched forward and turned sharply to the left as the propellers dug into the water. At that moment a huge wave crashed over the side of the vessel soaking the occupants and almost capsizing it. Thankfully the driver had pushed the throttle to full and the boat quickly turned and sped offshore into the darkness, pounding the waves violently as it went. Over the din of the motors and the howling of the wind, Samuel could hear a number of the passengers had started wailing in fear.

He pulled the huddled body of Lucia closer to him and covered her ears with his arm through her anorak. A minute later the boat finally hit a stretch of smooth water and the driver was finally able to open the throttle further and gain some speed. The motion of the boat settled into a repetitive and bone-jarring rhythm as it sped through the darkness. 15 minutes into the journey the pitch of the engines slowed and the stinging spray calmed somewhat. It was clear to Samuel that they had slowed for a reason and this was confirmed when the engines were brought to idle and Uday turned and shone a torch on the passengers.

Seemingly satisfied that all were accounted for, he pulled a mobile phone from his pocket and made a call. The conversation was brief and he placed the phone back in his pocket. Samuel Kisimba stared at the man from where he sat and wondered what the call could have been about. As far as anyone knew, the boat was to drop them on a remote piece of Spanish coastline and the job would be done. *Why then are we stopping halfway?* He wondered with growing concern. The question was soon answered when out of the darkness came the sound of another boat motor and a pinprick of light on the horizon to the North.

The driver reached down into the steering console and lifted a spotlight which he turned on and flashed in the direction of the approaching vessel. Both the driver and Uday stood there at the steering console gripping the chrome handrail to steady themselves from the lurching motion of the ocean swells. Within minutes the approaching boat arrived and Samuel saw it was identical to theirs and there were three armed men aboard. The vessel pulled up alongside and the men quickly tied a series of ropes along the gunwale to the next boat, effectively creating a single floating platform. Samuel cast his eyes around the faces of his fellow passengers and saw that their fear had now turned to confusion. *Why is this happening?* He thought. *None of us was told we would be meeting another boat.* Suddenly the seated figure of Elizabeth Nkulu turned and Samuel watched as she vomited with projectile force over the gunwale. Clearly, the swells and the violent motion of the boat during the journey had given her a serious bout of seasickness.

"What is wrong with Elizabeth, Daddy?" said Lucia in a small, frightened voice.

"It is just the boat moving, Lucia" he replied calmly. "She has seasickness. She will be fine..."

At that moment Uday stepped towards the passengers and addressed them.

"We are now at the halfway point!" he shouted over the howling wind. "All of you who wish to continue will now pay the sum of $1000.00 United States dollars each and you will then board the other boat. From here it is only 10 minutes to your destination in Spain. Those of you who do not pay will return with us to Tangier."

Silence fell over the passengers as they stared up at Uday in disbelief. He stood there still clutching the machine gun as he looked down on them with a smirk. At that moment a group of four young Senegalese men at the rear of the boat began shouting in protestation.

"This is bullshit!" shouted the larger of them "We paid you in full back in Marrakesh!"

The man's outburst fuelled the confidence of the others in the boat and most began jeering and shouting insults at Uday who stood there smiling calmly as he rode the swells. The atmosphere on the boat had changed from one of fear to pure outrage.

Samuel Kisimba glanced at Elizabeth who was already rummaging in her bag frantically for money. A cold sliding feeling filled his stomach and he felt the bile rising in his throat. He knew full well that there was only $1790.00 left in the money belt under his shirt. It was all that remained of his life's savings. His mind raced as he glanced from the tall figure of Uday with the machine gun to the seated crowd on his right. Their fury was growing by the second and their shouting and jeering becoming more and more defiant. One of the women near the rear of the vessel began wailing in anguish as the scene degenerated into confusion and chaos. At that moment Elizabeth Nkulu stood up and lifted her bag. She turned briefly and looked down to speak to Samuel and Lucia.

"God bless you, my dear friends!" she shouted over the wind "I must go now. I pray to see you both on the next boat!"

Samuel Kisimba saw the alarm and fear in her eyes as she began making her way towards the driver. She handed him a bunch of $100.00 notes which he counted quickly then stuffed in his pocket. Elizabeth Nkulu swung her bag over the gunwale and into the next boat. As she did so she slipped and fell face down onto the inflatable sides of both vessels. Uday laughed audibly and pushed her sprawling into the waiting boat with a boot to her backside. This only served to further infuriate the crowd of migrants who began to jeer and protest even louder. At that moment, one of the Senegalese men who had started the protest stood up at the rear of the boat. His confidence buoyed by the crowd, he challenged Uday directly.

"You bastards!" he screamed in English."We will not allow this!"

The crowd cheered his courage as he began to step forward. Uday's eyes narrowed as he watched the rapidly deteriorating situation at the rear of the boat. Emboldened by the cheering of the passengers, the Senegalese man began running up the length of the boat towards the steering console. Another cold chill ran down Samuel Kisimba's spine as he watched Uday casually raise his weapon with a single hand.

The three shots rang out in rapid succession and the bullets tattooed a diagonal line of black circles across the man's chest. His body was catapulted backwards in a series of violent jerks until he tumbled over the transom into the sea. There was a brief moment of quiet as the crowd took in the events. This was quickly followed by a cacophony of terrified screaming and wailing from the seated passengers. Samuel Kisimba watched as Uday spat out the butt of the cigar and stepped forward into the crowd.

"Anyone else?!" he shouted with a maniacal look in his eyes. "Is there anyone else who would like to argue with me?!"

As he looked over the seated passengers, the cruel grin returned to his face. He jerked his head to one side to flick the wet curly hair from his eyes.

"No...?" he said over the wind "I didn't think so. Now, I would ask you to step forward one by one with your money and then you will board the other boat..."

As instructed, the passengers stepped forward to pay the driver under the watch of Uday. Those who were unable sat with their heads hung low, some of them weeping uncontrollably. Samuel Kisimba's mind was racing. Lucia's body was shaking and she was crying softly in terror. *I don't have enough money for both of us! He thought. Perhaps they will allow me to pay half the amount for the child? I will wait until the rest have boarded and then I will ask the driver. Yes. That's what I'll do...*

"Darling Lucia," he said quietly "Don't cry. All will be well, I promise..."

Samuel's daughter looked up at him and he could see that her jaw was trembling and her face was streaked with tears. At that moment a rogue wave hit the gunwale behind them. No one could have seen it coming in the darkness and mist and it crashed into the boat, soaking everyone. Uday and the driver stood unmoved, gripping the chrome bar at the steering console. Samuel blinked the saltwater from his eyes and wiped Lucia's face with his right hand. Letting her shaking body go, he pulled his remaining cash from his money belt and began counting it.

The wind and the swells picked up as he did so, pitching and tossing the two vessels around violently. This sudden change had the effect of angering Uday and the driver. Both men began screaming at the remaining passengers to hurry forward with their money. Within minutes the majority had paid and crossed into the next vessel leaving only 4 dejected passengers who had been unable to pay sitting at the rear of the boat. Samuel stood up with his money in his right hand. Lucia quickly followed suit, clinging to his waist as her body shivered. As they stepped towards the steering console Uday recognized him from before and spoke.

"Ah..." he shouted "It is you, the baboon. Hurry up!"

"I have only $1790.00..." said Samuel, holding the cash out in front of him "Please allow us to cross. Please, have mercy. I have my child with me."

"$1000.00 each, Mr Baboon!" shouted Uday with a grin "Or you come back with us!"

Samuel Kisimba stared into the eyes of the man. In the pit of his stomach, he felt his hatred rise along with the bile. The man was tormenting him and enjoying it at the same time. At that moment, the voice of Elizabeth Nkulu called from the next boat.

"Samuel!" she cried "Send Lucia over! I will look after her until you can cross! It is the only way! Hurry!"

Another huge swell rose out of the darkness, threatening to overturn the two vessels. The driver shouted in Arabic to Uday in a panicked voice. Uday had clearly heard Elizabeth's offer. He lifted the rifle and pointed it at Samuel's chest.

"You have 10 seconds to make your choice, Mr Baboon!" he shouted "What will it be?!"

Samuel took his eyes from Uday and glanced across at the next boat. Elizabeth Nkulu knelt near the gunwale with her arms outstretched and her pleading face glistening with saltwater.

"Please, Samuel!" she screamed "I swear I will look after her! We will wait for you!"

Samuel Kisimba leant forward and handed the pile of notes to the driver. He did so without taking his eyes from the face of the sneering Uday. The driver quickly counted $1000.00 and handed the remaining notes back to him. Lucia, now realizing what was about to happen, began screaming and clinging with surprising strength to Samuel's midriff.

"No Daddy!" she wailed "I will stay with you! Please! All will be well, just like you always say! Please, Daddy!"

Samuel prised her arms gently from his waist and knelt on the wildly rocking floor of the boat. Lucia's face was a mask of pure terror.

"You are right, child..." he shouted over the wind. "All will be well, but you must go with Elizabeth now. I will be there with you soon. That is my promise to you, my child."

At that moment the driver stepped forward and ripped Lucia away from Samuel. As he did so she began screaming uncontrollably in terror. The driver shoved her over the gunwale and into the waiting arms of Elizabeth. Instantly the men on the next boat untied the three ropes that had bound the two vessels together.

From his kneeling position, Samuel Kisimba watched the tormented face of his daughter as the two vessels drifted apart. Her arms outstretched towards him, her frantic pleas were now being drowned out by the wind as the mist and darkness filled the space between the boats. Suddenly he was filled with an uncontrollable rage. A seething, animal fury that boiled over his normal senses and turned his vision red.

From his crouched position he leapt towards the sneering figure of Uday with the full intention of ripping the man to pieces. But Uday had anticipated this reaction and responded immediately. The bullet tore into Samuel's left shoulder just below the collar bone and the force of it knocked him back onto the floor of the boat. He lay there, winded, confused, and blinking as he heard the boat motor start. Through the mist, he saw the thin, cruel face of Uday coming down to speak to him.

"Good night, Mr Baboon..." he said with a grin as he brought the butt of the rifle down onto Samuel's forehead with savage force.

Then there was only darkness.

Chapter Two: London, Present Day.

"What the hell do I know about archaeology, Diane?" I said into the phone.

"Wow..." she replied. "Did you get out of the wrong side of the bed this morning, Jason? We don't need an expert on archaeology. It's a simple supply chain issue with an archaeological dig. Quite an important one at that..."

"Sorry..." I replied. "And you said the job is where?"

"Morocco" she replied. "I can send you the brief and the case file by email now. But the brass want your decision by lunchtime."

I glanced at my watch to see it had just gone 9.10 am. I had only drunk one cup of coffee and this was more than likely the reason for my irritable state.

"Sure..." I said reaching for a cigarette. "Please go ahead and send the email. Sorry for snapping at you..."

The sultry voice of my supervisor on the other end of the line chuckled then spoke again.

"No problem, Jason," she said. "But please, call me as soon as you've decided..."

The email came through immediately as promised. Still wearing nothing but a towel wrapped around my waist I printed it as I boiled the kettle and made a second brew. With the morning news muted on the television, I sat down to read the thin pile of papers I had collected from the printer. It made for interesting reading and I lit another cigarette as I began.

Ten months previously a significant discovery had been made in the High Atlas Mountains some 60 km south of the city of Marrakesh in the North African country of Morocco.

A local Berber herdsman had stumbled across what at the time had appeared to be an ancient burial site. The young man had seen some beads glittering amongst the rocks on a steep mountainside slope and had stopped to investigate further.

Scratching away at the rocky ground he uncovered a number of silver plates and scattered pieces of jewellery buried in the caked earth. Being young, and somewhat naïve, the herdsman reported his discovery at a nearby police post. Word soon got out to the landowners and the area had been quickly sealed off and the local ministry of antiquities informed. News of the discovery had spread fast through the global archaeological community and a team was soon despatched there by both the ministry and the landowners.

What was initially thought to be the simple burial site of a wealthy trader was soon excavated further to reveal something much more important. The discovery of hundreds of silver and gold ingots along with ceramic casks of gemstones proved this. Further ultrasound geophysical surveys of the mountainside showed that beyond the initial excavations there appeared to be an extensive network of man-made tunnels dug into the mountainside. If these tunnels were filled with anything like the treasures already recovered, the discovery would certainly be the richest and most significant in the history of Morocco.

But with global attention now focussed on it and the slow and methodical processes that must follow every archaeological dig, the excavations had been frustratingly slow. Each and every find, no matter how insignificant, needed to be meticulously recovered, cleaned, logged and recorded. Strict protocols had to be followed in every aspect of the dig, which was now anticipated to take more than three years to complete. Television crews from various global networks were permanently camped at the privately-owned site and the treasures being unearthed daily there had come to be known globally as part of The Zukman Hoard. So-called, because the land where the discovery had been made belonged to a Serbian conglomerate by the name of Zukman International. The company were mainly involved in the frozen meat industry and owned vast tracts of livestock grazing land with offices throughout North Africa.

Due to the sheer size and historical importance of the discovery, both the Moroccan ministry of antiquities and Zukman International had agreed to hire the services of a large commercial archaeological company. The UK based Oakland Archaeology Ltd had arrived soon after with a team of 40 qualified staff to begin the excavations. The scale of the hoard was unprecedented, with the value of the recovered gold and silver alone already running into tens of millions. This figure did not take into account the hundreds of priceless artefacts that were being dug out almost daily.

The reason I had been called by my principals at the insurance company was the fact that several items had gone missing during the process. Namely a large case of gold ingots and a trunk of priceless Berber chargers and ancient Jambiya daggers.

The job, if I took it, would be to inspect the security at the dig site, the subsequent transport procedures, and the security arrangements at the storage facility in Marrakesh. The leaks that had occurred had caused significant embarrassment to all involved and the claims had been substantial. This would explain the urgency indicated by my case supervisor, Diane, during her call. I placed the papers on the desk and took my cup of coffee to the large bay window that looked down on the Seven Sisters area in the borough of Tottenham, North London. It was late March and Spring was taking its time to appear. The winter had been long and bitterly cold and I had been cooped up for far too long. *Well, it's a different sort of job from the usual, Green. Could be interesting too. Why not?* I lit a cigarette and dialled the direct line to Diane at the insurance company.

"Hi, Diane..." I said when she answered. "It's Jason. I've just read the brief. I'll do it..."

The job was on.

Chapter Three: Recovery

Samuel Kisimba grunted as he shifted his tall frame on the concrete slab that jutted out of the wall in the 3 by 3-metre cell that had been his home for the past 21 days. He stared up at the tiny window in the wall above him. Through the thick steel bars, he saw the moon had risen and there were wispy clouds slowly blowing past it. With running water only flowing once a day, it was the only source of fresh air in the stifling heat of the cell and the stench of the single concrete latrine and sink nearby. The smell had been overpowering at first but by then he had become used to it. Directly beneath where he lay was a second slab that served as a bed for another unfortunate migrant detainee from Cameroon. A cheerful young man by the name of Pierre Lumumba, he too had been unable to meet the extra fee levied by the people smugglers during the crossing to Spain and had been forced to return to Marrakesh.

Despite the appalling conditions, Pierre Lumumba had remained upbeat and would often recite rap music lyrics and tell jokes. Sometimes he would even show off his dance moves and prance around the cell. These rare moments of humour were a tonic for Samuel and he had grown to like the young man. After the incident on the boat, Samuel had only regained consciousness while being attended to by a medic somewhere between Tangier and Marrakesh. The bullet had been removed from his shoulder and the wound treated with antibiotic ointment and dressings while he was shackled to the steel floor of the same truck he and Lucia had travelled in.

Upon arrival back in Marrakesh, he and the others who had been unable to pay had been taken to an unknown location and transferred under armed guard to the facility he had been in for the past three weeks. Samuel Kisimba suspected, however, that the location of the place he had found himself in was within the same industrial complex where he and Lucia had originally boarded the truck to Tangier. It had been a giant meat processing plant in an industrial area north of the city. At the time he recalled he had heard the constant sound of band saws in the distance and there had been a lot of flies and the distinct smell of an abattoir in the air. *Yes.* He thought. *It must be the same place. The sounds and the smells are identical.* Although his wound was healing well, Samuel Kisimba had been plunged into darkness and deep despair since the forced separation from his daughter.

Upon arrival at the facility back in Marrakesh, all of the remaining migrant's belongings, including phones, money, and passports had been seized for 'safe keeping. Those who had been unable to pay had effectively become prisoners. Worse still, they had become prisoners with no idea of their release date. Constant questions to the guards who patrolled the facility and delivered food went unanswered. It was as if their captors were trying to break them mentally. At least it felt that way to Samuel. A quiet sense of failure, loss, and hopelessness had descended on Samuel Kisimba like a thick fog and he had been unable to pull himself out of it.

The memory of his daughter Lucia had been his only light in the darkness of the weeks of isolation and had it not been for the distant hope of one day reuniting with her, he felt he might have simply given up and died. *All will be well, Daddy.* She had said. *All will be well.* Night after night he had been tormented by the same terrible dream. The vision of Lucia, her arms outstretched towards him as the two boats had drifted apart in the mist and darkness on that dreadful stormy night. Her terrified screams begging him to allow her to remain with him. He would awaken and shed silent tears of fear and worry for her. *Had she and Elizabeth made it safely to Spain? If so, where were they now? Would they wait as Elizabeth had promised? Would he ever see his beloved daughter again?*

There had been a doctor who had visited twice a week. A short, elderly Moroccan man who spoke English and had a kindly nature. He had treated Samuel's wound and administered pills that had helped with the pain and the healing process. The visits by the doctor were always done under armed guard and the fact they happened at all was somewhat puzzling to both Samuel and Pierre. The fact that he smelt of alcohol and had a slight facial twitch was not a concern. The man had treated him well and prevented his wound from becoming infected. And for that he was grateful. At first, he had felt a burning hatred for the man who had tormented and shot him. The man he knew only as Uday. He had seen Uday on many occasions since. The dark corridor outside the cell was constantly patrolled by armed guards and Uday was one of them. Thankfully the animosity that had prevailed that fateful night seemed to have passed. Uday seldom even glanced into the cell and when he did it was almost as if the man did not even recognize him.

Samuel was sure that there were several other cells down the same corridor. Just how many he could not tell, but he felt certain that they were occupied.

The food they were given was acceptable with meals consisting of boiled eggs with bread and mint tea in the mornings and either mutton or chicken stew with couscous in the evenings. This strange limbo in which he had found himself was puzzling to Samuel. *Holding migrants who had been unable to pay, would surely cost money?* This was not even taking into consideration the cost of having a doctor treating them as well. *Surely it would have made sense for the people smugglers to simply allow those left behind to* go free and to make arrangements to find the money to cross into Spain? What was the purpose of holding them all like this? To what end? It made no sense at all. Samuel Kisimba sighed and shook his head in dismay as he stared at the moon through the steel bars of the tiny window above him. *All will be well*. He thought. *All will be well*.

Chapter Four: Marrakesh.

The British Airways flight banked steeply to the left as it came down to land at Marrakesh Menara International Airport. I rubbed my eyes as I adjusted the business class seat to the upright position and looked out of the window. Below me, the parched and treeless landscape was the colour of milky coffee and it stretched away to the horizon under a perfectly blue sky. Although there were patches of green cultivated land dotted here and there, most of the countryside was an arid, barren desert. The early morning sunlight stung my eyes, and I blinked as I drank from the bottle of water I had stored in the side compartment of the seat. I had caught the 6.00 am flight from London Stansted Airport having left my flat in a taxi at 3.15 am that morning. I had fallen asleep within minutes of the flight taking off and had only woken 3 hours later when I had heard the pilot announcing our imminent arrival on the overhead speakers. The patches of green irrigated land became more frequent as the jet descended towards the city and I saw the scattered clumps of human settlements in amongst the olive and palm groves. As we approached the airport I saw a vast spread of low lying cream coloured buildings with terracotta roofs to my left. Tightly packed, orderly, and seemingly clean, it appeared the ancient city of Marrakesh was growing and encroaching on the airport.

The landing was smooth and the aircraft quickly slowed and turned right heading towards the squat but modern looking airport terminal. Eventually, the plane came to a stop and I watched as the moving walkway slowly inched towards the door behind me. I yawned and stretched as I stood to collect my hand luggage from the overhead compartment and headed for the door. The interior of the airport was clean, bright, and spacious and I followed the signs to the baggage reclaim as I walked the marble floors eventually descending an escalator to the reclaim area below. A bureau de change booth marked 'DMC Bank of Africa' reminded me where I was and it felt somewhat strange to find myself on the continent of my birth after such a short journey. I soon found the correct carousel and stood there wishing I could smoke as I waited for my two bags. Not knowing how long I was to be in Morocco, I had packed enough clothing and equipment for a lengthy stay. The benefits of flying business class proved true as several bags marked 'Priority' emerged from the rubber flaps in the wall.

I soon collected my own two bags, placed them on a trolley and headed towards the customs and immigration section at the far side of the building. After filling in a form I stood in the orderly queue near the immigration booths.

"Business or pleasure, Mr Green?" asked the young Moroccan official as I handed him the form along with my passport.

"Holiday..." I lied.

The young man yawned and stamped my passport after scanning it and I was on my way. I pushed the trolley through the 'Nothing To Declare' route under the watchful eyes of the waiting customs officers. As always, the surveillance equipment and the drone I was carrying was a worry as I had no idea of the laws regarding such equipment in Morocco. Thankfully I walked through into the huge arrivals hall without any problem. A massive skylight above with intricate geometric patterns ensured the building was well lit and welcoming and I followed the barriers towards the exit near the multiple automatic doors. Standing nearby were a number of men clutching printed and handwritten passenger name cards. One of them, a tall man in a black suit held up one with the words 'Mr J. Green' printed on it.

"Morning..." I said as I pushed the trolley towards him.

"Mr Green?" he said with a huge smile on his badly pockmarked face.

"That's me," I replied.

"Welcome to Marrakesh sir!" he said still beaming and offering his hand "My name is Ahmed from The Riad Sahari."

"Jason Green," I said as I shook his hand "Pleased to meet you."

The man insisted on pushing my trolley and we made our way out of the doors and into the fresh morning air. I quickly pulled the cigarettes from my pocket and lit up as we made our way to the pick-up point.

"Please sir," said Ahmed. "Kindly wait here while I collect the vehicle. I will be no more than a few minutes."

"Sure..." I said as I smoked.

The man walked off quickly as I stood taking in my surroundings. The temperature in Marrakesh in March had a pleasant average of 23 degrees Celsius and there was a cool breeze tinged with the smell of aviation fuel in the air. The morning sun shone brightly and I pulled my sunglasses from my pocket as I waited. All around was a mixture of tourists and locals all busily getting on with their business. Although I had done some research on the location of the actual archaeological dig, I had not had time to take a look at the hotel that the insurance company had booked for me. I pulled my phone from my pocket and did a quick Google search on 'The Riad Sahari'. It turned out that a Riad is a traditional Moroccan house. The term came from the Arab word 'ryad' meaning garden, but is applied to townhouses built around an inner courtyard or garden. I scrolled through several pictures and was pleased to see it had been awarded 4 stars and appeared to be fairly plush. From the brief conversation with Diane the previous afternoon, I knew she would be e-mailing the final details to me later that evening. Along with my itinerary and brief, it came through just after 7.00 pm and I had printed them off to read at a later date. I did know, however, that I was to be met by a certain Professor Tremblay from Oakland Archaeology at my hotel at 12.30 pm that day. I glanced at my watch to see it had just gone 9.50 am. *Plenty of time, Green.* The driver pulled up soon after in a Mercedes minibus and quickly stepped out of the front to open the sliding door. He placed my bags in the back and courteously gestured with his hand.

"Please, Mr Green," he said with a smile "Take a seat..."

The journey from the airport into the city was quick and we passed a multitude of modern shopping malls and hotels on the way. The clean, tree-lined streets were colourful and bustling with traffic of all kinds and on more than one occasion Ahmed had to brake to avoid one of the thousands of motorbikes that seemed to be everywhere. All of the modern shops and takeaways to be expected in an international city were represented. It was clear that the city fathers took great pride in their job and but for the lack of any skyscrapers I could well have been in Dubai or Abu Dhabi.

"First time in Marrakesh, Mr Green?" asked Ahmed from the driver's seat.

"Yes..." I replied, "Looks very nice so far."

"Yes sir!" he said proudly in his strong Arabic accent. "Riad Sahari is right inside the old medina souk. A very beautiful hotel indeed. We will be there soon."

As we continued, the traffic became more congested with horse-drawn carriages and mopeds and I noticed a long and ancient-looking wall to my right.

"These are the walls of the old city, sir..." said Ahmed. "Here I will park the vehicle and we will walk to the hotel."

"That's fine..." I said feeling somewhat puzzled that we would be unable to drive to the entrance.

Ahmed pulled up at a parking lot under a large tree near the ancient wall. Under it sat a number of local porters who were smoking and lazing around on their push trolleys waiting for work. On seeing the Mercedes van arrive, a scruffy looking young man wearing traditional Moroccan robes and dusty black sandals leapt to his feet and ran towards the vehicle.

He quickly opened the sliding door and beamed at me with bloodshot eyes and a mouthful of rotten teeth. A few words were exchanged with Ahmed in Arabic and my bags were quickly pulled out of the vehicle.

"This is our regular porter, sir..." said Ahmed. "We can now take the short walk to the hotel."

I climbed out of the vehicle as Ahmed locked it behind me. He waved cheerfully at the other porters lounging under the tree then motioned me to cross the street that ran parallel with the wall. Carrying only my hand luggage, I followed the porter with Ahmed walking beside me and we made our way across the street towards a large archway in the wall. Once through it, we turned left and walked on ancient flagstones towards a darkened, tunnel-like opening ahead. All around was a sea of humanity with blind beggars sitting up against the wall rattling pots for coins and donkey-drawn carts competing with pedestrians and mopeds. It took some time for my eyes to adjust to the darkness as we entered the souk but as soon as they did I found myself walking through a bewildering and exotic maze of darkened tunnels lined with kiosks and tiny shops selling everything from spices and ceramic tagines to carpets, silverware and antique daggers.

Hundreds of locals, some dressed in traditional Berber jillabas milled around as they went on their daily business seemingly oblivious to the organized chaos and bustle all around them. Wide-eyed European tourists could be seen politely fending off the persistent trinket salesmen as they made their way through the confusing maze of the souk. Intricate Moroccan metal ware lamps hung in their hundreds alongside richly woven carpets and traditional sweet shops and bakeries. On more than one occasion we had to step aside to allow donkey-drawn carts and mopeds to pass in the tight space.

"Don't worry, sir," said Ahmed over the hum of noise. "The souk can be overwhelming at first but you will soon get used to it."

I nodded as a group of dwarf-like men walked past. They wore heavy hessian robes the colour of mud and the hoods over their heads were pointed.

Jesus, Green. I thought to myself. *This is like a scene from Star Wars. You do find yourself in some strange places!* The walk through the maze of the souk continued for another 100 metres until we arrived at a seemingly unremarkable black door set into the rough and worn plaster of the wall on the left-hand side. Had it not been for the inconspicuous polished brass sign to the left of it that read 'Riad Sahari' I wouldn't have given it a second glance.

Ahmed stepped forward and turned the ornate brass handle to the centre of the door and stood back as it swung open. Standing there was a young hotel porter immaculately dressed in traditional robes with an embroidered silk fez atop his head. He smiled as he bowed and ushered me into the space beyond. I stepped up a few highly polished terracotta steps into the reception area of the hotel while my bags were quickly gathered and brought in behind me. The wooden door was closed, blocking out all traces of noise from the souk as I walked up to the ornately carved reception desk. Soft piped music played from hidden speakers in an atmosphere of tranquil luxury and grand opulence. Huge oil paintings of desert scenes and rich tapestries hung all around the heavy teak furniture which was adorned with plush, tasselled cushions.

"Welcome to The Riad Sahari, sir," said the male receptionist who was dressed in a sharp black suit and tie.

"Thank you..." I replied feeling somewhat overwhelmed. "Jason Green, checking in."

The process was quick and when I was done, the receptionist handed me a note.

"A message from Professor Tremblay, sir," he said.

I unfolded the small piece of hotel-branded paper to read a scrawled note in barely legible handwriting.

'Mr. Green. Welcome to Marrakesh. I will be here to collect you at 12.30 pm as arranged. Regards. G. Tremblay.'

In my mind, I pictured the man who had written it. A professor of archaeology, I imagined him in a tweed suit wearing horn-rimmed spectacles. I folded the note and pocketed it as I was led by a porter into the garden of the central courtyard. In stark contrast to the bustle and chaos of the souk, I found myself in a lush tropical garden shaded by giant palm trees. The floors, pillars, and plant boxes were covered in intricately designed blue and white mosaic tiles and flocks of colourful songbirds flitted and tweeted in the palm fronds above. In the middle of the courtyard stood a large circular raised pond with a fountain in its centre. The quiet gurgling of the falling water added to the atmosphere of exotic splendour and luxury. Positioned in the shade around the garden were several dining tables, some occupied by guests who sat talking quietly as they drank mint tea from dainty glass cups. Around all four sides of the open space, plastered terracotta walls rose up three storeys with open corridors on each level giving access to the rooms. Had it not been for the softly piped music I might well have been transported back in time to the age of sultans and princes.

"We have put you in one of our best rooms on the top floor, sir..." said the porter. "There is a private balcony with views over the old town and onto the Atlas Mountains. Would you like to go up now?"

I took one more look around at the magnificent surroundings before deciding I needed a cigarette.

"Yes, please," I said to the young man.

I was led through the gardens to a stairway in the building on the right. The bannisters were fashioned from twisted wrought iron and the steps themselves decorated with more mosaic tiles of blue and white. The stairs led to a sun-drenched mezzanine level with a perfectly blue rectangular swimming pool surrounded by loungers with crisp white cotton cushions. Another flight of stairs led to the top floor where we took a short walk down a tiled corridor with open archways looking down onto the lush green gardens of the courtyard below.

The porter stopped at the heavy teak door which he unlocked with a tap of a key card. I stepped into the hallway and down a short set of polished stairs into the suite below.

The room was vast with high ceilings and walls adorned with huge oil paintings and tapestries, in keeping with traditional Moroccan décor. To the left of the room a lounge suite was arranged around a low ebony coffee table and on the right was a massive king size bed with a fluffy white duvet and a multitude of pillows.

Hanging from the ceiling were three antique-looking overhead fans that spun slowly and silently giving the room an authentic, old-world feeling. Three tall arched windows looked out onto the roofs of the old city and the snow-capped peaks of the High Atlas mountains in the distance. The young porter made himself busy showing me the various amenities while I looked on nodding in approval. It was unusual for the insurance company to splash out on such blatant luxury but the fact that they had done so, coupled with the urgency that Diane had spoken of was testimony to the importance of the assignment.

"Well, I think that's everything, Mr Green..." said the porter politely as he handed me a personal card. "My name is Omar. If you need anything, please do not hesitate to contact me."

The young man had a fresh, likeable face with a cheeky grin and intelligent eyes. I liked him immediately.

"Thank you very much, Omar," I said handing him a $10.00 note. "I'll be sure to do that."

The young man's eyes lit up and he bowed graciously as he took the cash before making his way back up the stairs and out of the door. Finding a heavy brass ashtray on the table, I immediately opened the glass doors of the central windows. I stepped out onto the small balcony which looked down onto the pool and beyond across the old city to the mountains. A cool breeze was blowing in from the South and the mid-morning sun was pleasantly warm on my skin.

As I lit the cigarette the haunting and eerie notes of the Muslim call to prayer echoed over the rooftops of the ancient city. *My my...* I thought to myself as I exhaled a plume of smoke. *You certainly do find yourself in some strange places, Green.*

Chapter Five: Options.

"Which of you is Samuel Kisimba?" shouted the guard.

Samuel sat up, turned to his right on his concrete bunk and raised his left hand to identify himself.

"Come with me..." said the guard. "The doctor wishes to see you."

With the FN machine gun still strapped to his shoulder, the guard stepped forward and unhooked a large bunch of keys from his belt. The steel door squeaked loudly as it was opened and Samuel climbed down from his concrete bunk and glanced at his cellmate, Pierre, who sat watching with wide eyes.

"What is this about?" asked Samuel.

"No questions!" shouted the guard angrily. "Step out now!"

Samuel did as he was told and only then did he see the other guard who stood in the darkened corridor nearby, rifle at the ready. He watched as the cell was locked once again by the guard who then turned around and spoke.

"Walk this way..." he said pointing down the corridor with the muzzle of the rifle.

Samuel did as instructed, walking barefoot on the cool concrete through the gloom towards what appeared to be a guard station at the far end of the corridor. The small cubicle was lit by a single lightbulb that hung from a wire in the centre of the ceiling. Two tatty looking office chairs were positioned in front of an old desk with scattered papers, a kettle, and coffee mugs atop it. Mounted on the wall above the desk were four small closed-circuit television screens. Each one showed a live view of the cells in the corridor he had just walked down. Samuel had never seen these cameras which had been cleverly hidden in the darkness opposite the cells.

"Turn left!" said the guard from behind him.

Samuel did as instructed and as he made his way into yet another darkened passageway he heard the familiar abrasive sound of the band saws growing louder. Eventually, they arrived at a massive steel sliding door. One of the guards stepped forward and pulled it to the left to reveal a large, well-lit warehouse space filled with what appeared to be broken or defunct butchery equipment. There were refrigeration compressors, copper pipes, cold rooms, insulation material, wrapping machines, scales and scrapped forklifts scattered throughout the space.

"Walk on..." said the guard from behind.

Samuel's fears grew as he made his way through the centre of the warehouse past the piles of broken machinery. He glanced at a heavy steel railing that ran along the centre of the space at head height. Hanging from this rail were several large meat hooks. Designed to suspend the carcasses of fully grown animals, it was clear that the warehouse had once been used as a slaughterhouse or abattoir. At the far end of the building was a series of three offices with large glass windows that looked out onto the warehouse floor.

"The door on the right." said the guard from behind Samuel "The doctor is waiting for you inside..."

Samuel Kisimba stepped up to the door and knocked three times.

"Come in..." said a soft voice from within.

Samuel glanced behind him nervously then turned the handle on the door. The room was well lit with a desk in the centre behind which sat the kindly old doctor that had attended to Samuel on many occasions since his arrival.

"Ah, Samuel, it is you," he said with a smile that revealed nicotine-stained teeth. "Please, come in and take a seat..."

Samuel stepped into the office leaving the two guards standing in the warehouse behind him.

"Close the door behind you, Samuel," said the doctor with a dismissive wave of his hand. "The guards can wait outside."

Samuel did as instructed glancing briefly at the stern faces of the guards as he closed the door.

"Take a seat, my friend..." said the doctor gesturing casually towards the two wooden chairs that faced the desk.

Feeling somewhat frightened and confused, Samuel pulled out a chair and sat down.

"How is your wound healing, Samuel?" asked the doctor "Take off your shirt and let's have a look."

"It is almost healed now," said Samuel as he took off the khaki shirt that was the uniform of all detainees at the facility.

The doctor stood up and walked around the desk, placing a pair of spectacles on his nose with a shaky hand. He bent over to inspect the wound on Samuel's shoulder and grunted in satisfaction. Samuel could smell the alcohol on the man's breath and saw specks of dandruff on the collar of his dark suit under the white coat.

"Well..." said the doctor as he made his way back around the desk to sit down. "I think we can safely say the wound is healed now."

"Thank you for everything, Doctor," said Samuel. "Without your help, I'm not sure it would have turned out so well."

The doctor waved his hand once again in a dismissive gesture.

"Ah!" he said sitting back in his chair "It is my job after all. But tell me, how are you doing? In general, I mean..."

Samuel took a deep breath and looked around the small office.

"Well..." he said, "I'm not sure why I am being held here."

"I understand you were unable to meet the full crossing fee?" said the doctor with a look of genuine concern on his face.

"Yes...That is true, although none of us were told about the extra fee beforehand. I have been separated from my young daughter."

"I see..." said the doctor with a thoughtful look on his face. "This is not good."

Samuel leant forward and spoke to the man in a hushed tone.

"Why are they keeping us here?" he asked in a whisper.

"Well, I can only assume they are waiting for final payment..." replied the doctor with a questioning look on his face.

"But they have all of my belongings including my passport and phone..." said Samuel "How can I possibly raise this money while I am being held here? It just doesn't make any sense."

"Hmm..." said the doctor as he sat back in his chair. He brought a pen up to his mouth and twiddled it around in his fingers as if deep in thought.

The doctor placed the pen back on the desk, leant forward, and spoke in a hushed tone.

"Samuel..." he said quietly "it seems all you need is some money. Not very much either. Then you can quickly get across to Spain and be reunited with your daughter, yes?"

Samuel Kisimba felt a wave of joy and hope as he looked into the man's bleary eyes. This man who helped him with his wound was offering him a chance to be reunited with Lucia.

"Yes..." he replied.

"Well then, Samuel," said the doctor "I might just be able to help you..."

Chapter Six: Professor Tremblay.

A cool breeze blew in through the large arched windows and the room was bright from the warm late morning sunshine that shone down on the roofs of the old city of Marrakesh. I had been relaxing on the extremely comfortable bed having spent the past two hours reading the file from the insurance company and researching The Zukman Hoard on my laptop. Several websites had photographs of the gold and silver ingots and other relics that had been unearthed from the network of caves. The discovery had made worldwide news and it was clear there was a great deal of interest in it. One of the websites had photographs of the chairman of the company that owned the land, a Mr Darko Zukman of Zukman International, standing at the dig site with the Moroccan minister of antiquities.

The two men were pictured shaking hands near the mouth of the excavations and were clearly very pleased and smiling from ear to ear. In the background was a helicopter with the words 'Zukman International' emblazoned on the side. A map of the dig site on the same web page showed that the entrance to the tunnel was located on a steep and rocky mountainside. This would explain the need for a helicopter landing pad, specially constructed there to allow visiting dignitaries to inspect the site. 65-year-old Serbian businessman, Darko Zukman, was a short and morbidly obese man. Pictured almost bursting out of his black suit and tie, he stood there grinning as he shook hands with the much taller, traditionally dressed Moroccan minister of antiquities. Feeling sleepy, I stared at the picture on the screen of my laptop as my eyelids began to droop. The man reminded me of the character from Star Wars, Jabba The Hutt. Totally bald, his heavy jowls seemed to hang down over his collar and his thin-lipped smile looked like a wide gash across the expanse of his lower face. I took the computer from my lap, placed it on the bed next to me, and stared out at the snow-capped mountains in the distance. Feeling pleasantly tired, I was just about to drift off to sleep when I was jerked awake by the shrill ringing of the telephone on the bedside table. I reached over and lifted the receiver.

"Hello..." I said.

"Good afternoon, Mr Green," said the receptionist "Professor Tremblay is here to collect you..."

"Thank you" I replied glancing at my watch, "I'll be right down."

I sat up on the edge of the bed, rubbed my eyes and stretched. *Time to get to work, Green.* Not knowing what to expect, I pocketed my passport and phone, quickly washed my face, and headed out. As I walked down the stairs I noticed two women sunbathing in bikinis on the pool deck. Both in their 30's, they lay on their sun loungers, frosted glasses of iced drinks nearby. One of them, a tall blonde, turned and watched me as I passed and I saw her pull her expensive sunglasses down her nose to get a better look. *Well, well, Green.* I thought as I made my down the final set of stairs. *That is certainly of interest.* The lush green courtyard had several hotel guests seated at tables around the central fountain. I made my way past them under a date palm and headed towards the front office. The reception was busy with tourist arrivals but I immediately noticed a tall elderly man wearing spectacles standing near the front desk. He stood there with a frown on his face as he watched me enter. *Has to be him, Green.*

"Professor Tremblay?" I said.

The man's frown deepened and he appeared somewhat confused

as I approached him. It was only then that I heard the woman's voice coming from the low couch on the opposite side of the room.

"Hi!" she said, "Mr Green?"

Chapter Seven: Samuel.

———◈———

"Please, Doctor..." said Samuel, his voice desperate. "If you can help in any way. I *have* to be reunited with my daughter. It's been almost a month since we were separated and I don't even know if she and her guardian made it to Spain!"

Samuel Kisimba saw the kindly doctor as his only hope. His only way out of the harsh and confusing world he found himself in.

"Have you heard otherwise?" asked the doctor with a look of concern. "Did the guards mention any issues with their crossing?"

"No..." said Samuel with a wide-eyed look of exasperation on his face. "The guards have told me nothing at all. Not a word! I have begged them for information but they say nothing!"

"Then you can safely assume they are in Spain as we speak..." said the doctor with a reassuring smile. "I'm sure they will be waiting for you there as promised."

"Please, sir..." said Samuel sitting back in the chair "help me if you can."

The doctor studied Samuel and nodded as he opened a drawer in the desk. He pulled out a sheet of glossy paper and placed it on the desk in front of him.

"Samuel..." he said quietly "Have you ever heard of living organ donations?"

"No, sir..." said Samuel feeling slightly confused. "I have not. What is that?"

The doctor smiled, leant forward and placed his elbows on the desk with his spectacles sitting halfway down his nose.

"Samuel..." he said "As you know I am a medical professional. Here in Morocco, I have helped many people like yourself who need the money to make the crossing into Europe."

Samuel sat forward in his seat as a wave of hope and relief rushed over him. The doctor continued.

"Now apart from my work here in Marrakesh, I also run a private medical facility up North in Tangier."

"That is where we boarded the boat to cross to Spain," said Samuel.

"Correct..." said the doctor "Now, there are a lot of gravely ill people around the world who desperately need transplants. Minor transplants that is, but nonetheless life-saving for them."

Samuel frowned and shook his head.

"I'm not sure I understand, sir..." he said.

The doctor smiled and nodded once again.

"These are mostly kidney transplants..." said the doctor nonchalantly spreading his hands in an open gesture. "But some patients require corneas. For those who are going blind."

As the penny dropped, Samuel Kisimba sat back in the chair and stared at the doctor completely aghast.

The doctor chuckled and went on.

"Now Samuel..." he said "Before you become alarmed, which I can see you are, you must know that this is a completely voluntary and above board procedure. Those who wish to take part are taken up to Tangier and put into a hotel for two weeks. Of course, one of those nights is spent in the medical facility I spoke of. The procedure is 100% legal and carried out within the framework of the ministry of health here in Morocco.

Anyone who wishes to donate will first register as a voluntary donor and this registration is then approved by the ministry of health. As I said, this is all above board. A minor operation is done, and after a few days of recuperation, the donor is paid and goes on his or her way. The facility in Tangier is ISO certified and is state of the art. I have helped a good number of people who have sadly found themselves in a position similar to yours. Recipients are willing to pay $10,000.00 for a kidney or $5000.00 for a cornea. A great deal of money, I'm sure you will agree..."

Samuel Kisimba stared at the doctor as his blood began to boil and his fists tightened in rage.

"You want me to sell a part of my body?" he asked quietly.

"No, no, no, Samuel..." said the doctor, holding his hands up once again in a gesture of surrender. "This is not me. No, not at all. I am simply a humble doctor trying to help people. People like you..."

"What if I refuse?" said Samuel "What then? How long will I be held here?"

"Samuel..." said the doctor "I am not part of this and I can't answer that question. Look, I can see you are getting upset now. You must rest."

The doctor pushed the glossy paper he had taken from the drawer across the desk. With his left hand, he pushed a hidden button under the desk.

"Here..." he said "Take this brochure and read through it. I am always here if you wish to talk to me."

At that moment the door opened and the guards stepped in.

Chapter Eight: The Dig Site.

The real Professor Tremblay had been sitting on a low couch behind a giant pot plant in the reception. Feeling somewhat embarrassed that I had assumed it would be a man I was to meet, I took my eyes from the confused looking hotel guest I had initially approached and smiled at the tall woman who strode towards me. In her late thirties, she wore tight, dusty-looking jeans and a long-sleeved blue shirt tied around her midriff, revealing her tanned, shapely waist. Her long sandy blonde hair was pulled tightly into a ponytail on the back of her head. Her piercing blue eyes were smiling and welcoming and she tilted her head slightly to the left as I took her hand.

"I'm sorry, I didn't realise..." I said glancing at the older man at the reception "Jason Green, pleased to meet you."

"Professor Genevieve Tremblay," she said with a wide smile that revealed her perfectly white teeth. "Welcome to Marrakesh, Mr Green."

Although she spoke with a slight French accent, her English was perfect and as I looked into her face I saw her nose was slightly sunburnt from working in the glaring North African sun. At that moment I found it hard to decide if she was handsome, beautiful, or both. Her face was slim and symmetrical and her eyes were quick and intelligent.

"Well..." she said "My instructions are to take you up to the dig site. Are you ready to go?"

"I am..." I said. "Is there anything I'll need?"

"Nope..." she said looking me over and putting her hands on her hips. "Oh, you will need your passport to get into the site."

I tapped the pocket that held my phone and travel document.

"Got it..." I said.

"Well..." she said gesturing towards the door "Shall we?"

We stepped from the cool tranquillity of the hotel reception directly into the chaos and bustle of the souk beyond. Professor Genevieve Tremblay immediately turned right and walked ahead of me at a pace and I saw the straw cowboy hat that hung on a string between her broad shoulders. It was only then that I noticed the two-way radio, archaeological trowel, and other tools of the trade attached to her leather belt.

"So, Mr Green," she said turning to me with a smile as she walked. "What do you think of the old city?"

"Please, call me Jason..." I called out as I dodged a moped and struggled to keep up. "I have to say it's quite overwhelming."

"Don't worry!" she shouted with a chuckle as she leapt to the right to allow an overloaded donkey to pass. "You'll get used to it soon. And you can call me Gen..."

Eventually, we made it out of the maze of darkened passageways and emerged into the sunlight near the archway that led from the old city to the new. Across the busy street was the same group of porters I had seen on the way in with the hotel driver. Parked in the shade under the giant Argania tree was a brand new Land Rover with the words 'Oakland Archaeological Ltd' emblazoned on the side.

Genevieve Tremblay placed her cowboy hat on her head and strode out into the traffic as she crossed the street causing several vehicles to suddenly brake and hoot in indignation. She walked with the speed and confidence of someone on a mission with a serious job to do. I followed at a safe distance arriving at the Land Rover to hear her cheerfully greeting the lounging porters in fluent Arabic. It was clear she was a regular visitor and was well-liked by all. I climbed into the passenger seat once she had unlocked the vehicle and watched as she put the key into the ignition.

"Right..." she said looking at her Hamilton field watch. "It's about 45 minutes to an hour from here to the dig site. Depends on the traffic."

"Looking forward to seeing it..." I said as she reversed and then did a quick U-turn on the busy street.

Genevieve Tremblay was a fast and impatient driver. She wove through the traffic on the orderly streets of the new town eventually leaving the built-up area and emerging on the outskirts of the city at an industrial site. Here she took a left turn at a roundabout into a long straight road with the snow-capped peaks of the High Atlas Mountains ahead of us in the distance. The road surface was good and apart from a few tourist buses and horse-drawn carts, it was relatively free of traffic. On each side of the road were various small businesses from plant nurseries and vehicle sales yards to clay tagine manufacturers and builders merchants. The next 20 minutes were spent in pleasant small talk mainly about the Zukman Hoard and the dig site itself. It was clear to me that she was extremely enthusiastic about her job. It was the historical significance of the discovery rather than the monetary value that was important to her. I guessed this was true of most archaeologists. She went on to explain that the dig site had been transformed into a mini-city of sorts with a helicopter landing pad, incident rooms, catering trucks, a clinic, state power and water supply, and of course an elaborate security system. She spoke with an infectious air of excitement often using her free hand to emphasise points while turning in her seat to look at me. Given the speed at which she drove, this had the effect of making me somewhat uncomfortable.

"Have you any idea of the origin of this hoard?" I asked, gripping the door handle as she overtook a tourist bus. "Who put it there and why?"

"Well..." she said with a laugh "It's almost certainly the stock of a 15th-century trader. A very wealthy one at that."

"Why then was it abandoned?" I asked feeling somewhat foolish. "Something of such value..."

"Great question" she replied tapping the steering wheel impatiently. "This sort of discovery has turned up in the world of archaeology before. It is rare but it does happen from time to time."

"So what is the general theory so far?" I asked, feeling relieved my question was relevant.

"Well it can only be assumed that the owner and the people who put it there in the first place were killed..." she said with a half-smile. "There can be only one reason. There is no way that it would have remained undiscovered for so many hundreds of years if there had been anyone left living after the fact. Perhaps it was a battle between warring tribes. We simply don't know."

"Incredible..." I said shaking my head in amazement, "And it's only being uncovered now."

"Yep," she replied with a twinkle in her eyes. "And we're only just getting started. The indications are there is a whole lot more to be discovered in those caves."

I turned to look out of the window to see the countryside had begun to change as we arrived in the foothills of the mountains. We had passed through the dry scrubby flatlands and ahead of us were the rocky, rolling hills with scattered clumps of primitive-looking human settlements.

"Who lives in these villages on the hills?" I asked.

"They are modern-day Berber tribes people..." she replied as she took a sharp corner. "Nomads and herdsmen. We have a lot of them working at the dig site as well..."

The sun was bright and the sky a perfect blue above us as the journey took us over the foothills and down into a steep-sided valley where the road ran parallel with a raging river. The water was a bright red colour from the soil erosion as it made its way down from the towering snow-capped peaks above.

Along the watercourse at several intervals were tourist restaurants decorated with strings of bright coloured flags and umbrellas. I watched as several camera carrying groups crossed the rickety-looking bridges on their way to lunch.

"The water here is quite red as you can see..." said Gen. "It picks up soil particles as it comes down from the mountains. Up at the dig site, you'll see the river is clear and icy."

I nodded silently as the powerful vehicle swung around yet another corner and climbed further up the steep gradient. Some 10 minutes further on suddenly there was no sign of any more tourists and the road became thinner and more treacherous. This did nothing to slow the speed at which Genevieve drove as she powered the vehicle up towards the black, imposing snow-capped mountains ahead. The air had become decidedly cooler and thinner and the occasional stilted buildings we passed were ancient and weather-beaten.

"We are now in the High Atlas region, Jason..." she said. "We're near the site now."

I looked at the river below to my left to see it was no longer red in colour but was now a raging, frothing torrent of clear mountain water racing over massive shiny black boulders. Two minutes later we rounded yet another corner and the landscape levelled out into a plateau on the mountainside. Up ahead I saw what was clearly a modern high-security area to the left of the road. We pulled up to a car park near several shipping containers that had been converted into site offices. There were around 30 vehicles of all descriptions parked there in the sun. Some bore the colours of the local police service while others were marked The Zukman Group and Oakland Archaeology Ltd. Standing on the opposite side of the road were a group of 40 to 50 local men. Clearly waiting for work, they were traditionally dressed in thick hessian gowns and their weather-beaten faces were testament to their harsh outdoor lives in the thin air of the High Atlas range. Genevieve skidded the Land Rover to a halt in a cloud of dust near the rear of the parking area and turned to look at me with a smile.

"Right..." she said brightly "Here we are then."

I unclipped my seat belt gratefully and stepped out into the cool, thin air. The sun was warm on my face and there was a distinct feeling that I had arrived at a place of significant importance. I felt the urge for a cigarette but it appeared there would be no time for such vices. Once again, Genevieve took the lead and strode quickly towards the main site entrance which was marked with a yellow and black boom between two offices.

"Follow me, Jason," she said, "we need to get you cleared and organize an access pass."

I glanced down the valley to my left to see a tall fence stretching down to the river line, over a temporary steel bridge, and up the mountain on the other side. The top of the fence was crowned with razor wire and there were bright plastic signs placed at 3-metre intervals with the universal lightning symbol warning of high voltage. It was clear to me that this was the North boundary of the dig site and there would be another equally imposing barrier on the far side. As we approached the boom I saw several uniformed men standing near the office to the left. All of them were armed with FN machine guns and I noticed the words 'Zukman Group' printed on the breast pockets of their camouflaged uniforms. The sight of the weapons caused the hairs on my arms to stand up briefly and I noticed one of the guards, a tall, wiry man, scowling at me. I knew that from behind my sunglasses there was no way he could have known that I had seen him watching me, but there was no mistaking it. The man had been told to expect me. Genevieve greeted the guards cheerfully and handed them a piece of paper she had pulled from her breast pocket.

"This is your clearance letter, Jason," she said, turning back to me "They will need your passport now and then you'll get your gate pass."

"Sure..." I said handing her my passport "Looks like you have some serious security here." "Oh yes," she said handing the passport to the nearest guard. "There has to be. This is the most important archaeological discovery in the history of Morocco."

Two of the guards disappeared into the site office to the left, leaving the tall one who had been watching me standing alone. I pulled the packet of cigarettes from my pocket and walked off to the right, back towards the main road to try to get a look up the hill. It was only when I had passed the second site office that I saw the rough dirt road that led up the steep mountainside on the far side of the river. It wound around a few enormous boulders as it rose eventually flattening out at what appeared to be a man-made plateau.

Even from that distance, I could see the area was a hive of activity with lighting towers, scaffolding, and yet more boundaries and security marked off with bright red and yellow chevron tape. There must have been a hundred people up there all busy with their individual tasks. Most of them wore bright yellow hard hats but I could see several locals who had been hired as labourers. I put a cigarette in my mouth and cupped the lighter flame from the breeze as I lit it. The smoke billowed away in the wind as I stared up at the spectacle above me. At that moment, Genevieve walked up and stood to my left.

"Ah, you've seen it..." she said with a smile and a palpable sense of awe. "It takes my breath away every time. That, Jason, is the mouth of the excavation of the world-famous Zukman Hoard..."

Chapter Nine: Samuel.

Samuel Kisimba lay on the hard concrete bunk in his cell and stared up at the afternoon sky through the bars in the tiny window above him. Once again he heard the sound of a motorbike arriving outside and sat up to look out at the walled-off tarmac parking area. As usual, there were around 30 motorcycles parked there in a neat row against the warehouse wall opposite. He watched as the rider who had just arrived removed his helmet and hung it on the rearview mirror on the handlebars. Like all the others who came and went every twelve hours or so, the man walked up the tarmac and disappeared around the corner at the far side of the giant building.

During the first days of his incarceration, he had often speculated as to their purpose but had long since decided that they must be shift workers in the meat processing plant within the same complex. There were, after all, thousands of motorcycles in Marrakesh and it seemed they were the preferred method of transport for working-class locals. Once again he lay back on his bunk and stared out at the blue sky through the window. Samuel Kisimba was feeling a debilitating combination of furious anger and helpless confusion after his late-morning meeting with the doctor.

This was the man who had almost certainly saved his life and someone he had pinned all his hopes on until that day. In his mind, he tried to make sense of the juxtaposition between the harsh attitude of the guards and the seemingly kindly manner of the doctor. It was as if they were two completely separate entities. Samuel brought his hand up and touched his breast pocket where the brochure that the doctor had given him was folded up and hidden. He had not mentioned it to his cellmate, Pierre. *How can this be? Is this really happening to me?* he thought. Samuel Kisimba took a deep breath and exhaled as he thought of his young daughter, Lucia. He closed his eyes and mouthed a silent prayer for her well being and that of her guardian, Elizabeth Nkulu. In the bunk below him, Pierre Lumumba cleared his throat and yawned loudly as if just waking up from slumber. Samuel's thoughts went once again to his own fate and that of the other prisoners in the complex. Would Pierre be given the same option as he had just been? *Perhaps it was only him that had been offered this way out? But if so, then why?*

Hearing some more movement from the bunk below, Samuel sat up and leant on his right elbow.

"Pierre..." he said softly "Are you awake?"

"Yes, Samuel." said his cellmate.

"Have you been offered anything since you have been here?" said Samuel "A way to make money to get out of here..."

"No..." came the reply "Like you, Samuel, I am in the dark."

"How then we will ever leave?"

"My brother..." said Pierre resignedly "I do not know."

Samuel lay back on the bunk and closed his eyes to think. Through the mists of despair and desperation, he thought of the money. *$5000.00 for a cornea. A single cornea! That is a lot of money. And that would be it. Freedom! Or $10,000.00 for a kidney. That is a fortune... More than enough to set Lucia and me up in Europe. I could find a home and look for work. I'm fit and healthy. There is no doubt that physically, I could do it.* Samuel Kisimba lay there deep in thought until he heard the familiar sound of a motorcycle arriving outside some 10 minutes later. Quietly, he pulled the glossy brochure from his breast pocket, unfolded it, and began reading.

Chapter Ten: The Caves.

———⋅❦⋅———

Genevieve and I took the short walk back to the security gate where I was handed a laminated identification card on a nylon ribbon. I placed it around my neck as we walked through the cordon and onto the site. The ground was covered in a thick layer of fine brown dust from the constant foot and vehicle traffic that passed through. Once again I felt the eyes of the tall guard who had been watching me earlier following me. From behind my sunglasses, I studied him. He had a thin, cruel face with hollow cheeks and what appeared to be a permanent smirk. His eyes were set close to each other and his nose was large and aquiline giving him the look of a cross between an eagle and a weasel. It was as we walked past him that Genevieve spoke.

"Uday..." she said quietly to him in greeting.

The guard responded with a grunt and continued to watch us as we passed. Making a mental note of his face, I chose not to question my host about the man, preferring to leave any questions I had till later. Parked out of sight under a shade cloth shelter to the left beyond the portacabins were several quad bikes. All black in colour, they were covered with dust and had the words 'Oakland Archaeology' painted on their petrol tanks.

"Can you ride a quad bike, Jason?" asked Genevieve.

"Sure..."

"Great!" she said pointing to a trestle table nearby. "Grab a hard hat from the table and we'll head up to the dig."

I did as instructed then walked over to the parked motorbikes. Genevieve had already chosen her own and sat watching me with a half-smile on her face as I climbed onto the nearest machine. I pushed the electric start button and the engine roared to life.

"Ready?" she called over the clatter of the engines.

I responded with a thumbs up and watched as she kicked the bike into gear and revved it. The vehicle lurched forwards into the sunshine, kicking up a cloud of fine dust behind it. I did the same and soon enough we were both making our way down the rocky slope towards the steel bridge that spanned the raging white waters below. The steel girders of the bridge made a high pitched drumming sound as we crossed and I could hear the icy water crashing into the giant blackened boulders below. The road on the other side of the bridge was rough and steep and it wound around several huge boulders that had tumbled down the mountainside over the ages. At one point we met two more quad bikes driven by European men coming in the opposite direction. Fixed to the back of their bikes were large plastic crates and the riders waved at us as they passed. The cool mountain air was filled with fine dust from the road surface. The road became steeper still as we made our way upwards and passed a group of locals loading a tipper truck by hand with boulders. The work was hard and treacherous and they wore cotton scarves around their mouths and noses to protect themselves from the dust. The football-sized rocks were clearly being used to extend the man-made plateau at the mouth of the diggings above. A truck with the words 'Zukman Group' painted on the driver's door stood at an angle near the side of the track. Eventually, we made it up to the dig site and the rocky track levelled out onto the artificial plateau which was roughly the size of a tennis court. The borders of the site were heavily built up with site offices and numerous other temporary buildings. The perimeter was surrounded by scaffolding with powerful spotlights atop and cordons and chevrons below. There must have been a hundred people milling around busily and I noticed more armed security and what appeared to be a film crew lounging around on plastic chairs in the shade near a catering truck. In the side of the mountain at the far end of the area was a gaping hole with a number of pipes and heavy-duty cables feeding into it. I immediately assumed that this was the entrance to the famed caves of the Zukman Hoard. Far up above the cavernous opening was a team of two Europeans moving around carrying a rectangular white metal frame with two long spikes to the base. The frame was attached to a cable that ran into the backpack of the man who carried it, and he carefully placed the spikes into the rocky ground as he negotiated the steep and treacherous slope.

I followed Genevieve to a shaded parking area on the left and cut the engine on the bike. She leapt from her bike and smiled as she saw me staring up at the two men above.

"That's the geophysical team," she said while dusting her top. "They're using the radar machine to look for any more openings to the cave system."

"Have they found any yet?" I asked as I climbed from the quad bike.

"Not yet, but we have to check..." she replied, her face glowing with pride. "Now, Jason. Let's go and look at some real archaeology!"

The surface of the plateau was packed hard with cinder giving it the look of a tarred road. As we walked, Genevieve pointed out the various buildings and their purposes. There was a large storeroom, a laboratory, an incident room, a finds tent and a first aid station.

Most of the buildings had satellite dishes atop them and multiple cables and pipes ran across the area supplying electricity and other services. There were several Westerners of all races, both male and female, who greeted Genevieve as we walked. Most seemed busy and somewhat preoccupied with their jobs but the atmosphere was cheerful and pleasant.

"We're not all archaeologists here..." said Genevieve turning to me as she walked. "We have engineers, surveyors, electricians and plumbers to name a few. We all have to work together to keep the dig safe and secure. Tunnelling into a mountainside can be quite dangerous."

"I'm sure..." I said feeling slightly bewildered by it all.

By then it was abundantly clear that the site was of both national and international importance. I was under no illusion that the cost of setting up and operating an undertaking like this must run into many millions of dollars.

We soon arrived at the mouth of the excavations and there was a buzzing sound from the bright overhead lights and the activity within. I stared up at the roof of the cave to see it had been supported with concrete shuttering and thick wooden beams. The floor of the cave was covered with a thick, talcum like dust and several cables and pipes ran into it. It took some time for my eyes to adjust from the bright sunlight outside but by the time I had placed my sunglasses in my pocket, I could see clearly once again. Ahead of me was a large rounded open chamber that stretched ahead into the rock for roughly seven metres. The space was well lit and airy and at the far side, I saw a small crawl space that led further into the mountainside.

"This was the first cave we excavated, Jason," said Genevieve gesturing at the space with her hands. "We removed several tonnes of rock from the front to open it up. It took us three months to finish clearing the interior, working 24 hours a day, and there were some truly wonderful finds."

"And now?" I asked.

"Well..." she said pointing to the far side of the cave. "The geophysical reports show a number of other, equally large chambers further into the mountainside. We found a tunnel leading to the second chamber and excavated it. It's in this second chamber that we are now working. Would you like to see it?"

"Sure..."

"You might get a bit dirty" she replied with a grin. "We'll have to crawl through."

"That's fine," I said "Let's go..."

I followed Genevieve to the far side of the cave to the crawl space I had seen before. There were several shockproof lights set into the rock and a thick pipe that I imagined was attached to an extractor fan in the second chamber. Genevieve quickly got down on all fours and began crawling into the tunnel.

I could not help noticing her shapely bottom as she went. *Concentrate, Green. Concentrate.* I followed suit soon after and my hands and knees were instantly covered in the ultra-fine dust that seemed to coat everything. The tunnel was tight and surrounded by jagged boulders. It stretched ahead of me for a good three metres and I suddenly found myself overcome with an alarming sense of claustrophobia. Above me were millions of tonnes of rock and I was travelling deeper still into what felt like an abyss. This feeling stayed with me as I crawled along until I heard the sound of metal scraping on rock and soil ahead of me. There was also the familiar sound of the Fleetwood Mac song, 'You can go your own way', coming from the chamber ahead. *What the hell?* I emerged into yet another cavernous space with three people working at the far side. To the left and right of the cave were lighting rigs I imagined belonged to the film crew. Although the area was well lit, the archaeologists working at the far side of the cave wore hard hats with powerful lights mounted on them. They scratched and scraped with trowels at a large wall of hard caked soil and dirt that was a different colour from the surrounding rock. Lying on the rock floor nearby was a small blue tooth speaker that was the obvious source of the music. Genevieve greeted the archaeologists and they turned and waved as they worked. We walked over to the face of the diggings and it was then that I saw the golden hilt of the dagger protruding from the caked earth. Encrusted with jewels, its sheath was still buried deep in the dirt and the archaeologist who was working on it was carefully brushing the soil away with what looked like a toothbrush. Numerous other treasures were protruding around and above the dagger but they were covered in soil and grit and I could not identify what they were. Lying in the dust near where the archaeologist knelt was a canvas roll-up case with various picks, trowels and brushes. Genevieve leant over to study the wall and spoke.

"Nice find, Roy..." she said.

The bearded, bespectacled man who was working with the brush turned from his kneeling position and smiled.

"Not too bad, Gen," he said in a broad Yorkshire accent "Not too bad."

Genevieve stood up straight once again and turned to speak to me.

"Well Jason..." she said "This is what we do. What do you think?"

"Amazing," I said truthfully. "Am I correct in thinking that this whole wall of different coloured soil will have to be removed?"

"That's correct. The entire chamber is packed hard with this material" said Genevieve. "The items we are removing were stacked up high all those years ago. It's painstaking but rewarding work."

In my mind, I imagined how impatient I would get with such a task. I pictured myself setting to the wall with a pickaxe and removing great chunks of the caked earth with each blow. Of course, I knew that such behaviour would be sacrilegious in the meticulous and methodical world of archaeology. Genevieve went on.

"This caked earth you see here is the result of hundreds of years of seepage. Even in an area such as this, with very little rainfall, over the years the treasures that were stacked in these chambers were gradually covered with soil and this concretion has built up and eventually filled the space completely. No human has laid eyes on what you are seeing here in over 500 years. Added to that, our findings indicate the presence of a third chamber deeper within this cave system. We have no idea what was hidden there and will only find out once we have excavated it all. It is the discovery of a lifetime and privilege to be part of it."

Finally, I understood her passion for the job and realised the historical importance of it all. The thrill of exploration and discovery. I stared down at the gleaming golden hilt of the dagger that was embedded in the wall of dirt.

"It's incredible…" I said shaking my head "Thank you for showing me this, Gen."

"Pleasure…" she replied "Well, I could take you to see the finds tent and the incident room now if you like?"

"Sure" I replied "Yes, let's do that."

We crawled back through the tunnel and into the first chamber of the cave system. As we emerged into the afternoon sunshine we passed two members of the film crew who were making their way in with a microphone boom and camera. Clearly, they were going in to film the excavation of the golden hilted dagger. Genevieve greeted them as we passed and turned right towards the buildings near the perimeter of the plateau.

"We'll start with the finds tent," said Genevieve turning to me as she walked. "It's where everything goes to be logged before it is taken to the incident room."

"Sounds good," I said feeling the urge to smoke.

It was then that I saw the tall guard, Uday, lurking around in the shade near the catering truck. Still clutching his FN rifle, he watched us closely as we walked but once again I pretended not to see him. Ahead of us was a large white PVC marquee tent with a network of electricity cables running into it. Genevieve opened one of the entrance flaps and stepped inside and I followed soon after. The interior was brightly lit with rows of neon lights and two long rows of trestle tables along the length of the space. At the far side of the tent was a frame-mounted overhead camera and a lighting rig. Sitting on plastic chairs nearby were two more staff from Oakland Archaeology. Genevieve waved at them and then turned to speak.

"So, Jason," she said "All of the finds are logged by the archaeologists as they are removed from the chambers. They are then crated and brought here where they are photographed, numbered, and logged into the computer system. This process is fairly quick and once complete, the items are then moved into the incident room."

"I see..." I said looking around "And what happens in the incident room?"

"Well, the items are then carefully and thoroughly cleaned, examined, logged, and photographed once again. All of this information is uploaded to our servers and finally, everything is transferred to our strong room where it remains until transported to the secure warehouse in Marrakesh. If you like I can take you to have a look at the incident room. It's right next door..."

By then I was fully aware of the incredibly slow and extremely painstaking work that was going on at the site. Still, the entire operation appeared to be running like a well-oiled machine. The security arrangements I had witnessed so far were adequate as far as the initial processes were concerned and I wondered if my presence was bothering Genevieve. *I'm sure she'd much rather be getting with her job, Green.*

"Yes..." I replied, "I'd like to see that if I can."

We made our way out of the finds tent and into the waning afternoon sun. The incident room was made up of two conjoined porta cabins situated on the right-hand side of the tent. White in colour, they had wall mounted air conditioning units on the outside and no windows at all. We stepped up a set of metal stairs and Genevieve entered a six-digit code into a keypad near the door. She pushed the door open and we stepped into what I can only describe as a sterile, laboratory environment. The large room was cool and brightly lit and there were long white tables strewn with hundreds of glittering finds and an assortment of decorated ceramic pots and other earthenware. There were four staff members, all in lab coats, working on various artefacts. One of them sat behind a large microscope and was slowly cleaning a silver charger with an earbud. I imagined that process alone would take well over a day. Lining the walls of the room were shelves containing hundreds of bottles of chemicals, cameras and various pieces of laboratory equipment.

"As you can see, this room is sterile," said Genevieve proudly. "When our finds leave here they're pretty much as good as new. Perfectly preserved by the earth itself."

"Amazing..." I said nodding "Would it be possible to take a look at the strongroom?"

"Certainly..." she replied looking at her watch. "In fact, there will be a collection of finds this afternoon. We can watch it happen."

"You mean a load of goods is being taken to the warehouse in Marrakesh?"

"Yes," she replied "The truck comes every two days or so. We can watch it being loaded if you like."

"Sounds good..."

The sun was moving steadily down the sky as we walked out of the incident room and the air had cooled significantly. I followed Genevieve as she made her way to the right of the incident room towards what appeared to be a converted shipping container. Painted red and surrounded by tall electric fencing, there was an armed guard stationed nearby and I noticed numerous closed-circuit cameras positioned around it. The gate was made from wrought iron with spikes atop it and was secured by a chain and a heavy-duty padlock.

"As you can see," said Genevieve as we approached the guard "Our security is tight."

"Yes..." I replied, "And where is the control room for these cameras?"

"That's down at the entrance to the site" she replied "There are ministry officials, Zukman Group staff, and Oakland people manning it 24 hours a day."

The guard stood to attention upon seeing Genevieve and me approaching. She spoke to the man in French briefly and taking the two-way radio from his belt he called the guard station below at the site entrance. With permission to enter granted, he collected a logbook from his workstation and filled in our names and the time. Finally, we were asked to remove our watches and any metal objects from our pockets and place them in a tray at the guard station. As we did this the guard unlocked the gate and swung the gate open.

The three of us stepped inside and Genevieve entered a code into a keypad on the door to the strongroom. There was a loud metallic clunk and I watched as she swung the heavy door outwards. The interior of the room was well lit and lined with racks of steel shelving that went up to roof level. There were a number of heavy-duty plastic crates stacked along the middle shelf to the left. Beyond that were several open steel trunks.

"Most of the finds are wrapped in blankets and transported in these crates," said Genevieve. "The more delicate pieces are individually wrapped and placed in compartments in the metal trunks. That way there is no damage during transit."

"I see..." I said looking around for any weak spots in the space "And what about the gold and silver ingots? How are those transported?"

"We use the same method" she replied quietly as she lifted a corner of the blanket from a nearby crate to reveal a jewel-encrusted silver teapot within.

I watched as she ran her fingers softly down the spout of the ancient vessel. Like a lover's caress, it seemed as if she was entranced by the very sight of it. Suddenly she snapped out of her dreamlike state and replaced the blanket over the crate.

"Now..." she said with a smile "How about a cup of tea? We can go to the catering truck."

I took one final look around the space in the strongroom and spoke.

"That sounds like a good idea."

I watched as Genevieve and the guard secured the strongroom and I heard the metallic clang of the locking mechanism in the thick steel door. We stepped through the gate and the guard replaced the padlock on the heavy chain. Finally, he ran a handheld metal detector over our clothes to ensure that nothing had been removed.

Once done, he nodded politely and we collected our belongings from the tray and set off towards the catering truck which was parked on the right-hand perimeter of the plateau. The air had cooled even more and I stood to the side of the vehicle out of the wind as we arrived.

"Tea, Jason?" said Genevieve as she approached the counter.

"Coffee please..." I replied. "Black, no sugar."

I lit a cigarette as I waited and gazed at the busy activity all around the plateau. Up the mountain to the right, I saw the helicopter landing pad I had seen pictured online earlier that day. A set of neat concrete stairs had been built to allow VIP guests and visitors to access the site with ease. My mind went back to the photograph of the Moroccan minister of antiquities and the landowner, Darko Zukman, standing at the entrance to the cave system. Both men had been pictured looking extremely pleased with themselves. *I can see why now. This discovery must be worth a fucking fortune. Never seen anything like it.*

"Black coffee, no sugar..." said Genevieve as she walked towards me clutching two paper cups.

"Ah, thanks very much Gen," I said as I took the cup. "Well, I must say you have quite an impressive operation here..."

"Thanks!" she said brightly "We're all very proud of it.

We stood in silence as we drank and watched the various personnel moving around the site. Suddenly the two-way radio on

Genevieve's belt squawked and she brought it to her ear and nodded as she listened.

"The armoured truck is here..." she said replacing the radio. "It's just come through the lower gate and is on its way up now. We can take our cups over and watch it being loaded if you like."

"Yes..." I said crushing out the cigarette "Let's do that."

The vehicle was a standard cash in transit van with the Group 4 logo emblazoned on its sides. It trundled up the steep slope revving hard and kicking up small stones behind it as it approached.

The front and side windows were all covered with thick black mesh to prevent any attempts at smash and grab. The load bay at the rear had no windows at all. The driver arrived at the plateau and reversed quickly to a parking spot near the strongroom. The staff working at the mouth of the diggings never gave it a second glance and it was clear that this procedure was part of the daily routine.

As we walked over to watch the loading process I noticed the tall figure of the guard, Uday, lurking in the shadows at the rear of the incident room. The stub of a cigar was clamped between his teeth and he watched us as we approached. Ignoring this scrutiny, I followed Genevieve to a spot near the rear of the truck and we stood there in the sunshine to watch. The driver and two assistants emerged from the cab of the vehicle and walked over to the guard who had let us into the strongroom. I took some more photographs as the four men walked over to the guard station and began dealing with the paperwork. At that moment the site supervisor, a thin, ginger headed man with spectacles, walked over and greeted the driver and his crew. Under his arm, he carried a clipboard stuffed with papers. The formalities took a few minutes then the driver returned to the rear of the armoured vehicle to open it up. The guard then opened the gate and the supervisor stepped in to punch the code into the keypad near the door of the strongroom. My eyes darted from the truck to the strongroom and to the lurking figure of Uday as I watched in silence. Once the door was open, the supervisor stepped back to watch and the two assistants from the truck stepped in and began lifting the plastic crates. They carried them carefully, under the watchful eye of the supervisor, and placed them in the rear of the truck. Once they had returned to collect more crates, the driver climbed into the back of the truck and began securing the crates with load straps. It was obvious they did this to prevent any movement or shifting of the load during transit. The entire process of loading the crates took less than 10 minutes and finally, the guard stepped forward and locked the strongroom once again. He ran his handheld metal detector over the uniforms of the loaders and finally the gate was locked once again. I watched as the driver jumped from the load bay of the truck and waited for the supervisor to inspect his work. Seemingly satisfied, he nodded and the door was closed and locked once again.

The supervisor pulled a bunch of plastic zip tie seals from his pocket and logged the serial numbers on his clipboard. Once done, he stepped forward and attached them to the heavy bar that housed the locks for the load bay. The group of men walked back to the guard station to complete the paperwork for the handover and two minutes later the job was done. I watched as the site supervisor waved at the driver and his assistants and turned back to his work at the dig site. The exhaust pipe of the armoured vehicle puffed a cloud of blue smoke as the engine started and the vehicle trundled off down the slope towards the front gate.

"The operation runs like this 24 hours a day..." said Genevieve "Soon all these floodlights you see around the perimeter will turn on and the night shift staff will arrive."

"Well," I said looking at my watch "I must say, it looks like you're doing a great job."

"Thanks. Is there anything else you'd like to see, Jason?" she asked.

"No..." I said "I don't think so. I think I've seen enough for today."

"Great!" she said "Well, let's head back to the car and get going then."

The air was cold as we descended from the dig site and crossed the steel bridge on the quad bikes. I rode alongside Genevieve to avoid the clouds of dust thrown up by her tires. We parked the vehicles where we had found them and walked around to the boom gate at the site entrance.

The drive back to the city was hair raising but the setting sun cast a beautiful pink glow on the rugged, earthy slopes of the High Atlas mountains. It was 45 minutes later and the sun had almost set when we arrived at the same parking spot under the giant Argania tree near the ancient walls of the old city of Marrakesh. The porters we had seen earlier were still lounging around, smoking and waiting for work. Genevieve cut the engine of the Land Rover and I turned to speak to her.

"Thank you very much for everything, Gen," I said as I unbuckled my seatbelt. "It's been an education. I'm sure I'll see you again at some stage during my visit."

She turned to look at me with a slightly bemused look on her face.

"Um, I'm coming in with you..." she said.

"You are?" I said, feeling somewhat confused.

"Yes..." she said with a smile. "I'm staying in the same hotel as you. I've been there for months."

Chapter Eleven: Samuel.

Drips of sweat fell to the concrete floor of the cell from Samuel Kisimba's forehead. His arms ached and he grunted as he counted down the last of the 100 press-ups that were part of his daily exercise routine. When he was done he stood and splashed his face with the cool water from the bucket near the latrine. Still panting heavily, he climbed up to his bunk, took a perfunctory look out of the tiny window above, and sat on the edge. The sweat on the naked skin of his muscular upper body glistened in the sunlight. It had been a full hour since the guards had come for his cellmate, Pierre.

Samuel had no idea where they had taken him but in the back of his mind, he suspected that he had been taken to see the doctor. Samuel's strength had returned and the bullet wound on his shoulder was all but healed. It had been two days since his last run with the guard who had shot him, Uday, but his hatred for the man still burned deep in his soul. He had kept the brochure he had been given hidden from Pierre and never mentioned a word of the offer the doctor had made to him. Night after night he lay awake staring up at the stars through his tiny window and contemplated this offer.

In his mind, he pictured his reunion with his beloved daughter, Lucia, and what a joyous day it would be. But these happy thoughts were tainted by the ever-present dark clouds of worry and dread. On many occasions, during the loneliest hours of the night, he had been tempted to call for the guards and ask to be taken to the doctor. To go ahead with one of the medical procedures he had been offered and simply get it over and done with. But Samuel Kisimba was a devout Christian. A man of principles and honour. The cruelty he and Lucia had been subject to surely could not continue.

Night after night he had prayed for guidance and mercy but it had been to no avail. Fear and worry were eating into his very soul and he wondered how long he could continue in this cruel world of isolation and limbo. Still seated on the edge of his concrete bunk, Samuel Kisimba closed his eyes, took a deep breath, and exhaled. At that moment he heard the clatter of the steel door to the right beyond the guard station.

There were mumbled voices and laughter he imagined was from the guards. Soon after, the guards and his cellmate Pierre arrived and the door to the cell was unlocked.

Pierre was bright-eyed and clearly excited about something. He stood staring at Samuel silently as he waited for the door to be locked behind him and the guards to leave. Once they were beyond earshot, Pierre stepped forward with a grin on his face and spoke in an animated whisper.

"I have a way out of here my brother!" he said pulling the folded brochure from his pocket. "Look, Samuel. Look at this!"

Samuel took the brochure and nodded as he examined it. It was identical to the one he had been given only days beforehand.

"I was given the same paper, Pierre..." said Samuel with a sigh as he handed it back.

"But you never told me, my brother. Why?"

"I needed time to think about it," said Samuel quietly.

"Well," said Pierre "I'm going to do it. It's my ticket out of here. It's money for nothing!"

Samuel smiled sadly at his young friend.

"Pierre..." he said quietly "Think about this very carefully."

"What is there to think about my brother?" said Pierre with a wide grin. "I can live without eyesight in one eye..."

"Pierre..." said Samuel "What these people are doing to us is appalling. In fact, it's disgusting. Can you not see that? Think about it, please."

"Oh I've thought about it, my brother!" said Pierre "I have told the doctor I am ready. I can smell the ocean already and soon I will be eating paella in Spain!"

Chapter Twelve: Green.

I walked with Genevieve through the archway and into the hustle and bustle of the souk. The lights in the darkened alleyways had been turned on, making the thousands of metal trinkets on sale glow like gold and silver. The air was filled with the aroma of spices and still, there was no let-up in human and animal traffic. It was a relief to finally step through the heavy door into the calm and serenity of the Riad Sahari. Genevieve stopped at the reception but turned to speak to me as I passed.

"See you later, Jason..." she said with a smile.

I thanked her once again and made my way out into the courtyard. Cleverly designed subtle lighting had been turned on, bathing the entire area with a cool green glow. This, coupled with the bubbling and gurgling of the central fountain added to the atmosphere of exotic opulence.

The tables had been set for dinner and each one had a series of candles placed in the centre. I made my way to the right under the palms and headed up the two flights of stairs past the now-empty pool deck. Finally, I stepped into the cool of my suite and lay on the bed feeling tired. The laptop was still on the duvet next to me and I opened it to check my emails. It turned out there was one marked urgent from Diane at the insurance company. I clicked on it to see there was a file attached with about 30 pages of text. I stared at the ceiling and blinked my stinging eyes deciding I would print the file rather than read it on the screen.

Stepping out onto the small veranda I could see the lights and roofs of the old city stretching away into the distance. The call to prayer sounded and echoed eerily in the darkness as I lit a cigarette and stared up at the stars as they began to prick through the black shroud of the night sky. Still feeling tired from the long day I took a shower, picturing in my mind the golden artefacts being dug out of the caves as I stood under the powerful jets of hot water.

It was just before 7.00 pm when I saved the file on the email to a flash stick and made my way downstairs to the reception. The manager on duty led me to a business centre down a corridor where I printed and bound the file for reading later.

Finally, I made my way out into the courtyard and chose a table near the waterfall for dinner. Several guests were eating at the time and I ordered a beer from a waiter as I browsed the menu. I settled on the B'ssara soup followed by the Kefta tagine. Both were excellent and I washed this down with two more beers. As I sat back to smoke after the meal the young porter, Omar, approached me.

"Good evening Mr Green," he said with a smile "How is your stay so far?"

"Very good thanks, Omar..." I replied, "I have no complaints at all."

"Excellent," he said with a grin and a wink of his left eye "Please remember, do call me if you need anything. Anything at all. You have my card..."

"Yes I have your card" I replied feeling slightly bemused as I reached for the ashtray. "I'll be sure to remember that."

I watched as the young man made his way back to the reception. *What is he referring to? Anything at all? Certainly can't be prostitutes. Not in Morocco. Must be hashish. Looks like the youngster has a sideline. Cheeky little bastard.* I shook my head and smiled at the young man's entrepreneurial spirit. It was impossible not to like him.

I glanced at the pile of papers I had printed lying on the table and decided to head up to my room to read them. It had been a long day. But as I was on my way back to the stairwell I saw Genevieve. She had been sitting having dinner alone at a table in the corner of the courtyard and it was clear that neither of us had any idea that we had dined at the same time. She wore an elegant evening dress that shimmered in the green light and her blonde hair freed from the ponytail now hung long and full around her naked shoulders.

The transformation from her field clothes was more than surprising and I realised then how extraordinarily beautiful she was.

"Jason..." she said as she saw me "Have you been here all along?"

"Yes," I replied, "I just had some dinner at a table near the fountain."

"Oh, that's a shame," she said "Sorry, I had no idea. We could have had dinner together."

"Another time perhaps..." I said.

I watched as a frown formed on her forehead.

"Will you join me for a glass of wine?" she asked "I have discovered an excellent Merlot from Tuscany."

I looked down at the large glass on her table. It was still half full and she ran her finger down the stem as if to tempt me.

"Sure..." I said, pulling out the seat opposite her. "Why not?"

She motioned to a waiter who was standing nearby and spoke in French as she ordered more of the wine. The waiter returned within minutes and filled our glasses. The wine was indeed superb with hints of black cherry, vanilla, and mocha. Relaxed from the meal and the wine, Genevieve sat back twisting the stem of her glass slowly on the crisp cotton of the tablecloth as she spoke.

"So, Jason..." she said "Tell me about yourself."

"There's not a lot to tell really," I said as I lit another cigarette. "As I'm sure you know, I'm with the insurance company. My trip out here was a bit rushed but I've been asked to take a look at the security arrangements."

"Ah, yes..." she said as a small frown formed on her forehead. "The unfortunate incident of the missing ingots and artefacts."

"That's right," I said taking another sip of wine.

I tapped the file of papers I had just printed which lay on the table in front of me.

"My head office in London has just sent me some more reading material. I guess my next set of instructions will be in here."

"Well..." she said "I'm here to assist you in anything you wish to see or do. You have full access to every part of our operation. You just have to say the word."

"Thank you, Gen. I appreciate it. Your work is fascinating..."

"Hmm..." she said with the same dreamy look in her eyes I had seen earlier at the dig site. "It certainly is."

The conversation continued for another 30 minutes until our glasses were emptied. Genevieve Tremblay brought her shapely hand up to her mouth and yawned.

"Excuse me, Jason. I think I'm going to head up to my room."

"No problem," I said gathering the file. "I'm going to do the same thing."

We both stood and I walked behind her as she made her way to the stairwell. The elegant evening dress hugged her shapely figure and the muscles in her back stood proud from her straight spine.

"Are you staying in this wing of the hotel as well?" she asked turning to me as she walked.

"I am..." I replied, "On the second floor."

"We're almost neighbours in that case," she said smiling with a flash of perfectly white teeth. "I'm on the first floor."

It was when we arrived at the pool deck level that she stopped and turned to speak once again.

"Good night, Jason..." she said quietly.

"Good night, Gen" I replied with a smile and a polite tilt of my head.

She walked a short distance down the corridor and opened her room with a key card from her dainty handbag. Once again I was struck by the transformation from the tough, hyperactive field archaeologist I had met earlier to the polished and graceful woman I had just been sitting with. I glanced up the stairwell and realised that my suite was directly above hers. *So near but so far, Green. So near but so far.*

By the time I made it into my room I was dog tired and I lay down on the bed to read the file I had just printed. As expected it was a series of instructions detailing the next part of the assignment. It turned out that stolen ingots and artefacts had gone missing from the secure warehouse in Marrakesh. This was at least the theory of the insurance firm but it was clear that a lot more work was necessary to confirm this. The security procedures I had witnessed at the dig site were thorough but by no means foolproof. My eyelids began to droop as I read and I placed the file on the bed next to me. *One more cigarette and then it's time to go to sleep, Green.* I yawned deeply and stood up to walk out onto the small balcony. The night air was cool and there was a soft breeze coming in from the South. As I lit the cigarette I heard the music. At first distant and muffled, it grew in volume and clarity as I listened. It was the sound of a single violin and a tune that I recognized immediately as the theme from the movie, Schindler's List.

It was a sad and haunting sound played with emotion and intensity, and this was no recording. The music was being played live. Of that, there was no doubt. The exquisite music was coming from below and I leant over the steel railings to try and ascertain where it was coming from. It was then that I saw the tall figure of Genevieve silhouetted in the reflection of her balcony door below. She stood barefoot, a metre from the doorway, clad only in a silk nightdress. She held the neck of the violin in her left hand with her head slightly tilted, her jaw touching the chin rest of the instrument.

Her head and upper body swayed gently to the sombre tones of the music and she played with her eyes closed as if in a trance. I stood there transfixed at the sound and vision of beauty in the reflection of the door below but all too soon the piece was over and Genevieve disappeared back into her room.

"My, my..." I whispered to myself as crushed out the cigarette and headed back into my room.

Chapter Thirteen: Samuel.

It had been three days since Pierre Lumumba had visited the doctor and agreed to go through with his procedure. During this time he had paced the cell constantly telling Samuel what he planned to do when he arrived in Spain. The day after he announced that he was going, he was again taken to the doctor and told when he was to leave for the medical facility in Tangier. That day was today. Pierre had tried and tried again to convince Samuel to join him but he had remained steadfast. His morals, scruples and Christianity would not allow him to go through with it.

Samuel felt a degree of happiness that his friend actually believed he was going, and late at night when Pierre finally slept, he had prayed for his safety in whatever awaited him. Of course, there was always the possibility that all would be well and Pierre would have his operation successfully and actually get to Spain. *Yes, that would be wonderful for him.* But he had a sneaking suspicion that all was not as it seemed. That, and the brutal and inhuman way they had been held to ransom in that stinking hellhole. Held with no real recourse or way of escape other than to agree to some barbaric and almost medieval procedure.

At 9.00 am sharp two guards arrived. One of them was the tall one, Uday. He stood there with a cigar clamped between his teeth and a permanent grin on his face as he stared at the seated figure of Samuel.

"Good afternoon, Mr Baboon," he said with a sneer. "Why are you not going to Spain with your friend?"

At that moment Samuel relived the seething rage he had felt that fateful night on the boat when he had been separated from his beloved daughter Lucia. Samuel glanced at the FN machine gun and he had to physically fight the urge to leap from his bunk and rip the man to pieces with his bare hands. Uday's glaring and unwarranted hatred was like a laser beam burning into Samuel's very soul. Instead, Samuel set there placidly and watched as Pierre readied himself to leave while gathering up his meagre possessions.

A minute later, Pierre stood up to say goodbye.

"My brother," he said shaking his head with a sad smile "I wish you well. Thank you for your companionship. We will stay in touch on Facebook."

Samuel climbed down from his concrete bunk and shook hands with the young man.

"I will pray for you, my brother," said Samuel "God speed and safe travels."

Samuel watched as Pierre was led from the cell and taken down the corridor to the right. Uday was left and he stepped forward to lock the cell door once again. After doing so he stood there grinning at Samuel while chewing the cigar in his teeth. With the FN rifle strapped to his shoulder, he taunted Samuel once again by waving his arms around like a monkey.

"Goodbye, Mr Baboon!" he said before laughing and walking off.

Chapter Fourteen: Green.

I glanced at my watch to see it had just gone 7.20 am. The bright morning sun shone through the glass patio doors onto the wooden surface of the desk where I sat drinking coffee and reading from the file I had printed the previous evening. I had awoken at 6.30 am with the memory of hearing and seeing Genevieve playing the violin in the reflection of her patio door below. I could still hear the sublime tones of the instrument in my ears and the memory had stayed with me as I took a long shower. I had tried to read the new file as I lay down on the bed the previous night but exhaustion had overtaken me and I had fallen asleep with the papers on my chest.

However, my instructions were clear. I was to be taken to the main storage facility in Marrakesh where the world-famous Zukman Hoard was being held. There was further mention that it was suspected that the missing artefacts and gold ingots had been stolen from here. I was to take a detailed look at the security arrangements there and report back to head office later in the day. At exactly 7.30 am there was a shrill electronic ring from the telephone on the desk. I lifted the receiver wondering who would call at such an hour.

"Hello?" I said into the mouthpiece.

"Good morning, Jason..." said the female voice on the other end. "It's Genevieve. Hope you slept well?"

"Hi Gen" I replied, thinking immediately of the violin. "Very well, thanks."

"Great!" she replied enthusiastically "I believe I am to take you to the main storage vault in the city today. I wanted to check if you'd be ready to leave at say, 9.30?"

"Yes..." I replied. "I got the same instructions. That sounds perfect."

"Meet you at the reception then?"

"Sure..." I replied, "I'll see you there at 9.30 sharp."

We said our goodbyes and I hung up the phone. Grabbing my cup of coffee I opened the glass door to step out onto the patio for my first cigarette of the day. The air was fresh and crisp and in the background, I could hear the hustle and bustle of the old city as the new day began. The curved orange and terracotta roof tiles on the roofs of the ancient buildings stretched away below me and in the distance, I could see the jagged peaks of the High Atlas range. The mountains had a blue tinge to them while their snow-capped peaks resembled the creamy white tips of ice cream cones. The sky was perfectly blue and the sun was warm on my skin. *Not such a bad day at the office, Green.* I thought as I lit the cigarette. At that moment I noticed the young porter, Omar crossing the tiles on the pool deck below. He glanced up at me, smiled and waved.

"Good morning, Mr Green!" he said.

"Morning, Omar..." I said as I exhaled a plume of smoke.

The young man winked and brought his hand up to his ear and held it there as if he was clutching a phone.

"Yes..." I said, "I'll call you if I need anything."

The young man smiled again and I watched as he made his way down the stairs towards the courtyard below. *Cheeky little bastard.* I thought with a smile. When I was done I walked back into the room and ordered a full English breakfast from room service. I sat at the desk in the sunlight as I waited and went over the papers once again. In my mind, I went through the processes I had seen the previous day at the dig site. There was no doubt it was an extremely thorough and well-run operation. I recalled the site manager securing the load of the armoured van with numbered zip ties.

The security company providing the transport of the goods from the dig site to the city was world-class and I was sure the handover at the storage facility would be thorough. *There will be a weak point in the chain, Green. There has to be. Keep watching and you'll see it.*

My breakfast was delivered by a waiter pushing a trolley not long afterwards and I watched the news on the television as I ate. It was at 9.15 when the phone rang once again. It turned out to be Diane calling from the head office in London.

"Hi Jason..." she said sounding somewhat anxious. "How's it going there? Is everything going to plan?"

I replied telling her that I had visited the dig site as arranged the previous day and had received my instructions for the day ahead.

"Do you think you might be able to get us your initial impressions of the situation soon?" she asked "The top brass are quite edgy about it all..."

I replied telling her I would email later with an initial assessment of the overall security but explained the complexity of the processes and the fact that I would need some time to form an opinion on where and how the leaks were occurring. This seemed to satisfy her and we said our goodbyes.

It was 9.25 am when I grabbed my identification card and cameras, left the room and made my way downstairs to the courtyard. Several guests were eating at tables near the central fountain, with groups of tiny, colourful Mousierre's Redstart birds tweeting in the shaded fronds of the palm trees above. The gurgling water of the fountain was crystal clear and the green and white tiles surrounding it had been mopped and cleaned until they sparkled. I made my way through the lush gardens and into the reception to find Genevieve standing with her back to me chatting to the hotel manager.

She wore similar khaki field clothes with her usual tool belt around her waist and her long blonde hair pulled back into a ponytail. She turned as I walked in and greeted me with a wide smile. Although she wore no makeup at all, I could see the radiant beauty in her face. It had been something I had been unsure of when I had first met her but I realized then how exquisite she actually was.

"Hi, Jason!" she said "Are you ready to go?"

"Yup..." I said, "Let's do it."

Chapter Fifteen: The Road To Freedom.

Twenty-five-year-old Pierre Lumumba was feeling a mixture of elation and excited anticipation as the black Toyota people carrier sped through the desert towards the port city of Tangier. Since leaving the cell, his belongings and every cent of what remained of his money had been returned to him. It seemed certain that his freedom had been restored and along with that, his human dignity. It felt good to be wearing his own clothes again which had been laundered and pressed to perfection. Even the fake Nike trainers he had treasured so much had been cleaned and fitted with new laces. After all the weeks of inexplicable detention, he now felt he was finally being treated like a human being again. Even the guard who sat in the front seat next to the driver was relaxed and making jokes with him. There was also music from the vehicle's radio and an endless supply of snacks and Coca Cola.

Soon after his belongings had been returned to him, he had been taken to see the kindly doctor who had helped him. There he had been told what to expect when he arrived in Tangier. The doctor had been calm and reassuring and had quickly allayed any worries that he had had about the minor medical procedure he was to have the following day.

Pierre smiled and looked out through the window at the desert landscape. The late afternoon light and the tinted windows gave it a blue-grey tinge. But along with this feeling of exuberance, there was a certain melancholy and sadness that he had left his friend and cellmate, Samuel, back at the detention centre in Marrakesh. Pierre Lumumba frowned and shook his head. *Why had he been so adamant that he would remain there and not join him? Why had he not grasped the opportunity and taken the simple, quick and easy way out like him?* Pierre took a deep breath and reached for the can of Coke he had stored in the sidewall of the door. The drink was sweet and cold and it tingled as it went down his throat. It was 5.30 pm and some four hours after leaving Marrakesh that they approached the port city of Tangier. Pierre's excitement grew as they entered the rush hour traffic and made their way through the outskirts of the city towards the ocean front road near the port.

He watched as the vehicle passed the rows of plush hotels and restaurants on his left. To his right was the ocean and not far from the shoreline was his destination. Spain. To Pierre, it was now so close. Almost within touching distance, and the very thought of it filled him with a thrilling buzz of euphoria. It was dusk by the time they arrived at the ocean front hotel that was to be Pierre's home for the next few days. By that time the pink and blue neon lights at the front of the posh looking establishment were illuminated. Pierre Lumumba never imagined that he would ever stay in such a wonderful place. The guard in the front passenger placed his pistol in the cubbyhole and turned to speak.

"Well, Mr Lumumba," he said "Here we are. We can now go and check-in..."

Leaving the driver parked at the front, Pierre grabbed his only bag and the two climbed out of the vehicle and made their way up the steps into the grand entrance. A smartly dressed concierge greeted them and swung open a heavy glass door for them to enter. Pierre and the guard made their way across the carpeted foyer to the reception where once again they were greeted politely by the hotel staff. The guard completed the check-in process talking in Arabic to the receptionist as he filled in the necessary forms. The paperwork took less than five minutes and a porter arrived to carry Pierre's bag. At first, this alarmed him, but the guard smiled and spoke.

"It's fine. This is his job. You are a guest here."

Pierre reluctantly handed his bag to the young man and he and the guard followed him across the foyer to the lifts. The porter pushed a button and the polished aluminium doors opened silently. The three men stepped inside and the doors closed behind them. Pierre Lumumba had never been in an elevator. His home in rural Cameroon had been nothing but a simple and peaceful village until the rebels had come and slaughtered half of the people. The walls of the lift were mirrored and there was a whisper from the air conditioning. This was another wonder Pierre had never experienced.

Soon the doors opened again and the three men stepped out into the corridor. Pierre's room was opened with another wondrous device known as a key card. The interior was as luxurious as many he had seen on television but unlike anything he had ever seen in real life.

He followed the porter around as he was shown the many facilities and the curtains were opened to reveal a majestic view of the ocean frontage. Finally, the guard paid the porter a small tip and the two men were left alone.

"Well, Mr Lumumba..." said the guard "This is where we part company. You are free to order as much food and drink as you like while you are here."

He pointed to the desk where there was a telephone and a black leather file.

"The menu is there by the phone," he said with a smile. "But there are two very important things you must not do..."

"What is that?" asked Pierre.

"You must not leave the hotel for any reason..." said the guard, his face now serious. "Also, you must not eat anything at all tomorrow morning. Doing so can complicate the mild anaesthetic you will be given by the doctors. I will collect you and take you to sign the forms in the morning, then afterwards we will go to the medical facility for the procedure. This will only take a few hours and you will be brought back here afterwards. Your money will be given to you in United States $100 bills. You should rest here for 48 hours and then you will be free to make the crossing over to Spain on any night you choose. You will be given a phone number to call when you feel you are fit to make the journey. Call that number when you are ready, and you will be collected and taken to the boat that evening. That is all, but these instructions are important..."

"No problem..." said Pierre cheerfully "I understand."

The guard stepped forward and smiled as he offered his hand.

"See you tomorrow," he said.

"Thank you, sir," said Pierre as he shook the man's hand vigorously. "Thank you!"

Finally, Pierre was left alone. He put his hands on his hips and smiled broadly as he looked around the plush hotel room once again. He picked up the television remote, found a music channel and turned up the volume. Next, he walked up to the large bay windows and stared out at the now dark ocean. *This is amazing! Soon I will cross that short stretch of water and I will be free!* Pierre turned and looked at the large flat-screen television. He brought his hand up and covered his left eye as he imagined what his vision would be like after the procedure. *It's perfectly fine!* He thought. *I can see everything!* Then he walked over to the desk and browsed the menu. He made a call to room service and ordered three cheeseburgers and a large portion of chips. Another wonder he took great pleasure in. Finally, Pierre stretched out on the comfortable bed and lay with his hands behind his head. *Yes!* He thought. *This is just perfect.*

Chapter Sixteen: The Storage Facility.

I followed Genevieve through the reception and out of the hotel door into the now familiar but ever-bustling souk. A number of the locals recognized us as residents of the hotel and were not overly aggressive in attempting to lure us into their stalls and shops, but of course, there were still a few persistent ones who were determined to make a sale no matter what. Eventually, we made it through the hustle and chaos and out into the sunlight. Apart from the usual pedestrian and animal traffic, an old woman was sitting against the ancient wall to the left. Emaciated and blind, she wore tattered rags and rattled a rusty tin cup as she wailed forlornly, begging for coins.

Finally, we made it to the grand archway and crossed the busy street. As usual, the traffic was heavy with cars, motorbikes and horse-drawn carts and carriages. The group of porters who waited under the giant Argania tree were greeted as usual by Gen as we climbed into the Land Rover to make our way to the storage facility. Just like the previous day, Gen was full of energy and enthusiasm. She revved the engine and did a quick U-turn onto the street resulting in a lot of hooting and general chaos. She smiled cheekily as she changed gear and sped off.

"So, Jason..." she said "We are going to the main storage facility today. It is on the outskirts of the city in an industrial site and it houses all of the treasures we have found since we began the excavations."

"Apart from the stolen ones..." I said quietly.

She raised eyebrows from behind her sunglasses and a flush of red ran up her neck.

"Yes," she said "Apart from those, sadly..."

Her enthusiasm returned immediately and she went on.

"The vault was specially built within the Zukman Group premises. Of course, it's climate-controlled and has all of the security one would expect for such an important collection."

Okay. I thought. *Well, I guess it makes sense given the land where the discovery was made is owned by the company. But why was there no insistence on there being an independent storage facility? Perhaps one of the banks or government buildings would have been better suited?*

"Do you have any idea why the storage facility was built on the premises of the Zukman Group?" I asked.

She shrugged her shoulders once again and shook her head.

"I guess it was an arrangement between the department of antiquities and the Zukman Group..." she said as she overtook a taxi. "It was done before I arrived. I'm not too sure, Jason."

I accepted this explanation and gazed out of the window at the passing buildings. Some 10 minutes later we left the tidy and orderly part of the city and entered what appeared to be the outskirts of an industrial site.

Here the buildings were shabby looking and there were no longer any grass verges and palm trees. Up ahead I saw the factories and chimneys and I immediately noticed there was a lot more motorcycle traffic.

"No tourists here..." I commented.

"No," said Gen "This is the Sidi Ghanem industrial zone. You won't see many tourists here. Just a lot of trucks and motorcycles as you can see."

I nodded as I watched the chaotic scenes ahead while we travelled deeper into the area. Eventually, we came upon a tall orange coloured wall to our left. It seemed to stretch ahead for at least 400 metres and was topped with lines of electric fencing. We were slowed down by an open truck moving slowly in front of us. Loaded with live sheep, it trundled along with its steel livestock cage bars rattling noisily in their sockets.

Genevieve tapped the steering wheel impatiently as the vehicle slowed further and indicated it was turning left. I looked ahead to the gate it was turning into and immediately noticed a large painted sign on either side that read 'Zukman Group'.

The entrance to the premises was paved with heavy-duty interlocking concrete pavers to cater for heavy vehicle traffic. It appeared we had arrived. The truck turned and stopped at the gate boom and I noticed several motorcycles leaving the premises through the exit at the same time. There was also a distinct, animal smell of an abattoir in the air.

"Shift change at the factory..." said Gen.

I nodded as I looked inside and noticed a refrigerated lorry making its way out as well.

"Busy looking place..." I said.

"It sure is," said Gen.

Finally, we were able to speed up once again and we drove on for another 300 metres with the same tall orange wall to our left.

Eventually, Genevieve slowed the vehicle and indicated she was about to turn left as well. Up ahead was what was clearly the corporate entrance to the facility. There was a central guardhouse with tinted windows and a large yellow and white boom at both the entrance and exit. Painted on huge signs on either side of the entrance were the words 'Zukman Group'.

Genevieve turned left into the entrance and pulled up near the guardhouse. The tinted window was pulled aside and a uniformed guard with a peaked hat leaned out to greet us. I handed my identification card to Genevieve who in turn handed both of ours to the guard. He examined them and typed our names into a computer. Then I noticed him turning to look at my face. He glanced at the card once again then picked up a phone. I could not hear what he said to whoever was on the other side of the line but the conversation was quick. *Looks like they were expecting me.* I thought. The cards were handed back to us and the mechanical boom was lifted.

Genevieve drove slowly into the corporate headquarters of The Zukman Group. Ahead of us was a wide, modern double storey building painted in the same orange colour as the perimeter wall. Again, the building had tinted windows and a flat roof. To the front of the building was a large rectangular fish pond with a fountain in the centre of a similar style to the ones found in most Moroccan riads. On either side of the pond were rows of shaded car parks surrounded by neatly manicured lawns. It looked to me like a standard corporate head office one might find in any country.

To the left, in the distance, I could see the factories I had noticed when we had driven past the service entrance. It made sense, given the noise and smell, that the head office would be separated from the working end of the operation. Between these two sections was a squat, flat-topped and windowless building surrounded by green lawns and an electric fence. *That'll be it, I guess.*

"Well, Jason," said Gen as she pulled into a parking space "Here we are. I'm sure you know that The Zukman Group is a meat processing company. They have vast tracts of livestock grazing land all over Morocco and are the largest wholesale meat suppliers in the country."

"Yes..." I replied, gazing around the complex "I read about it in my files. I can smell it in the air..."

"That's from the abattoir," she said pointing at the factory buildings to our left. "They also have major facilities in Algeria and Egypt. The building you see in between is the storage facility we have come to see today."

"Quite a big operation..." I said as she cut the engine.

"Yes, it is," she said. "I believe they're the biggest meat processing company in North Africa. Well, shall we go on in?"

We both climbed out of the vehicle and walked down the paved walkway towards the office building in the fierce sunshine. I looked into the pond as we passed it and saw several prize Japanese Koi fish swimming around lazily.

From the pristine gardens, palm trees, and immaculate buildings, it was clear there was no shortage of money in the meat business in Morocco. We climbed a set of stairs and two automatic doors opened as we entered the cool interior of the reception. The floors were marbled and soft classical music played in the background. The large room had a high ceiling and at the centre stood a huge abstract statue in the form of a rearing horse fashioned from wrought iron. Once again it was clear to me that this was a thriving and extremely profitable business. Two young Moroccan men in immaculate black suits were waiting for us near the sandstone reception desk. As we entered they walked up and greeted us warmly. I shook hands with each in turn as they introduced themselves. Once the introductions were made, we were invited outside into the sunshine once again. The men paused near the fish pond and the taller of the two spoke.

"Mr Green..." he said with a smile "Allow me to familiarise you with our premises before we make our way to the storage facility."

"Sure..." I replied.

"Behind us, as I'm sure you gathered, is our head office. At the far end of the property to our right is our main abattoir and processing plant."

I turned to look at the distant buildings and once again I could smell the bloody, slightly metallic odour of raw meat. There was also the faint sound of band saws and other butchery machinery in the distance. The man went on.

"When the great discovery was made, and the significance and scale of it became apparent, The Zukman Group, with the cooperation of the Moroccan department of antiquities commissioned the building you see between where we are standing and the factory complex. That building houses our vault and this is where our national treasures are stored once they are processed by the archaeological team."

The young man was enthusiastic and proud of his involvement in the discovery and the company as a whole. I liked him immediately.

"Now..." he said "If you are ready, we will go and check-in through security and we can show you the world-famous Zukman Hoard."

Genevieve stood there in the sun with her hands on her hips and a half-smile on her face. Her hair glowed like strands of silk and although she had obviously seen it many times, I could tell she was excited.

"Sure..." I said, "I'm looking forward to seeing it."

We made our way down a paved pathway between the green

lawns and palm trees towards the building. As we walked, the young man who had done most of the talking went on to tell us about the historical significance and astounding value of the discovery. He noted that it had now become a national treasure as well as being one of the most important global archaeological events in decades.

The excitement was real and I found that even my own need for a cigarette was being rapidly negated by the prospect of what I was about to see. We followed the pathway until we reached the boundary of the building near the electric fence and turned left to follow the route around to the entrance. It was as we turned the corner and headed towards the front that I saw him. There was no mistaking his tall, wiry stature and hawkish, sneering features. It was the guard who had been watching me the day before at the dig site. The same one who had followed us around from the site entrance at the road to the excavations and thereafter until we left. I had forgotten about him until that moment but it all came back to me rapidly. It was the man Genevieve had greeted as we had entered the dig site. The man she had called Uday. He stood there near the steel entrance gate in his same uniform, FN machine gun strapped to his shoulder. Another armed guard in the same uniform stood near him with a slightly bored look on his face. Although Uday had no cigar at the time, the sneer on his face was still there and for some reason, the very sight of him sent shivers down my spine. From behind my sunglasses, I watched the man as I turned my head and pretended to listen to the young man who was talking animatedly as he led us towards the gate.

As we arrived I removed my sunglasses and looked Uday in the eye for the first time. I held his gaze for a split second longer than I should have and I saw the slight flinch in his thin, sun-bronzed face. The second guard typed in a code on the keypad on the steel gate and a loud electronic buzzer sounded as the lock disengaged.

Leaving Uday and the other guard at the gate, we were led across a thin perimeter and into yet another reception area. The room was cool and quiet with the same marble floors as the head office. I immediately noticed the security cameras that had been placed in the corners of the room facing the entrance. Sitting behind a tiled reception desk to the right were yet another two guards. They stood and smiled politely as we approached them but their faces left me in no doubt as to their qualifications. These were hard ex-police or military men with an extremely important job to do.

Genevieve, myself and the two young men from head office handed them our identification cards and one of the guards set to work typing our details into a computer. We waited as our tour guide went on to proudly tell us how the building had been commissioned in record time and was built to be totally impregnable.

Finally, the security formalities were completed and our cards were handed back to us. One of the guards walked around from behind the reception and invited us to follow him down a short corridor towards what looked like an airport metal detector. Here we were all asked to remove any metal objects and place them in a series of plastic trays. The process took less than a minute and when we were done I handed the guard my cameras so he could return them to me once we had passed through the metal detector.

I half expected him to protest but he took it without question. Clearly, he had been told before our arrival that I was to be allowed to take it into the vault. The four of us passed through the metal detector without any problem and the guard handed back my cameras before leading us down another short corridor to the large, rectangular vault door. In the centre of the heavy grey steel door was a large chrome wheel. Above this was yet another camera with a flashing red light next to it. The guard stepped to the left of the door and lifted a telephone receiver that hung next to a miniature flat television screen set into the concrete wall.

He spoke a few words in Arabic to a nameless face on the screen and then typed yet another code into a nearby keypad. Suddenly the chrome wheel in the centre of the door began to spin slowly in an anti-clockwise motion and I saw Genevieve twitch slightly and snatch a sharp intake of breath with excitement. Finally, the guard stepped forward and pulled at the heavy steel door using the chrome wheel. It swung open to the right on its huge hinges revealing a stark, brightly lit room beyond. The young man who had brought us to the building smiled and beckoned Genevieve and me to enter with his right hand.

"After you..." he said quietly.

The room was 20 by 20 metres in size with plain concrete walls and a ceiling made of the same. The floor was clad in neat white ceramic tiles and bright neon lights ran along every section of the roof. The lights were so bright I felt my eyes ache slightly as they adjusted from the comparative dim of the reception and the corridors. Near the ceiling on each wall were small air conditioning ducts with heavy steel bars set into the concrete. Their size was such that not even a small child could get through them. As expected, there were cameras placed at each corner of the room and they too flashed red as their motion detectors were activated by our presence. There were three rows of shelving running down the length of the room on each side. To the centre of the space were two long concrete tables that also ran the length of the space. They appeared to be covered with green felt. At first, the sight was somewhat underwhelming but as I stepped to the left and looked down the length of the room I saw that only half of it had been filled so far.

The rows of shelving and tables nearest where I stood were bare but the second part of the building was crammed with glittering objects. A tingle ran down my spine as I realized the true scale of it.

"Well, Jason..." said Genevieve. "There we have it."

She stepped forward and began walking along the space between the table to the left and the first row of shelving. I followed feeling slightly awed as we approached the section of the building that had been filled so far.

The sight of it all was staggering at first and I was rendered speechless as I took it all in. There were literally thousands of items ranging from tiny pieces of jewellery and beads to massive silver chargers and platters. There were gem-encrusted goblets and daggers, golden shields and silver hilted swords. There were rows upon rows of intricately designed ceramic pots and earthenware alongside piles of thousands of gold and silver coins. One shelf alone housed several hundred golden decanters, teapots and cups while another was filled with fantastic statues and figurines. Alongside all of this were thousands of pieces of cutlery and priceless pots of gemstones and rubies. Glittering bangles and headpieces stood alongside funerary wares and strange-looking religious artefacts. I took my eyes from the spectacle around me and looked at Genevieve as she walked slowly in front of me. She turned to check my reaction and her expression was one of pure elation and rapture.

"What do you think?" she asked quietly as she studied my face.

"I think I'm going to need some time to take this all in..." I replied truthfully.

She nodded knowingly and walked on. We spent the next 10 minutes wandering through the shelves on both sides of the room. Genevieve pointed out items of specific interest while speaking in whispers. The two young men who had brought us to the vault stood quietly and politely near the door and allowed us free reign as we wandered the aisles.

Finally, Genevieve led me to the rows of concrete tables in the centre of the room. Laid out along their tops were 40 modern steel crates the size of ammunition boxes. None had locks and Genevieve paused near one of them to allow me to catch up with her.

"This should impress you, Jason," she said, lifting the hinged lid of one of them.

The box was filled to the brim with thumb-sized gold ingots. Perfectly rectangular in shape, each had the design of an eagle in flight stamped onto it.

I stared at them and tried to imagine the weight of the single box. The ingots were as fresh and shiny as if they had been cast only the day before. Leaving the lid of the box open, Genevieve led me further down the row of tables to the next set of boxes. She lifted the lid of one to reveal it was just as full, this time with silver ingots. The stamp in each was the same.

"My God..." I said quietly "This is unbelievable."

"And to think we still have another one and a half caves to excavate..." she replied. "These we know exist, there could be more."

I shook my head and took a deep breath. *Do your job, Green. Concentrate. Get on with taking the photographs and videos. This is not a tourist trip to a museum.*

"Well..." I said, "As much as I'd like to stay for hours just looking at this collection, I'd better get on with my photographs."

"Of course," said Genevieve "Please go ahead. I'll just wander around while you get on with it."

I took one final look at the rows of steel crates of gold and silver ingots and spoke.

"Right..." I said, "Let me do that."

It was at that moment that I heard someone clear their throat at the door to the vault. I turned to see the guard, Uday, had arrived and was standing near the door with our hosts, watching us. He was without his gun and I immediately assumed he was not allowed to bring it past the metal detector. *Ignore him, Green.* I began taking pictures of the room from every possible angle. I gave special emphasis to the air conditioning ducts above and the walls behind the artefacts on the shelving units that stood against them. I moved down each and every aisle taking photographs and videos in 4K as I went. The lighting in the room was so bright I knew the clarity would be perfect.

The exercise took a full ten minutes and all the while I was aware of the glare of Uday burning a hole in the back of my head. Finally, I did a last round of the perimeter of the room taking a video with a wide-angle setting on the camera. I held the camera at chest level knowing it would capture exactly what I was seeing, so my own eyes were free to roam. As I arrived at the far left corner of the room between the first and second rows of shelves, I noticed something.

The entire floor of the room had been set with large white ceramic tiles similar to the ones seen in most modern medical facilities. I realized then that I had not given them much attention but something caught my eye as I approached. The thin line of grouting between the tiles was a standard pale grey colour throughout, but in the far left corner, there was a small section that appeared ever so slightly different. It was barely visible, but it seemed somehow, to be a shade darker than the rest. The section of floor was roughly 1-metre square and the grouting to the centre tiles was exactly the same as the rest of the room. But it was the grouting around this square metre section that caught my eye. *That's a bit unusual.* Fully aware I was being watched and not wanting to draw attention to the fact that I had spotted it, I stopped and lifted a silver goblet from the shelf nearby. As I did so, I dropped my right hand that held the camera and rotated it slightly to capture this anomaly on video. I stood there for 30 seconds pretending to study the goblet, then placed it back on the shelf and took a further set of photographs of it.

I moved off casually and spent the next five minutes taking more photographs of the concrete roof of the building. Finally, I joined Genevieve who was squatting near a shelf in the centre of the room admiring a silver and enamel amulet on a chain. She replaced the item and stood as she saw me approaching.

"Sorry, Jason," she said with a smile "I can't help admiring my work."

"Not at all..." I replied, "I must say it's quite an achievement."

"Thank you," she said "Are you finished with your inspection?"

"Yes, I think I am," I said "I may need to return at some stage but for now I think I'm done."

Genevieve took a final, wistful look around at the astonishing collection of treasures.

"Okay then..." she said "Shall we go?"

I followed her towards the vault door. The two young men from head office still stood there politely but thankfully Uday had left.

"I hope you have enjoyed seeing our collection so far, Mr Green?" said the taller of the two.

"Very much" I replied "Thank you."

"It's been a pleasure, sir," he said with a curt bow "Mr Zukman is actually in the country at the moment and is here at our head office. He is aware of your visit and I do know he is free this morning. If you have the time, perhaps you would you like to meet him?"

I glanced at Genevieve who raised her eyebrows and nodded amicably.

"Certainly..." I said, "We can do that."

"Excellent," said the young man "Shall we go?"

The four of us walked out of the vault door and waited while the guard pushed it closed and called through for it to be locked once again. The large chrome wheel spun slowly and eventually we heard the heavy bolts strike as it locked. The guard made a quick call on the telephone near the door and we made our way back towards the rows of plastic trays and the metal detector. The process took less than two minutes and we were through to the reception once again.

We made our way past the reception towards the exit and I followed from behind as Genevieve chatted to our host.

As we approached the exit to the building I saw the lurking figure of Uday once again. He stood in the sunshine with his machine gun strapped once again to shoulder and watched as we approached. His obtrusive and arrogant attitude had grated me by then and I felt my anger rising slowly. The doors slid open and I followed Genevieve and our two hosts out into the sunshine towards the perimeter gate. Pretending to fiddle with the bracelet of my Omega watch, I paused at the exit less than a metre from where Uday stood leaning against the wall. Without looking at him I spoke.

"What seems to be the problem?" I asked quietly.

"Problem?" he replied in perfect English "There is no problem..."

"Oh, I think there is..." I said.

At that moment Genevieve had arrived at the exit gate and turned to look for me. She immediately saw I was struggling with my watch. I pulled the sunglasses from my pocket and put them on my face. Again, without looking at the tall man who stood near me, I spoke.

"I see you, Uday..." I said quietly as I walked off into the blazing sunshine.

Chapter Seventeen: Pierre Lumumba.

———•❦•———

Apart from some mild heartburn from the vast quantities of food and soft drink he had consumed the night before, Pierre Lumumba awoke feeling happy and rested. He stretched his body and yawned lazily on the comfortable bed as he reached for the remote control for the television. The large flat screen flashed into life and the luxurious hotel room was filled with rap music from the same channel he had been watching when he had finally fallen asleep. On the tables at either side of the bed were the remnants of his many calls to room service. Piles of plates, glasses and empty cans littered both and he smiled at the memory of such unlimited indulgence. It had been something he had never experienced and he was eagerly looking forward to more. He glanced at the telephone and the room service menu nearby but then remembered the warning he had been given by the guard the previous evening.

'You must not eat anything at all tomorrow morning. Doing so can complicate the mild anaesthetic you will be given by the doctors.' He had said.

The man had been clear and had made a special effort to warn him about this. The memory of this conversation caused a slight twinge of concern and worry in Pierre Lumumba's mind. He sat up and burped loudly as he did so. This immediately cleared his heartburn as he stood up and walked across the room to open the curtains. It had been dark when he had arrived and he was eager to take a look at the view that lay beyond the hotel front. The morning was clear and bright and there was not a single cloud in the North African sky. Across the road, the rippling, vibrant blue waters of the Mediterranean sea stretched out to the horizon and several working and leisure boats bobbed around lazily in the harbour. Pierre Lumumba slid the large windows open and breathed in the cool sea air. Above a fishing trawler in the harbour to the right, a flock of seagulls squawked noisily as the previous night's catch of sardines was unloaded. He placed his hands on the window sill and leant out to gaze at the magnificent view. *Spain is just across those waters.* He thought.

After the procedure today, I will relax in this amazing hotel for a few days. Maybe I will take a walk and visit a few restaurants. Then, when I am ready, I will make the journey across those waters to Europe. I will arrive with a pocket full of money and I will start my new life. Pierre Lumumba took a deep breath of the cool, salty air and exhaled as a smile formed on his face.

Chapter Eighteen: Darko Zukman.

I was still bristling from the passive confrontation with Uday as we were let out of the main gate and back onto the paved pathway towards the Zukman Group head office. But the midday sun was warm on my skin and our host was entertaining and congenial as we walked and I did my best to put the tense moment out of my mind. We were led once again past the fish pond and fountain and up the stairs into the giant reception area of the building. The shorter of our two hosts bade us farewell while the other had a quick word with one of the receptionists. He returned smiling and invited Genevieve and me to follow him past the giant horse statue and up the grand set of stairs to the rear. The thick chrome bannisters on either side gleamed and the steps were fashioned from the same polished marble as the rest of the building. *Marble floors everywhere except for the vault.* At the top of the stairs, the building split into two wide corridors with yet another small reception desk at the centre. The young woman manning it was expecting us and nodded with a smile as we made our way down the corridor to the left. On either side of the corridor were large glass-walled offices with minimalist furniture and decor. The senior staff members, both male and female, working here sat at modern looking desks behind computers. A few of them averted their gazes from their screens and nodded at our host who led from the front. It was clear we were making our way towards the office at the end of the corridor which, instead of having glass frontage, was fashioned from magnificently carved marble slabs. Glorious images of horses running and musical notes set against mountainous backgrounds had been painstakingly etched into the facades on either side. To the centre of it all was a huge polished double door fashioned from solid ebony with two massive chrome handles on each. Once again I was reminded that this was the nerve centre of an extremely successful business. This was corporate opulence on a grand scale. I thought back to the pictures I had seen of the man I was about to meet and a half-smile formed on my face as I remembered that they had reminded me of the character, Jabba The Hut, from the Star Wars movies. Our host knocked twice on the door as we arrived and immediately opened the door on the right.

Genevieve and I followed the young man through into an enormous office with floor to ceiling windows at the rear that looked out onto a tropical landscaped garden with palms trees, hibiscus, birds of paradise, and bougainvillea plants. At the far end of the room was a large antique French mahogany and ormolu desk. The walls on either side of the room were entirely covered in mahogany bookshelves crammed with leather-bound books and classical statues and bronzes. On the right, near the desk, stood a plinth with a marble bust of a man atop. Clearly, it took pride of place within the office and I stared at it as I walked in. It was only when I took my eyes from the bust that I noticed the two green oxygen bottles next to the blob-like figure seated behind the desk. *Does this man have breathing problems?* The strange-looking man stood up slowly as we approached and only then did I realize how short he was. He could not have been taller than 4 feet, 8 inches and his body appeared as wide as it was tall. Wearing a black suit similar to the one I had seen in the pictures, the man began to walk slowly around the desk to greet us and as he moved I could hear his chest wheezing with each step. The man's huge bald head seemed to meet his shoulders without any neck in what instead appeared to be great, ever-widening rolls of flesh. Across his face was a broad grin that resembled the open gash of a machete wound rather than a smile. His eyes were dark and set deep within the shiny, meaty tissue of his face. It was then that our young host spoke.

"Mr Zukman," he said, "Allow me to introduce Professor Tremblay, whom you know, and Mr Jason Green."

I nodded politely at the approaching man but the sight of him was somewhat disconcerting and slightly alarming. He resembled a toad and even his eyelids seemed to be made up of folds of heavy skin. Eventually, he made it around to where Genevieve stood towering over him and offered his hand.

"Genevieve..." he said in a deep laborious voice. "Always a pleasure my dear."

Next, the man turned to me and once again I heard the gurgle in his chest as he approached.

"Mr Green," he said in a strong Serbian accent, offering his hand once again "Welcome to Morocco."

"Hello Mr Zukman," I said as I shook his hand. "It's a pleasure to meet you. Thank you."

The man's hand was small, warm and clammy even in the crisp, climate-controlled air and I felt the urge to wipe my hand on my shirt as he motioned us to sit down and turned to make his way back around the desk. Genevieve and I took our seats as the man began the long journey back around the desk to his chair. His progress was almost painful to watch and once again he puffed and wheezed as he went. I realized then why the helipad had been built at the dig site. Walking any great distance was clearly a problem for the man. Eventually, he made it back to his seat and I glanced at the marble bust on the plinth to his left.

"Ah, Mr Green..." said Zukman slowly "I see you are admiring my statue of the great Ludwig van Beethoven."

"Yes..." I replied, "I thought I recognized it."

The man smiled once again and the folds of flesh in his eyelids drooped as he blinked slowly.

"A great man indeed, Mr Green," he said "A genius..."

I smiled politely and nodded, not knowing quite how to respond. *Explains the classical music playing in the reception, I guess.*

"I would like to wish you a successful trip, Mr Green," said Zukman "Of course you will have our full cooperation in anything you wish. Are you satisfied with what you have seen so far?"

"Yes..." I replied "Although I don't think I will be done for some time. It is quite a discovery. Incredible."

The man nodded slowly and once again his entire body seemed to move as if he had no neck.

"Yes..." he replied, blinking once again "It is *quite* incredible. And may I ask if Professor Tremblay is looking after you in your endeavours?"

I turned briefly to look at Genevieve who sat with a half-smile on her face.

"Oh, yes..." I replied "She has shown me a great deal. From what I have seen so far, your security arrangements are good."

"Good..." said Zukman as he nodded slowly "Good. Yes, we are very proud of what we are doing here..."

There followed an extended and awkward period of silence during which the strange-looking man appeared to be studying me with his dark, porcine eyes. I felt the urge to shift in my seat and avert my own eyes but I held them in place and waited for him to go on.

"I believe you have visited the dig site and seen the transport arrangements, and today you visited our vault?"

"That is correct..." I replied.

"What will you be doing next?" he asked.

I shifted slightly in my seat and spoke.

"Well..." I said, raising my eyebrows "I think I might like to travel with the armoured vehicle from the dig site to the vault. Perhaps watch the finds as they are transported into the vault. I may want to visit these sites again, but after that, I'm pretty sure my work will be done."

Darko Zukman nodded slowly once again and paused.

"You can be assured of our complete cooperation as I have said, Mr Green. It has been a great pleasure to meet you and to see you again Miss Tremblay. Now, if you will forgive me, I have much work to do."

The man's mouth was downturned and he was wheezing once again.

"Of course..." I said turning to look at Genevieve "Thank you very much."

At that moment I heard our young host moving behind us. I turned in my seat to see him walking towards the door.

Genevieve and I stood up to leave.

"Forgive me for not standing..." said Zukman quietly.

"Not at all," I said "Thank you again, Mr Zukman..."

With a final smile from Genevieve, we turned and made our way towards the door. Our young host stood there and held it open as we left.

Chapter Nineteen: Pierre Lumumba.

The sharp knock on the hotel room door came at exactly 9.30 am. Not knowing exactly what to do, Pierre sat up in his comfortable bed and reduced the volume on the flat-screen television. Before he could speak, the door opened and in walked the same guard who had accompanied him on the drive from Marrakesh to Tangier the previous day. It was immediately clear to Pierre that the man's demeanour had changed. He appeared stressed and slightly anxious.

"Have you eaten or drunk anything today?" said the guard.

"No, sir..." replied Pierre "As you told me, I have not had anything at all."

"Are you sure?"

"Yes, sir..." said Pierre "I have brushed my teeth and that is all."

The guard cast his gaze around the room and noted the empty plates, bottles and cups. Pierre watched as the man visibly relaxed. It was clear that the man believed him.

"Good..." he said "Very good. You can eat and drink as much as you like after the procedure. What have you been doing? Have you left the hotel at all?"

"Not at all, sir," said Pierre "I have not even left the room."

The man nodded and finally the smile formed on his face once again. He pulled a large brown paper envelope from under his left arm, walked towards the desk, and sat down.

"Now, Pierre..." he said "We have one minor formality to complete. You were told about it I'm sure?"

"What is this formality?" asked Pierre, looking somewhat confused.

"It is the papers you must sign for the ministry of health," said the guard. "To register yourself as a donor."

Pierre Lumumba felt a twinge of anxiety. Until that moment he had forgotten about this although he had been told by the doctor that he would need to do it.

"Sorry..." said Pierre "I had forgotten about that."

He paused as he stared at the guard while he removed the papers from the envelope and placed them on the desk.

"What about the money, sir?" asked Pierre. "When will I get it?"

The guard turned in his seat and smiled warmly.

"Don't worry..." he said "I will give it to you personally on the way back here after the procedure. Everything has been arranged."

Pierre Lumumba paused and thought about the money. *A whole $5000.00 United States dollars. Money the likes of which I have never seen.*

He took a brief look around the luxurious hotel room then stood up.

"Of course..." said Pierre "Where do I sign?"

Chapter Twenty: Anomaly.

The fierce midday sun burned my skin as Genevieve and I walked down the steps past the fish ponds and fountain towards the car park of The Zukman Group head office. As I walked I struggled to come to terms with the somewhat shocking and extremely peculiar appearance of the man I had just met. *Jesus, he was ugly! A real-life troll with an egg-shaped body. That would certainly take some getting used to.* I made a conscious effort to put it out of my mind as we climbed into the Land Rover and made our way through the exit boom and back into the busy roads of the dusty, polluted industrial sprawl beyond. Feeling the urge to smoke, I stared dreamily out of the passenger window and thought about the subtle but strange change in the colour of the grouting in the floor tiles in the corner of the vault. It would have been so easy to miss had I not been scrutinizing it in such minute detail. I blinked as Genevieve swerved to avoid a moped that had strayed into our lane. *The photographs and the video will answer all of that, Green. It's probably nothing after all.*

"So, Jason..." said Genevieve "Where would you like to go now? I'm at your disposal as you know."

I glanced at my watch and remembered the urgency of the call from Diane that morning.

"I have some work to do back at the hotel, Gen," I said. "My firm is eager to hear my initial impressions of the operation, so I had better go and get on with that."

"Oh that's a pity" she replied "I was hoping you would come to the dig site again."

"I'd love to..." I said, "But sadly I don't think I'll make it today."

"Well in that case I'll head out there for the afternoon and perhaps see you later?" she said as she took a sharp and fast left turn.

"Sure..." I said, "I'd like that."

"I could take you to the famous Jemaa el-Fnaa square in the old city this evening. We could have some real authentic Moroccan food in the market stalls. It's quite an experience."

"That sounds perfect..." I said.

With the evening planned, we left the grubby industrial area and made our way through the new town towards the archway at the wall of the old city. Genevieve pulled over on the left-hand side of the road and I immediately lit a cigarette after we said our goodbyes. The street was busy as I crossed and made my way through the arch and left towards the souk. It took some time for my eyes to adjust to the darkness of the busy maze of the market place but by then I was confident about finding the entrance to the hotel. With only a few bold salesmen making their pitches, I arrived at the heavy doors and made my way into the cool serenity of the reception.

I nodded at the staff as I made my way into the lush green gardens of the courtyard and up the stairs to my suite. With the strange anomaly in the tiling still playing on my mind, I immediately opened my laptop and sat down at the desk. I plugged in the USB cable from the camera and uploaded the images and videos I had taken since arriving. I had forgotten how many I had taken and it took a full 10 minutes to scroll through and find the pictures and videos I had taken towards the end of my visit to the vault. The afternoon sun shone through the tall windows in front of the desk and I pulled the curtains closed to cut the glare and study them with better clarity.

I sat there with a frown on my face as I studied each and every photograph, zooming in on each one in an effort to spot what I had seen earlier. But it was only in the video that I had surreptitiously taken whilst pretending to study the silver goblet on the shelf, that I found what I was looking for. It appeared as it had done when I had seen it with my own eyes. It was minute to the point of being almost imperceptible. But it was there, and of that I was certain. Although I had been rotating the camera blindly as I had filmed it, I had managed to capture it well. I paused the short video six times and saved a screenshot of each image. The 4K camera had served its purpose well and I zoomed in on each image and took a further screenshot of each.

There, in front of my eyes was what I had suspected. Hidden in the grouting surrounding a 1-metre section of the tiles was a thin black line that could have been no thicker than a single human hair. I shook my head in dismay as I stared at the screen. *It's there, Green. Just like you saw it. What the fuck?* I sat back in my chair and closed my eyes as I gathered my thoughts. At that moment the late afternoon call to prayer sounded over the rooftops of the old city.

I stood up, opened the curtains, and stepped out onto the balcony to smoke. Standing in the sunshine staring out at the blue horizon of the Atlas mountains, I wondered. *Could it really be? A trapdoor? What else would it be? If it is, it would be an extremely sophisticated and cleverly built piece of engineering. How the hell could such a thing have been constructed without the knowledge of the many hundreds of locals who would have been employed during the building of it? Architects, builders, engineers, plumbers, electricians, labourers. Anyone involved would know of its existence! It's impossible, Green!* I crushed out my cigarette and walked back into the cool of my room with a frown on my forehead. I spent the next 15 minutes composing an email to my own head office telling them of my initial impressions of the operation. I made no mention of the anomaly in the vault preferring to keep it short and simple and informing them that I would need a lot more time to come up with anything concrete. Finally, I clicked the send button, took a deep breath, and sat back in the chair once again. *If it is a trapdoor there is only one way you can prove it, Green. Prove it beyond a doubt. You'll feel a damned fool if you're wrong but there's no other way. Do it!* I sat forward once again and did a Google search for a modern hardware outlet in Marrakesh. It turned out there was a builder's warehouse within 10 kilometres of my hotel. I lifted the receiver of the telephone on the desk and dialled reception.

"This is Mr Green," I said "I would like a taxi immediately at the archway please..."

Chapter Twenty One: Pierre Lumumba.

The waterfront road in front of the hotel was busy with traffic. The chrome on the passing vehicles gleamed in the morning sunshine and there was a strong salty smell in the warm breeze coming in from the ocean. To the right, over the harbour, a flock of seagulls swooped and squawked above a fishing boat that was busy offloading its catch. The burly guard led Pierre down the pavement to the same vehicle they had travelled in the previous day from Marrakesh to Tangier. Climbing into the back seat once again, Pierre noticed it was also the same driver. The guard had seemed to relax somewhat after Pierre had officially signed the papers in the hotel room. His pleasant, cheerful demeanour from the previous day had returned. As the driver started the engine, he turned from the front passenger seat and spoke.

"Are you feeling okay?" he said.

"Fine..." said Pierre "Just a bit thirsty."

"Don't worry" said the guard with a smile "As I said, you can eat and drink as much as you like after the procedure."

The driver pulled out and headed West down the waterfront road. Once again they passed several expensive-looking hotels and restaurants. After 15 minutes the driver made a left and headed into what appeared to be a less affluent part of the city. Here the buildings were somewhat shabby looking and there were mule pulled carts and piles of litter on the street corners. Pierre sat in silence staring out of the windows as they drove deeper and deeper into the maze of streets. It was some 10 minutes later when they finally arrived and parked at the front of a five-storey block. The building was mustard brown in colour and there were peeling paper notices plastered around the dingy looking entrance. Once again, the guard turned in his seat and spoke.

"We have arrived..." he said.

Pierre Lumumba frowned and looked up at the dilapidated facade of the building.

"But this is not the facility I saw on the brochure back in Marrakesh..." he said nervously.

"No..." replied the guard. "There is some construction work going on at that building. But the very same medical staff and equipment are here. It is only a temporary move whilst the work is being done. Are you ready, Pierre?"

Pierre stared out of the window once again at the front of the building. Suddenly he felt the same twinge of anxiety and fear he had experienced when he had awoken that morning. Despite the air conditioning in the vehicle, his hands were sweating and he rubbed them vigorously on his jeans. *Think of the money, Pierre. $5000.00 United States dollars. That and the hotel room. All the food and drink you like as well.* He nodded as a smile formed on his young face.

"Yes..." said Pierre "Let's go."

Chapter Twenty Two: Feeler Gauge.

It was 5.25 pm when I finally made it back to my room from the busy streets of Marrakesh. After visiting three separate hardware outlets I had finally found the piece of equipment I needed. I pulled the small device from my pocket and sat down at the desk to study it. A feeler gauge is a small tool mostly used in engineering and is used to measure gap widths between two parts. A compact metal device similar in size to a small penknife, it houses several flexible steel blades of ever-decreasing thicknesses. The thinnest blade being only 0.02 millimetres. I pulled out the thinnest of all the blades on the device and felt it between my thumb and forefinger. *There's no doubt, Green. If there is a gap between those tiles, this will fit between them and you will have definitive proof that there is a trapdoor there.* I sat for the next five minutes contemplating how I would actually go about it. Eventually, a plan that I thought was credible formed in my mind and I opened the laptop to type an email to my head office. It took only 10 minutes to compose and I explained that the SD card in one of my cameras had malfunctioned that morning and that I had only discovered this upon returning to my hotel. I sent the email along with all of the relevant apologies for my equipment malfunction and told them that I would need to return to the vault once again the following day to take new photographs.

I knew full well that they would accept this explanation and immediately arrange for me to return as requested. The job was too important for them to ignore or delay this. I also knew that the people at The Zukman Group would not argue with a second visit caused by this minor mishap. They did, after all, seem extremely keen to be as accommodating as possible and my request was not out of the ordinary. I would also use the opportunity to attempt to glean some more information about the construction of the vault itself. I clicked the send button and immediately grabbed my smaller camera and opened the battery compartment. I breathed a sigh of relief when I saw there was ample space to conceal the thin blade from the feeler gauge inside it. My cameras had passed through the metal detector at the vault once already and they would go through again the following day.

Only this time, one of them would have the blade hidden within. Feeling satisfied, I sat back in the chair and began working the blade on the feeler gauge, bending it back and forth repeatedly.

It took only a minute for the metal near the hinge to heat up and snap off. Finally, I slipped the severed blade into the battery compartment of the camera and replaced the plastic cover. It snapped back in place with no issues. The blade was now completely hidden within the body of the camera. I sat back in the chair and stared at the cameras as I thought through my plans for the following day. *This trip to the vault will take no more than three hours, Green. That will be in the morning. If you prove that there is a trapdoor in that vault, what next?* I closed my eyes as I thought it through and soon enough an idea formed in my mind. I pulled the business card I had been given by the cheeky porter, Omar, from my top pocket. Using the hotel phone on the desk in front of me I called his number. It rang three times and I recognised his voice immediately as he answered.

"Omar..." I said "This is Jason Green. I'm hoping you may be able to help me with something. Please come up to my room as soon as you can..."

Chapter Twenty Three: Pierre Lumumba.

"You look nervous, Pierre..." said the guard as they made their way in the blazing sun from the vehicle into the entrance of the building.

The interior was gloomy and to the left was a single lift while on the far side of the lobby were a set of dusty windows, two of which were broken. At that moment a young boy ran out of a darkened corridor to the right. He could not have been more than six years old and he was barefoot and had dried mucus between his nose and his top lip. The boy paid them no attention and laughed as he continued his run out of the building and onto the sun-baked street. Somewhere further down the corridor, a radio played loud Arabic music. The place was unkempt and there was a strong musty smell in the air. This did nothing for Pierre Lumumba's nerves which were frayed by that point.

"I'm okay..." he said quietly as they approached the lift.

The guard pressed the button near the lift doors and they opened immediately. The two men had to step up a few inches as the base of the lift was uneven with the dusty floor of the lobby. The guard turned and pressed the button for the 4th floor and Pierre watched the doors close with a growing sense of alarm and trepidation. His hands were still sweating profusely and he wiped them on his jeans as he stood there rocking on the balls of his feet. The old lift laboured upwards for what seemed an eternity before finally there was a loud metallic bell sound and the doors opened once again. It came as something of a relief to see the floor they had arrived at was in stark contrast to the lower section of the building with freshly painted walls and a sparkling white tiled floor. Pierre and the guard stepped out of the lift and into the reception of what appeared to be a modern medical facility. Clean and well lit, there was a Moroccan nurse in a crisp white uniform sitting behind an open window in the reception partition to the left while on the right was a well-furnished waiting area near a bank of windows.

There was a low glass table covered with glossy magazines which was surrounded by plush looking black leather and chrome chairs. Soft music played through hidden speakers and there was a faint smell of air freshener and antiseptic in the air. The nurse lifted her eyes from her work and smiled warmly at the two men as they entered.

"Why don't you take a seat in the waiting area over there, Pierre?" said the guard with a smile. "Relax, I'll take care of the paperwork. It won't take long..."

Pierre Lumumba walked over towards the windows and picked up a magazine as he passed the table. To the left against the wall was a water cooler with a set of sparkling crystal glasses on a small table nearby. Thousands of tiny droplets of condensation had formed around the clear perspex that held the chilled liquid. He glanced at it briefly then remembered that he was under strict instructions not to drink anything before the procedure. His mouth was dry and at that moment he wished he had drunk more water the night before. He stepped up to the large bay windows and stared out across the city. In the distance, he could see the blue of the ocean on the horizon. There was no doubt that the shabby looking entrance to the building had given him second thoughts initially, and it had come as a great relief to find himself in what was a clean and modern facility. The smile from the nurse and the plush fittings had further abated his fears. Pierre took a deep breath and exhaled with a quiet whistle as he stared out at the distant ocean.

"Don't worry..." he whispered to himself. "It will be fine."

Chapter Twenty Four: Plans.

The knock on the door came within minutes of my call.

"Come in..." I called out.

"Hello, Mr Green," said Omar with a smile and a glint in his eye as he opened the door.

"Come over here and sit down..." I said, motioning to him from where I sat near the coffee table.

The smartly dressed young porter made his way down the short set of stairs and sat on a chair opposite me. I studied his face as he did so. His jet black hair was cut to a modern style and his short, youthful beard stubble was trimmed to perfection. Once again I noticed the cheeky, knowing look in his dark eyes. It was difficult not to like him although I made sure he was not aware of that.

"Omar..." I said sitting back in my chair "What do you know about drones?"

"Ah, drones..." he replied "Yes sir, I know about them. I watch many videos on Youtube, but they are illegal here in Morocco."

"I see..." I replied, "And you are sure about that?"

"Yes sir.." he replied "One hundred per cent. Why do you ask?"

I took a deep breath and exhaled slowly. This was news to me and I had not been aware of this rule when I had brought the machine into the country.

"To be honest, I didn't know they were illegal here..." I said, "Otherwise I would not have brought my own drone into the country."

The young man sat forward in his seat and spoke.

"You have one, sir?" he said with clear excitement. "I would love to see it!"

"Hmm..." I said, "Perhaps you will."

The young man blinked expectantly.

"Listen here, Omar," I said "I don't want any trouble with the police. I am interested in an area within the Sidi Ghanem industrial zone. All I want is to take a few photographs and videos. My machine, the drone, is fairly powerful and has a 4K camera. I can fly it at such an altitude that it will not be seen or heard by anyone at ground level. These photographs are for my work and I have to get them done, but as you know, I had no idea about the drone laws here in Morocco."

"What about taking them at night?" said the young man.

"No..." I replied, "This must be done in daylight, and I want it done tomorrow afternoon."

"Okay, sir..." replied the young man looking thoughtful.

"Look here, Omar," I said sitting forward in my seat "What if I hire a vehicle and we both go to this Sidi Ghanem industrial zone. Surely we could find a block of flats or a similar building and pay the owner or the tenants for access to the rooftop? We could simply explain that we are photographers and they would not have to know that we have the drone or wish to fly it."

"Yes sir..." the young man replied with a glint in his eye "That is very possible. Money talks, as I'm sure you know."

"Yes, Omar..." I said "I do know that, and I can see that you do too. So if I was to hire a vehicle, would you be able to take the afternoon off and accompany me? Then if we find a suitable building near the site I wish to photograph, you could then act as my translator. I would then give the building owner, or whoever is in charge, let's say $100 for 30 minutes in private on their rooftop. A substantial amount of money."

"Oh yes, sir..." replied Omar "It is a lot of money here in Morocco. I think it could be done quite easily and I am certainly available to assist you."

Once again I noticed the glint in his eye and the cheeky half-smile on his face.

"Of course I would pay you the same amount for your own time..." I said. "I do not want to bring any attention to you or myself. I simply want you to explain that I am a photographer who would like to use the viewpoint to take a few photographs of the area. That is all. We keep it simple and we would be there for no more than 30 minutes."

"Yes sir, Mr Green..." he replied, "I can do that, no problem at all."

"Right..." I said sitting back in my chair "Tell your boss that something personal has come up and that you will need to take the afternoon off tomorrow. Okay?"

The young man smiled broadly, stood up and offered me his hand.

"Yes sir..." he said "I will do that right away."

Chapter Twenty Five: Pierre Lumumba.

The nurse Pierre had seen as he had walked into the facility made her way across the polished floor to where he sat nervously trying to read a magazine.

"We are ready for you now, Mr Lumumba," she said in a calm, reassuring voice. "If you would like to follow me, we will now go to the preoperative unit and we can get you out of these clothes so you are comfortable and ready for the anaesthetist."

Pierre cleared his throat and stood up. The guard, who had been sitting nearby having finished the paperwork, smiled and spoke.

"Don't worry, Pierre..." he said "I'll see you shortly."

Pierre took a deep breath and followed the nurse through the waiting room and into a corridor on the right. *I am about to lose the eyesight in one eye. Dear God! But why must I change my clothes?* The nurse opened a door on the right and stood there smiling as he approached.

"Come in please..." she said.

Pierre stepped into the room which had white and grey walls and a modern wash station and cupboards. To the centre of the room was a tall, chrome frame single hospital bed on wheels with an electric control pad to adjust the angle for the comfort of the patient. It was tightly covered with a crisp white cotton sheet. Nearby was a set of tall green gas bottles with clear plastic hosing and a face mask attached.

The sight of this caused a cold shiver to run down Pierre's spine and although his mouth was as dry as the desert sand, he gulped audibly. On the far side, near the windows, was a portable screen fashioned from chrome piping and green canvas.

"Um..." he said looking around nervously "Why must I change my clothes. After all, it is a minor procedure is it not?"

"It is a standard medical practice, sir..." said the nurse calmly "You can change back into your clothes after we are done and you come around."

"How long will I be out for?" asked Pierre.

"No more than 40 minutes, sir," said the nurse "It is a very simple and quick procedure. You will feel a bit groggy for a while, but you can rest here until you feel ready to return to the hotel."

The thought of the luxurious hotel room was comforting to him and it steeled his resolve.

"Okay..." he said quietly.

"Now..." said the nurse "If you would please step behind the screen near the windows you will find a gown hanging there for you to change into. Please do so now and then make yourself comfortable on the bed here. The anaesthetist will be through shortly."

Wishing he could take just a tiny sip of water, Pierre stepped behind the screen and began to remove his clothing. As he did so he was aware of the presence of the nurse as she worked near the wash station on the far side of the room. He removed his shirt and the air conditioning felt icy on his bare skin. Next, he sat on a nearby single chair and removed his trainers. Finally, he removed his jeans and stood there naked apart from his underwear.

"Everything off or can I leave my underwear on?" he asked softly.

"Everything off please, Mr Lumumba..." said the nurse.

Chapter Twenty-Six: Green.

It was 6.10 pm when the phone on the desk rang. I had just stepped out of the shower and was wearing only the towel around my waist as I walked across the room to answer it.

"Hello..." I said as I picked it up.

"Hi Jason, it's Genevieve" came the reply "How was the rest of your day?"

"It was good thanks, Gen..." I said as I sat down on the chair.

I had decided not to tell her my story of the camera malfunction preferring to leave it till later. As we spoke I opened my emails on the laptop to see there was a reply from Diane at my head office in London. It was brief and to the point, informing me that she would arrange another visit to the vault immediately and to expect another email within the hour. A half-smile formed on my face as I minimised the screen and stared out at the distant mountains in the fading light. *They're not wasting any time on this, Green. They want it done and fast.*

"Now..." said Genevieve "What about that dinner in the square that we planned earlier? We could have a glass of wine and then go."

"Yes, I'm keen" I replied "Will be interesting to see it as well."

"Excellent!" she replied "Shall we meet downstairs in the courtyard at say 6.45?"

"Sure..." I said, "I'll see you then."

I took my time getting dressed then stepped out onto the balcony for a cigarette. The night was cool and the rising full moon cast a pale grey sheen over the rooftops of the old city. I leant on the railing and stared out into the night. I had spent the entire afternoon preoccupied with the strange anomaly in the grouting of the tiled floor of the vault.

That and my worries about how exactly I would go about testing it with the blade of the feeler gauge. There was also a niggling fear that I was completely wrong and there would be a perfectly good explanation as to why it was there. *You'll certainly feel like a fool if that's the case, Green.* I shook my head and crushed out the cigarette. *Time will tell, Green. Time will tell. At least you have a plan and you would never forgive yourself if you didn't carry it out.* I glanced at my watch to see it had just gone 6.40 pm. *Time to go.* I grabbed my wallet and key card on the way out and headed downstairs past the pool deck to the courtyard. I found Genevieve at the same table where we had sat the previous night. She wore tight jeans and a loose-fitting white cotton top embroidered with silk and tiny multicoloured beads. Her freshly washed blonde hair shone like gold in the subtle green lights and she wore open-toed sandals on her slender, tanned feet. Once again I was reminded of how astonishingly beautiful she was and she flashed her perfectly white teeth in a wide grin as I sat down.

"Professor Tremblay..." I said, "You look lovely tonight."

"Why thank you, Mr Green!" she said with a giggle. "I have made an amazing discovery..."

"At the dig site?" I asked.

"No..." she replied as she lifted her glass "This wine. A wonderful Bordeaux. Would you like a glass?"

"I would..."

I watched as she poured a generous amount of the dark red liquid into my glass. The wine was indeed superb with aromas of black current, plums and an earthy note of wet gravel. I sipped it and immediately it burst with fruit notes that led into savoury, prickly, mouth-drying tannins. We sat talking quietly in the tranquil gardens for the next ten minutes until Genevieve could take it no more.

"Jason!" she said out loud "I'm starving. Shall we go?"

I motioned to the waiter who stood nearby. He arrived promptly and greeted us politely.

"Would you mind looking after this bottle of wine until we return?" I asked.

"Certainly, sir..." he replied "I will have it ready for you."

Genevieve and I walked past the fountain and through the green-lit courtyard past the other diners who sat at candlelit tables talking in hushed tones. The reception was quiet as we made our way through the door and into the souk.

"Tonight we're turning left, Jason," said Genevieve "Deeper into the maze..."

Even at that late hour, the human and animal traffic was busy and the wily traders were eager to make a sale to the passing locals and tourists.

The air was filled with aromas of spices and there was loud Arabic music blaring from a number of speakers as we walked. We passed countless souvenir shops festooned with brass and silver trinkets. The tiny shops and kiosks were crammed to the ceiling with goods of all kinds and I could see why I had initially been overwhelmed by it all. Genevieve strode ahead with her usual confidence and vigour as she dodged the sea of animal and human traffic in the narrow alleyways. We passed a tea shop with several tourists and locals relaxing as they puffed on gurgling hookah pipes while sipping from tiny glasses of mint tea. Although she successfully ignored most of the hawkers, Genevieve was stopped by an old man in a hessian gown. He beckoned us into his tiny shop and proudly showed us his wares. The man was not your run of the mill souvenir trader but was an extremely skilled silversmith. In the cramped and dark confines of his tiny store, he proudly showed us photographs of the various Hollywood celebrities that had passed through his doors over the years. Genevieve was particularly taken by a tiny wall mirror that was surrounded by finely engraved pewter.

The two of them haggled until the shrewd old man skilfully negotiated a 'special' price of 500 Moroccan Dirhams. Genevieve handed over the cash and stuffed the mirror into her tasselled leather handbag.

We left the shop and continued through the maze of the souk for another ten minutes until finally, I saw the moon in the open sky ahead. The Jemaa el-Fnaa square is vast and located in the centre of the old city or medina. Despite its ancient origins, it remains the main square of the city of Marrakesh and this was clear from the many thousands of locals and tourists who wandered the cobbled surface. It came as something of a relief to escape the confines of the souk but Genevieve was instantly approached by an old lady in dark robes who insisted on giving her a henna tattoo on her hands. She skilfully dismissed this advance and made her way off to the right past a line of orange juice stalls. The square by night was a bustling hive of humanity and I saw a number of snake charmers and youths with chained Barbary apes jostling for the attention of tourists.

"Whatever you do, don't photograph them..." said Genevieve as she strode past them "They'll charge you a fortune."

The square was surrounded by ancient buildings, bazaars and restaurants and a selection of entertainers from dancing boys to magicians, storytellers and peddlers of traditional medicines. To the centre were dozens of makeshift food stalls and as we made our way towards them I could hear the rattling of pans and the sizzling of roasting meat. Each food stall had a dedicated tout standing at the entrance. Their job was to woo potential customers in for their meal and they tried their best to shove their laminated menus in our faces as we entered. Genevieve, however, knew exactly where she was going and I followed her through the various stalls until we arrived at her preferred spot. The waiter smiled and beckoned us to take a seat at the wooden bench table. As soon as we sat down we were handed menus and offered a soft drink.

"Sadly there's no wine on offer here..." she said, "But the food is sublime."

"In that case, I'll leave the ordering to you," I said, as I placed the menu back on the table.

Genevieve wasted no time in placing the order and we sat taking in the vibrant if somewhat hectic atmosphere. The food arrived within minutes and we started on our mini chicken shawarmas and grilled kefta kebabs with savoury potato cakes. The main meal was a steaming lamb tagine spiced with ginger and saffron with flatbreads and this was washed down with fresh orange juice. By the time the dessert of candied peanuts and sweet Moroccan ghoribas was served, I could eat no more.

"That was delicious, Gen..." I said "Superb."

"I told you..." she said with a grin "I know all the best spots."

It was at that moment that her phone rang. I watched as she opened her bag and brought it out to see who was calling. A frown formed on her forehead as she stood up to take the call.

"Excuse me, Jason..." she said "Looks like a work call. I'll be right back."

"Sure..." I said as I finished the last of my orange juice "No problem."

Genevieve stepped out of the food stall away from the shouting and laughter of the place and took the call just beyond the entrance. Clearly struggling to hear whoever was on the line, she blocked her right ear with her free hand to drown out the din. I lit a cigarette as I watched her talk and saw the frown was still on her forehead. *Maybe some problems at the dig site? Who knows.* The call was quick and she returned soon afterwards.

"Sorry about that, Jason," she said as she took her seat opposite on the bench table. "That was my site director. He said you had some problems with your camera equipment and you need to visit the vault again."

"Oh, yes..." I said as I exhaled a plume of smoke. "My SD card had a problem and I only found out once I got back to the hotel. Sorry, I had no idea at the time."

"I don't mind at all..." she said cheerfully. "We'll go back tomorrow morning. I could spend days in there."

"Great..." I replied, "This time I'll make sure my equipment is working properly."

We spent another ten minutes chatting and soaking up the atmosphere in the square. The food had been delicious and I felt content and relaxed. But soon enough I saw |Genevieve drumming her slender fingers on the surface of the bench.

"We should go..." she said "We have an appointment."

"We do?" I said raising my eyebrows.

"Yes..." she replied, "With that gorgeous bottle of Bordeaux."

"Ah..." I said as I pulled the wallet from my pocket and nodded at the waiter for the bill "In that case, we had better get going. We certainly don't want to be late for that."

The walk back through the square and the souk was calmer than it had been on the way there. It seemed the storekeepers and traders were winding down for the day and I recognised the route we had taken and many of the shops and kiosks I had seen earlier.

Eventually, we arrived at our Riad and made our way into the serene tranquillity of the courtyard gardens. By then most of the guests had retired and we took our seats at the same table where we had sat earlier. The waiter made good on his promise and appeared with our bottle of Bordeaux and two fresh glasses as soon as we arrived. It was some 30 minutes later that I ordered another bottle of the fine wine and the conversation was flowing and pleasant. All the worries that had plagued me during the day were forgotten and we both sat back in our chairs relaxing and enjoying each others company. Mellowed by the alcohol, Genevieve sat with a half-smile on her face and stared at me while she twiddled and caressed her glass. It was then that I remembered the vision of her playing the violin the previous night and I decided to bring it up.

"I heard some violin music last night..." I said, "You play very well."

Suddenly she was overcome with embarrassment and I watched as she blushed visibly.

"Oh, I'm sorry, Jason..." she said quietly "I didn't mean to disturb you."

"You didn't..." I said, "It was beautiful."

"Thank you..." she said "I used to play with a small orchestra in Toulouse. But then my work got in the way. I do try to stay in practice."

"I'm not surprised," I said "You're very talented."

The conversation continued for another half hour until Genevieve stretched her arms out and yawned. She covered her mouth as she did so then smiled at me with a dreamy, wistful look on her face.

"You're tired..." I said, "I'll walk you up to your door."

I could see at that moment that she was considering inviting me into her room and as we climbed the stairs she clung on to my left arm gently. As we reached her floor she stopped and swung me around firmly. She stared me in the eyes fiercely and I could feel the tension and electricity between us. *Don't go there, Green. She's had a bit too much to drink. Another time.* Suddenly she blinked as the moment passed. She leant towards me and kissed me on each cheek in the true French style.

"Goodnight, Mr Green..." she said quietly.

Chapter Twenty Seven: Preoperative.

Pierre Lumumba stepped out from behind the blind in the preoperative room. He was barefoot and wearing nothing but the light cotton hospital gown he had been told to change into. With his left hand, he clutched the open back of the garment to protect his naked behind from being seen.

"Now then..." said the nurse "Please make yourself comfortable on the bed here, the anaesthetist will be through shortly."

Although he was suddenly overwhelmed by crippling waves of terror, he fought the urge to run and did as he was told. The tight white sheet was crisp and clean and through the windows, at the far side of the room, he could see the bright morning sky. Shivering slightly from the cool air conditioners, he realised that his heart was pumping furiously, his hands still sweating, and his breathing was quick and ragged. In an effort to calm himself he stared out at the sky and forced himself to take long, deep breaths. Suddenly a door to his left opened and a tall Moroccan man wearing spectacles and a green surgical gown stepped in.

"Mr Lumumba?" said the man with a smile.

"Yes, sir..."

"Welcome!" said the man as he picked up a clipboard from a nearby counter.

He studied it for a moment, lifting papers as he did so. Finally, he nodded and spoke.

"Well..." he said with a smile "I'm going to give you a little shot of midazolam. It's a mild sedative that will help you relax and feel comfortable. Then, once we're ready, we'll get on with the procedure. All good?"

"Um, yes..." replied Pierre quietly.

"Great!" said the man.

The anaesthetist turned and busied himself near the wash station and cupboards behind the bed. Pierre could hear the man talking calmly to the nurse but the conversation was in Arabic and he could not understand a word. However, the quiet, pleasant tone of the conversation served to calm him somewhat. The man reappeared soon after, pulling a small trolley on wheels. On top of it was a silver dish with a single syringe lying inside it. Pierre stared at it with wide, fearful eyes.

"Right..." said the anaesthetist "If you could please stretch out your left arm so I can tie a tourniquet around it. This is so we can see your veins. Of course, I will remove it once you've had your shot."

Pierre did as he was told and the man gently tied the cloth tourniquet around his biceps then pulled it tight and fixed it with strips of velcro.

"Good," said the man "Now if you would please open and close your hand making a fist. We will then see the vein and get the shot done."

Pierre did exactly as he was told and sure enough, the veins in his arm stood proud.

"Good healthy veins there, Mr Lumumba..." said the man as he lifted the syringe from the silver dish "You will feel a tiny prick in your arm. That's all, please relax."

Pierre watched as the needle was skilfully inserted into the vein and the plunger slowly depressed. Finally, the man pulled the needle out and immediately applied a small piece of cotton wool that had been soaked in surgical alcohol. It felt cold on Pierre's skin and he continued to watch as the man removed the tourniquet from his upper arm.

"Excellent..." said the man "All done."

Almost instantly, Pierre Lumumba was overcome by a sensation unlike any he ever experienced in his life.

Suddenly the chill of the air conditioners was all but gone and he began to experience great waves of calm and relaxation washing over him. His head moved back slowly until it came to rest on the pillow and he let out a deep sigh of pleasure. In his now addled mind, he was happy once again. *This is not bad at all. This is fine.* He thought.

Chapter Twenty-Eight: Revisit.

"Sorry about this, Gen..." I said as we climbed into the land Rover.

"Not at all, Jason" replied Genevieve "As you know, I love visiting the vault. I could spend weeks in there."

It had just gone 9.00 am and the morning sun was bright and warm through the windscreen. I had awoken with a slight headache from the wine the previous night but that had disappeared after a shower and the breakfast I had ordered to my room.

Genevieve had called at 8.30 am sounding as sprightly as ever and we had met in the reception before making our way through the souk to the vehicle. I was carrying both cameras including the smaller one that held the blade from the feeler gauge within its battery compartment. Foremost on my mind was exactly how I would create a suitable diversion that would enable me to stoop and conceal what I had planned to do with the blade. I had been worried about this since I had woken up but as we entered the traffic I did my best to put it out of my mind. *Cross that bridge when you come to it, Green.* The roads were busy and it was some twenty minutes later that we arrived on the outskirts of the vast Sidi Ghanem industrial zone. As usual, there were thousands of motorcycles and heavy haulage trucks plying the roads and I used the slow pace of the traffic to scout for a suitable building from which to fly the drone later that day. Of course, I said nothing of my plans to Genevieve who chatted away merrily as we drove.

As we were approaching the Zukman Holdings complex I found it. Situated on the corner of an intersection was a shabby looking five-storey building with a grocery store on the ground floor. The walkway around the shop was cluttered with tables of fruit and vegetables and dusty looking plastic wares hung on the walls around the entrance. It was clear that the floors above the store were flats as I could see washing hanging from the burglar bars on the balconies and satellite dishes mounted on the walls. The building also had a flat top which was exactly what I was looking for. I glanced further up the road to see the walls of the Zukman Holdings complex in the distance.

That will be perfect, Green. That's the spot for sure. Soon we arrived at the main gates of the complex and went through the same process of handing in our identification cards at the guardhouse. Once again a phone call was made and our cards were handed back to us before the mechanical boom was lifted and we were finally able to enter. Genevieve parked the Land Rover in the same spot as the previous day and we made our way on foot towards the central fountain in front of the head office building. We were met by the same young man who had hosted us the day before. He greeted us with his usual polite charm.

"Sorry to hear about your equipment malfunction, Mr Green," he said "Shall we go straight to the vault?"

"Yes..." I replied, "Let's do that."

We made our way towards the vault down the same paved pathway as before and once again I could smell the raw meat and hear the faint buzzing of the band saws from the abattoir buildings beyond.

Although the main gate to the vault was manned by two uniformed men, it was a relief to see that the guard I had confronted the previous day, Uday, was nowhere to be seen. We entered the cool reception area of the vault and were greeted by the same burly men who had let us in beforehand. I began to worry as we walked down the corridor towards the metal detectors. My first concern was that the blade of the feeler gauge would be discovered. *Just take it easy, Green.* I handed the two cameras to the guard and watched him put them through the machine as I removed the watch from my wrist. It was with great relief that I saw him casually place them on the table beyond for me to collect once I had stepped through the large metal detector. Once we were all through, the guard typed in a code on the keypad near the giant rectangular door and spoke quietly on the nearby video phone. I watched as the heavy chrome wheel spun and the thick steel door of the vault swung open. Genevieve and I stepped into the bright interior of the vault while our host stood back near the entrance chatting in Arabic to one of the guards.

My eyes immediately went to the cameras positioned in the corners of the room and once again I felt a pang of anxiety. Genevieve, however, was in her element.

"Well..." she said with a grin "I'll leave you to it."

I began at the central tables and took numerous photographs and videos of the gold and silver ingots and other treasures that had been stored there. Next, I moved off down the first walkway to the left taking as many pictures as I could and squatting down on my haunches at times to capture close-ups of items that had been stored on the lower levels of the shelving. Eventually, I rounded the corner at the far side of the vault and began working my way back up towards the entrance. Our host was still happily chatting to the guard near the door and I used the opportunity to squat down once again and slide the battery cover off the back of the smaller camera.

Quickly, and without looking up, I removed the thin steel blade of the feeler gauge and slipped it into the top of the sock on my right foot. Once secured, I stood up and continued my charade.

With the cameras clicking away, I made my way slowly around the left-hand side of the vault until finally, I arrived at the far corner where I had spotted the anomaly in the grouting of the floor tiles. I glanced down to check my position and sure enough, I could see it below me. At that moment I heard our host and the guard laughing at some joke and I knew it was time to make my move. *Do it now, Green!* Once again I squatted down and lifted the smaller camera to my face as if I was taking a picture. At the same time, I removed the feeler gauge blade from my sock using my right hand. Glancing down, I placed the rounded side of the blade into the barely visible black line in the grouting. It slipped in without a problem and to double-check I pulled it down a good length of it to be sure. The blade glided through like a hot knife in butter. *You were right, Green. Fucking hell! You were right all along!* With my mind buzzing, I quickly replaced the blade in my sock, stood up, and continued my journey along the lines of shelving. It was as I rounded the next corner that I squatted once again and slid the battery cover off the smaller camera.

I pulled the blade from my sock but it was as I was replacing it in the battery compartment that Genevieve stepped around the corner and looked down at me. It was in that split second that I was unsure if she had seen what I was doing. *She wouldn't have noticed, Green. Photographers are constantly fiddling with their equipment.*

"Everything alright?" she asked with her eyebrows raised.

"Yes, fine..." I replied as I stood up "Going well, almost done."

The charade continued for another 20 minutes until finally, I announced that I had finished. The host was gracious as we made our way out of the vault and through the metal detectors. Once again, my cameras passed through without any issues. It was as I was putting my watch back on that I decided to question him about an issue that had been bothering me.

"I believe this vault structure was built in record time to house this incredible discovery..." I said.

"That's correct, sir" replied the young man.

"Impressive..." I said, "I would be interested to know a little about the actual construction."

"Ah..." said the man "The vault was built by a specialist Serbian company. They were flown in with all of their own staff and the section of land around the vault was sealed off. It was only at the grand opening that we all got to see their amazing work. As you can imagine it was quite an occasion."

"I'm sure..." I said "So you mean to say that no locals were involved in the construction at all? Not even labourers?"

"That is correct, sir," said the man "The company was brought in by Mr Zukman himself. As I mentioned, a specialist construction company. They erected temporary walls and spotlights between the head office and the factories and their team worked in shifts, day and night to finish it. It was all completed within two months. An amazing achievement."

"Indeed..." I said as we made our way towards the exit "Do you recall the name of this company?"

"Yes, sir," said the man as he nodded his thanks to the guards "Petrovic Engineering Consultants was the name."

"Thank you..." I said as we stepped out into the midday sunshine and walked towards the security gate.

"Will that be all, sir?" asked the young man.

"One more thing..." I said as we stepped through the gate "I would like to take a look at the air conditioning plant for this building if possible."

"Certainly, sir..." said the man before speaking a few words in Arabic to the guard "It is situated in a room just around the building. Please follow me."

We followed the man around the corner and down to the small extension that jutted out of the side of the vault building itself. The guard opened the padlock on the simple steel door and we stepped into the dark interior. A switch was flicked and suddenly the room was illuminated by bright neon lights. As expected there were the compressors, cooling tower, ducting, and pipework that one would expect for such a room. But my focus was not on the machinery but rather on the floors and walls. *There is a trapdoor in that vault, Green, and the tunnel that leads to it must start somewhere. This would be the obvious place.*

"I'll need a few minutes to take some photographs if that's okay..." I said to Genevieve and our host.

"Of course, sir," said the young man with a smile. "Please, take as much time as you need."

I spent the next 10 minutes examining every inch of the room and taking multiple photographs and videos. Apart from the obvious narrow ducting that pumped the cool and purified air into the building, I found nothing to suggest a hidden door or opening anywhere. The walls, floors and ceilings were cast in solid concrete. If anything, the room resembled a bomb shelter. Feeling somewhat perplexed, I walked back to the door and spoke.

"Thank you very much..." I said, "I'm done with this room."

"If there is anything else you would like to see Mr Green, you need only to ask..."

"No..." I said "You've been very patient. Thank you."

We made our way around to the front of the building near the gate to the reception. It was only then that I noticed the small concrete structure across the lush green grass at the far end near the boundary wall of the complex. Flat-topped and barely visible, it stood only three feet tall and was no bigger than two metres square. From behind my sunglasses, I saw a set of steps that led down beneath it. It was at least forty metres away from where we stood and appeared unimportant and unrelated to the vault building itself.

"What is that over there?" I asked at the last moment.

"I believe that is the pump house, sir..." said our host. "It is part of the plumbing system that supplies the vault with water for the bathrooms and the kitchen. It is connected to the main water supply for the entire complex. Would you like to see it?"

I glanced at my watch to see it had just gone 12.45 pm.

"No..." I said looking at Genevieve "I think I need to get back to my hotel. I now have all the photographs I lost yesterday. Thank you once again for your time."

"A pleasure, Mr Green..." said the man with a curt bow "Please feel free to return at any time."

We made our way back past the fountain where we bade farewell to our host. Genevieve and I walked back into the shade of the carports.

"I'm sorry it's been so frustrating for you, Jason," she said as we climbed into the Land Rover. "As an archaeologist, I know how annoying it is when equipment fails."

"Not at all..." I said cheerfully "It's just part of the job. Plus I got to spend some time with you, Professor Tremblay."

She shook her head as a wide smile formed on her face and I watched as a flush of red ran up her neck.

"Mr Green!" she said with mock outrage as she started the engine "You are very cheeky..."

Genevieve drove out of the car park, exited the main gate, and took a right on the busy road heading back towards the city. Still feeling somewhat puzzled by what I had seen, I sat in silence until we came up to the intersection with the building I had chosen for the drone flight. *Yes.* I thought as I stared up at it. *That'll be perfect...*

Chapter Twenty Nine: Midazolam.

It had been 10 blissful minutes since the anaesthetist had administered the shot into Pierre Lumumba's left arm. With his breathing now calmed, he lay there happily staring out at the sky with his eyelids drooping every few seconds. The conversation between the nurse and the anaesthetist at the workstation behind him had continued but it seemed somehow distant and irrelevant now. At that moment another man wearing a green surgical gown walked into the room from the doorway to his left. Pierre watched him with mild interest as he passed the bed and joined in the conversation that was going on behind him. Pierre tried to lift his head but it kept falling back onto the soft pillow as the warm waves of relaxation washed over him. Pierre Lumumba had smoked his fair share of weed over the years but this was a feeling unlike anything he had ever experienced. *Oh yes*. He thought. *I could get used to this*. It was at that moment that the anaesthetist appeared at his side once again.

"How are you feeling?" he asked with a smile.

"Fine..." said Pierre with a lazy grin "I feel fine."

His voice sounded distant. It was as if it was not his own and he found this somewhat amusing.

"Good." said the anaesthetist "We are now going to transfer you to the operating room. You relax right there where you are. We will push the bed through now. Okay?"

"Sure..." said Pierre with a long sigh.

Chapter Thirty: Preparation.

"Omar," I said into the telephone receiver "This is Mr Green. Where are you now?"

"I am waiting near the archway to the old city, sir..." the young hotel porter replied in his strong Arabic accent.

"So you're all set to go then?"

"Yes, sir"

"Good..." I said glancing at my watch "I'll see you in half an hour. Look out for me."

It had just gone 2.00 pm and I had been busy since returning from the vault at midday. As soon as I had made it back to the hotel I had booked a hire car to be dropped off. The receptionist had assisted me and I had messaged my own head office in London to expedite it. The receptionist had recommended a local car hire firm and assured me it would be arranged within the hour and the representative would be awaiting me at the car park near the archway.

I had spent the next 45 minutes checking over the drone and making sure the three lithium batteries were fully charged. Once done, I had laid out the equipment I would be taking with me on the bed. The idea was to appear as if I was a photojournalist so my two cameras were included. There was no way anyone would know that one of the carry cases contained a drone, so my only obstacle would be to secure access to the rooftop of the building alone. If I could manage that then I could see no reason why I shouldn't be able to make a successful flight. The Zukman Holdings head office was no more than a kilometre from the building I had chosen so it was well within the range of the drone.

Equipped with a zoom lens and a powerful 4K camera, I planned to fly the machine to a safe altitude and take numerous photographs and videos of the vault and the surrounding buildings. I checked my wallet to see I had just over USD $500 in cash. *More than enough, Green.* All that was left was to meet Omar, pick up the vehicle, and make our way across the city to the building I had chosen in the Sidi Ghanem industrial zone. I felt sure I would find it easily enough as I had memorized the route taken there with Genevieve. Failing that, I would use Google maps.

The next obstacle would be to obtain permission to access the rooftop of the building. *Hmm. That might be an issue.* I glanced down at my wallet once again. *Money talks, Green. Money talks.* I sat there drumming my fingers on the table as I waited. At that moment the phone rang. It was the receptionist informing me that the hire car had arrived and was waiting for me at the archway as arranged. I thanked him and hung up. With 20 minutes to kill, I stood up and walked out onto the balcony to smoke and gather my thoughts. My mind was buzzing with the events of the morning. My suspicions had been confirmed. There was now no doubt in my mind that there was a trapdoor in the corner of the vault. It had been ingeniously hidden and must have taken a great deal of specialized work to engineer. The implications of my discovery were huge. It would suggest that the very people that were supposed to guard the vault were the ones who were stealing from it. *Who will police the police?* It would also explain why there had been a specialist company brought in to carry out the work. A company that brought their entire staff quota in from abroad and who had worked day and night, sealed off from the rest of the world. I had been told that very morning that not one local was involved. Not even casual labourers. *It's hard to believe.* I thought. *There would have to be some kind of hydraulic system to open the trapdoor. Then there would have had to have been some advanced civil engineering and tunnelling done. That and a whole lot of earthmoving equipment. It would involve massive amounts of steel reinforcing and continuous pouring of concrete. And all of this before any real construction took place. It's genius. You make one of the most important and valuable archaeological discoveries in recent history and then go on to appoint yourself as the guardian of it all.*

"It's fucking crazy but brilliant..." I said under my breath as I crushed out the cigarette and headed back into the room.

With a few minutes to spare, I opened my laptop and Googled the name of the company that had been commissioned for the construction of the vault. The result came up immediately. Petrovic Engineering Consultants was a Serbian company. *Just like Zukman himself.* Their website was flashy and modern and had numerous language options. I clicked on the English one and it came as no surprise to see immediately that they specialized in engineering and mining construction. I clicked through the various pages quickly until I landed on one that showed several tunnelling projects they had completed in a gold mine in eastern Siberia. The pictures were right there to prove it. *Well, well, Green. Tunnelling. This is all starting to make sense now.*

Chapter Thirty-One: Panic.

One of the wheels on the preoperative bed squeaked as Pierre Lumumba was pushed towards the swinging double doors of the operating theatre. The sound caused him to chuckle but it was what he saw next that caused distant alarm bells to start ringing in some far vestige of his midazolam addled mind. All around were the bright lights, pinging machines, cold surfaces, and strange smells of an aseptic operating room. The walls and ceilings were a strange green colour and giant circular lights hung like UFO's over the cloth-covered table to the centre of the room. Four burly men in surgical gowns and masks stood watching him ominously from the corner. They stepped forward as the preoperative bed was positioned near the operating table and this only served to cause him further alarm. Even from behind their masks, Pierre could see that their expressions were dark and malevolent.

"We are going to lift you onto the table now, Mr Lumumba," said the nurse "Relax..."

But relaxing was the last thing on his mind. Despite the drug coursing through his veins, his body tensed up as he was lifted from the soft warmth of the bed and placed on the cool, hard surface of the operating table. Suddenly he felt cold once again and the bright circular lights above shone painfully into his eyes. Pierre Lumumba lay there for a few seconds as the grim reality of the situation he had put himself in suddenly became all too real. *This was a mistake.*

What am I doing? Samuel was right! This is madness! Blind panic began to fill him as he lay there listening to the mumbled conversation and tinkling of surgical tools around him. Suddenly he thought of getting up and making a run for it. He lifted his arms slightly and moved his legs. Could he do it or would he fall? *Calm yourself, man!* He told himself. *Everything has been fine so far. It's only the cornea of one eye! Think of the money and freedom. Freedom and a new life in Europe.* But the anxiety and terror would not subside and he lay there with an ever-increasing sense of icy dread. It was then that the anaesthetist stepped forward once again.

Standing next to him was one of the men who had lifted him onto the operating table. He had wheeled the two gas bottles he had seen in the preoperative room and positioned them nearby.

"Now, Mr Lumumba..." said the anaesthetist, "If you just relax, we will now give you some gas that will put you to sleep."

Wide-eyed with terror, Pierre Lumumba frantically looked from left to right as he tried to think of an escape route. Seeing this, the four burly men who had lifted him onto the operating table stepped forward. It was all becoming very real indeed and suddenly the animal instinct that is stress response hyperarousal or 'fight or flight' kicked in.

"No!" said Pierre "I have changed my mind!"

"Now there, Mr Lumumba," said the anaesthetist, his voice rising "Just relax..."

He nodded at one of the men as he lifted the mask and hose from where it hung on the gas bottles. Blind horror filled Pierre's mind as he watched the transparent mask coming down towards his face. Suddenly he sat up and tried to swing his legs off the table to make a run for it. But this move had been anticipated by the men who surrounded him. They quickly pinned his legs and arms with vice-like grips and held him fast on the cold table as the gas mask came closer and the lights blinded him. Knowing there would be a struggle, the anaesthetist slammed the mask onto Pierre's face, covering his mouth and nose. The gas was cold and sweet-smelling but this only added to his terror and he began to thrash his head from side to side as he started to scream. Suddenly a pair of strong hands clamped down on his head from behind and held it firm. Unable to move, Pierre Lumumba's screams slowly decreased in volume as the sevoflurane gas was inhaled. Gradually his senses began to dull and his struggles became weaker. The cold, bright lights above him began to fade as he was plunged into a dark world of nothingness.

Chapter Thirty-Two: Aerials.

I spotted Omar within seconds of leaving the hotel and stepping into the souk. He was standing near a souvenir stall not far from the door. He appeared wide-eyed and excited at the prospect of what we were about to do. *It's probably just the $100 he's about to earn.* I thought.

"Are you ready to go?" I asked as I walked up to him.

"Yes sir" he replied enthusiastically "All set..."

We made our way through the crowded confines of the souk, ignoring the hawkers and tradesmen before finally emerging in the warm afternoon sunshine near the archway. The street beyond was busy, but as promised, the car hire representative was waiting in the parking lot holding a sign with my name on it. The handover was quick and efficient and once done, Omar and I climbed into the small Honda Fit sedan. The engine started on the first turn of the key but there were numerous rattles from the engine and bodywork as I pulled out onto the street and headed in the direction of the Sidi Ghanem industrial zone. As we drove I told Omar exactly what I wanted from him. I told him I had already identified the building and that it would be up to him to secure access to the rooftop. I told him that his job would be to explain to whoever we met that I was simply a photojournalist who wanted to take some pictures of the area. Nothing more needed to be said. The young man understood completely and promised he would do his best to get us both up there.

"If you don't you will only get half of the money I promised you..." I warned.

Once again I saw the cheeky grin on his face return.

"I'll do it, Mr Green..." he replied in his strong Arabic accent "Don't worry about that."

Feeling slightly more confident that my plan was finally in action, I drove on until we left the manicured streets of the city and entered the shabby and overcrowded outskirts of the Sidi Ghanem industrial zone.

Some 10 minutes later we arrived at the crossroads with the building I had chosen for the drone flight on the right-hand side. Up ahead in the distance I could see the walls of the Zukman Group complex. I made a right turn and parked behind an overloaded donkey-drawn cart. The exhausted, mangy looking animal stood there in its harness with its head hanging low. I grabbed the three camera cases, one of which contained the drone, and we climbed out of the vehicle. The smell of exhaust fumes and rotten vegetables filled the air and the street was dusty and littered. This was a side of Marrakesh that few tourists ever got to see. We crossed the street and walked up to the entrance of the shop that made up the ground floor of the building.

"Right, Omar," I said "Go do your thing, and remember, we *must* be alone up there."

The young man nodded and made his way into the gloomy interior of the shop. I lit a cigarette and stood there smoking as the afternoon sun burned pleasantly on my skin. My mind was still buzzing from the discovery I had made in the vault that morning and I was itching to get the drone into the air. It was three minutes later when Omar came out again with a short, fat man with a long grey beard and a skull cap. He wore a grey tunic and smiled at me with a toothless grin as he shook my hand.

"Mr Green..." said Omar. "This is Mr Abdullah. He has kindly permitted us to access the rooftop. We can take as long as we need."

I thanked the old man in English which Omar translated immediately. I then pulled out my wallet and handed the old man a crisp $100 bill.

His grin grew wider and he bowed as he took the note with both hands. The old man beckoned us to follow him and we walked into the darkened interior of the shop through the stacked shelves until we reached the staircase at the rear. Dark and filthy, it appeared the place had last seen a coat of paint when it had been built. The man pulled a key from a pocket beneath his tunic and handed it to Omar. We thanked him once again and he immediately made a gesture with his hand as if to say 'help yourself'. Omar and I climbed the stairs making our way up the five floors of the building until we finally arrived at the roof access door.

There was a rusty padlock hanging from a clasp hinge. Omar unlocked it and we stepped out into the bright afternoon sun once again. Apart from some plumbing fittings and ventilation pipes, the rooftop was bare and covered with dust and bird droppings. It appeared that no one had set foot up there for many years. The boundary of the rooftop was surrounded by a simple waist-high wall that was painted in the same grubby colour as the exterior of the building. Closing the door behind us, Omar and I walked over towards the wall and I looked out towards the Zukman Holding premises in the distance.

"Perfect..." I said under my breath "This will do just fine."

I walked back a few paces, squatted down, and placed my equipment on the dusty floor. I opened the drone case and began preparing the compact machine for flight. Omar stood nearby watching with great interest as I did so. After placing the battery into its compartment I extended the rotor arms and fitted my phone into the remote controller. The drone emitted an electronic beep and I stood up watching the screen on my phone as the camera began transmitting and the device picked up 7 satellites for GPS location settings.

"Right..." I said to Omar "Stand back please."

The propellers spun into a blur and the drone flew up to a height of 5 feet. I held it there for a few seconds to make sure everything was functioning correctly. Omar stood there watching with wide eyes as the small machine hovered in front of us. Without warning, I lifted the left toggle and the drone sped upwards at speed until it was barely visible.

"Wow!" said Omar in amazement.

Ignoring him, I continued powering the machine upwards until the screen indicated it had reached an altitude of 400 feet. From that height, it was impossible to hear or see. I turned my body to shade the controller from the glare of the sun and flew the machine in a straight line towards the Zukman Holdings premises.

The drone flew off at 40 km per hour and in no time it was directly above my target. I immediately recognised the head office building behind the fountain with the green lawns surrounding the vault to the left. Knowing full well it was at a safe altitude, I flew it to the far front corner of the premises and began taking photographs. Once done, I flew back 100 metres and repeated the process. I carried on repeating this until I had reached the near side of the property, then moved the machine inwards. I planned to continue until I had covered and photographed every square metre of the property. This would ensure I had a complete grid of high quality 4K pictures to study. The entire process took only 15 minutes and I had to move to the shade of a plumbing pipe to avoid the glare of the afternoon sun on the screen.

Omar stood nearby, clearly enthralled. With the battery showing only 20 per cent remaining, I pressed the home button and waited for the machine to return to the GPS spot above us from where I had begun the flight. This took no time at all and I brought the drone down quickly, landing it in the same spot I had taken off from.

"Go take a look around the building, Omar," I said "Make sure we haven't attracted any attention."

I quickly replaced the battery and repeated the process only this time with a 50% zoom on the camera. The process only took only 10 minutes to complete so I decided to do another complete grid sweep, using just the video. Finally, I pressed the home button and brought the machine down in front of us once again. I stepped forward, removed the battery, and began packing the machine back in its case.

"Is that it?" asked Omar, looking somewhat crestfallen.

"That's it..." I replied, "All done."

With the machine safely packed away, I stood up and looked at the young man.

"You've been very helpful, Omar..." I said, "Thank you."

I took my wallet out and handed him a fresh $100 bill. This seemed to cheer him up and we made our way back through the door and down the stairway to ground level.

We emerged from the darkened interior of the shop and crossed the filthy street to the waiting vehicle. I glanced at my watch as I started the engine to see it had just gone 4.00 pm.

"Will you be needing me for anything else, Mr Green?" said Omar.

"Not right now" I replied as I drove off "But if I do, I'll let you know..."

Chapter Thirty-Three: Samuel.

It had been 24 hours since the guards had led Pierre Lumumba away for his operation in Tangier. Samuel Kisimba had spent this time alone in his cell, unable to sleep and in a state of morbid reflection and deep depression.

In his mind, he had an aching longing to be reunited with his beloved daughter who had been so cruelly ripped from him that fateful night so long ago. Now there was not even anyone to talk to in the bare confines of the cell and he was left alone with his ever-darkening thoughts.

Although he had been consistently steadfast in his refusal to accept the offer that had been made to him by the kindly doctor, he had begun to have a creeping suspicion that perhaps he had made a mistake by not agreeing to it all and joining Pierre.

He pulled the now crumpled brochure from his pocket and stared at it for the thousandth time. If what was written on it was indeed true, Pierre Lumumba would by now have had his procedure, been paid, and would be recuperating in a luxury hotel awaiting the transfer to Spain. Samuel Kisimba had no idea that the steady and consistent torment he was suffering each and every day of his confinement was deliberate, and it was beginning to break him both physically and mentally.

His entire world had become one devoid of hope and now his only companion was a deep sense of despair. *Perhaps Pierre had* been right all along? Perhaps his youthful sense of bravado had served him well in this instance? He had repeatedly insisted that he could easily go through the rest of his life with the use of just one eye. *Perhaps I could too?* With his fingers intertwined behind his head, Samuel Kisimba took a deep breath and exhaled slowly as he lay there on the bunk staring at the concrete ceiling of the cell.

He took his left hand from behind his head and once again brought it to his face, covering his left eye. He lay there for a good five minutes looking around the cell and imagining what it would be like to live with the use of only one eye.

Drifting through the small window above him was the constant, distant buzzing of the band saws and the revving of the mopeds and motorcycles as they arrived and left the facility. *All it will take is to say yes. If you just say yes, perhaps this nightmare will come to an end and you will be free once again and reunited with Lucia.* His anguish and longing were becoming a profound physical ache. He was now unsure how long he could endure this appalling torment and suffering. The temptation to simply ask to see the doctor and agree to the procedure was becoming more and more appealing with every hour.

Chapter Thirty-Four: Discovery.

It was 5.30 by the time I made it back to the hotel and walked into my room at the Riad Sahari. The afternoon traffic getting back from the Sidi Ghanem industrial zone had been appalling and I had finally dropped Omar at the car park near the archway. I was desperate to get the memory card from the drone into my computer and have a look at the photographs and video footage I had taken.

Omar had been perfectly professional and had made no enquiries as to why I was so interested in the Zukman Group premises. It seemed he was more fascinated by the drone itself rather than what I was filming. I was also hugely relieved that the flights had been successful and had not attracted any unwanted attention. All in all, the afternoon had been a success.

I placed the equipment on the bed and wasted no time opening the drone case and removing the memory card from the camera. I immediately opened my laptop and inserted the memory card as it booted up. The phone rang as I opened the files and was about to start studying the pictures.

"Hi Jason..." came the familiar voice "It's Genevieve. How was your afternoon?"

"Not very exciting" I lied "You know, work, work work..."

"What are your plans for dinner tonight?" she asked.

"I have no plans..."

"Would you like to join me in the courtyard in that case?" she asked.

"Sure" I replied "I'd like that very much, but I still have a pile of work to get through. Can we make it a little later? Say 8.00 pm?"

"Perfect..." she replied "See you then, at the usual table."

Feeling relieved that I would have some time to study my footage I set about it immediately. The first pictures were of astounding clarity and as I viewed them I set about stitching them together one by one into a grid pattern using a website I found online.

Designed for farmers to map their fields, it allowed a free trial of an area of up to 60 acres before the user would then have to pay for their system to be downloaded. The Zukman Holdings premises was far smaller than this so I knew I could effectively build a detailed aerial map of the entire property. This would enable me to zoom in and study the area around the vault that I was most interested in. The program was advanced and allowed unlimited waypoints, adjustable height, and automatic area calculation.

Within an hour I had completed the first grid map and I sat back to look at my work. Of course, there was the car park, the main head office, and the fountain with the vault building to the left. Further to the left of that were the numerous buildings that made up the meat processing plant. I zoomed in randomly on the various structures looking for any signs of a tunnel or anomaly near the vault but I could see nothing unusual or out of the ordinary. Feeling somewhat crestfallen, I stepped out onto the balcony to smoke. By then it was dusk and there was a pink hue on the Atlas mountains and a rustic red glow intermingled with the twinkling lights over the old city. *Keep going, Green, there are a lot more pictures and videos to process*. I returned to the computer and began working on the second set of photographs I had taken with the zoom lens on 50 per cent. This time there were fewer pictures in total but it still took a good 45 minutes to go through the laborious process of stitching and cropping them together into the grid pattern. Only when I had finished and finally sat back to open the whole picture did I see it. There it was, in the form of a thin line of green grass that protruded from the vault building itself. The grass was a shade lighter than the rest of the surrounding lawn in a stretch that could only have been two metres wide. It ran from the front left of the vault building directly to the small concrete pump house I had seen when we had left the air conditioning plant of the building that very morning.

At the time I had dismissed it, but now it was quite obvious that there was something a lot more substantial than water pipes running under that particular section of ground. At roughly two metres wide, it would be more than enough for a tunnel. Although every effort had been made to conceal it beneath the lawn with constant irrigation from the sprinklers, the grass was of a visibly lighter shade than that of the surrounding lawn. To me, this was a clear indication that there was something underneath. Of course, it was not visible from ground level, or even from the top floors of the head office, but from the aerial perspective from the drone pictures, it was revealed as clear as day.

There it was, an underground structure running from the pump house near the boundary wall directly to where I knew the trapdoor in the floor of the vault to be.

"My, my, will you look at that..." I said under my breath "Bingo!"

A pulse of adrenalin raced through my body as I studied it again and again, but there was no question about it. There was something there. My doubts had been vindicated and all of my suspicions had turned out to be true. All that was left was to prove it.

Feeling the desperate urge for a cigarette, I forced myself to go on to study the video footage I had taken. This was much easier to view and once again the strip of lighter coloured grass between the vault building and the pump house was there. I paused and replayed the footage, again and again, to be absolutely sure, until I needed no more convincing. *There is something there, Green. That is for fucking sure.* I glanced at my watch to see it had just gone 7.30 pm. I needed to shower and get ready for dinner with Genevieve, but I also needed to plan my next move. I would have to get into the Zukman Holdings premises under the cover of darkness and take a look at that pump house myself. *But how? The entire property is surrounded by a huge wall with an electric fence on top of it.* Unable to fight the urge any longer, I stepped out onto the balcony for a cigarette. The lights of the old city twinkled in the darkness and there was the smell of spices in the cool breeze.

The first problem would be getting in. That place is heavily guarded as you well know from the security at the gates. But the pump house is near the boundary wall. That's an advantage, although there's bound to be a whole lot of additional security at the tunnel entrance. Then again, maybe not. The whole thing is designed to be concealed. Concealed from everyone, including the everyday staff that work there. Perhaps it's a lot more simple than it looks? I crushed out the cigarette, walked back into the room and picked up the phone to make another call to my young helper, Omar.

"Omar..." I said when it was answered "It turns out I need your help once again. Where are you now?"

"I am at home, sir" he replied "But I can be there at the hotel within the hour. How can I assist?"

"I need you to get me a few things, unusual things..." I said slowly.

"I can help, Mr Green. What do you need?"

"I need you to get me three things. A five-metre section of nylon rope, an aluminium step ladder, and a common garden rake..."

There was a pause on the line as he struggled to understand my request.

"A rake?" he said, sounding puzzled.

"Yes, a rake..." I replied "You know the sort I'm talking about. Wooden handle with a rounded plastic head. The same thing the gardeners here at the hotel use to gather fallen leaves."

Once again there was a long pause.

"Ah, yes Mr Green..." came the reply "I can get you these things. There is a market near my house."

"I need them urgently, Omar..." I said, "How soon can you get them here?"

"I can bring them within an hour..." he replied.

"Are you sure? If you can do it, I will pay you another $100." I said.

"I will not let you down, sir..." he said confidently.

"Remember this..." I said "The rake *must* have a wooden handle and a plastic head. Is that clear?"

"A wooden handle and a plastic head." he said "That is clear, sir. I will call you when I am at the archway."

"Good man..." I said before hanging up.

Chapter Thirty-Five: Awakenings.

It was 11.27 pm when Pierre Lumumba first stirred. The powerful anaesthetics he had been given were still coursing through his veins. He had no idea that after the operation, he had been injected with huge doses of profopol, diazepam, anxiolytics and pain killers. The combination of these potent drugs had the effect of putting him in an extended, almost zombie-like state.

Even the simple effort of opening his eyes was impossible, let alone moving his arms or legs. One thing he was vaguely aware of, however, was his raging thirst. When he finally succeeded in opening his mouth, his tongue was swollen to twice its usual size and his mouth was as dry as the baking sands of the Sahara.

But this minor discomfort did not bother him at the time as his brain drifted in and out of consciousness. During the brief and confusing periods he was semi-awake, he had been aware of strange noises around him. There was the sound of Arabic music in the distance and on one occasion, the shouted voices of a man and a woman having a very loud quarrel nearby. The argument had been in Arabic so he had no idea, neither did he care what it was about.

In reality, Pierre Lumumba was so intoxicated that he barely knew who he was, nor could he recall the events of the day. His world was one of comfortable darkness occasionally pierced by strange, but not unpleasant flashes of reality. There was really only one thing that stayed in his mind. He was thirsty. Parched and desiccated.

More thirsty than he had ever been in his entire life.

Chapter Thirty-Six: Dinner Date.

"Good evening Mr Green," said Genevieve with a smile as I sat down at the table.

The garden was bathed in soft light and the air was filled with the scent of jasmine. Genevieve wore a black, tight-fitting cocktail dress that exposed her broad shoulders and upper back. Her long hair was loosely tied up in a bun at the back of her head and strands of it hung around her cheeks like fine golden gossamer. It was clear that she had made an effort and I was more than impressed. The results were breathtaking. In that moment she was the most exquisite creature I had ever seen. I wished then I had delayed Omar and waited till the next day to gather the equipment I needed. But it was too late, and by then I knew he would be on his way.

"You look stunning, Gen," I said as I sat down.

"Why thank you, Mr Green!" she said lifting her glass "I couldn't help it..."

"What?"

"I ordered the same wine as last night...." she replied with a cheeky grin.

"Good choice," I said as I reached forward and poured myself a glass.

The conversation flowed amiably and we spoke about her

afternoon as starters of olives and pitta bread with dips were delivered to the table. Some time later, the waiter stepped forward to take our dinner orders and I glanced at my watch as Genevieve browsed the menu. It had just gone 8.30 pm and I was expecting Omar to call at any minute. *Fuck. You screwed this one up, Green.* In an effort to do some damage control before his call, I decided to warn Genevieve that I would have to step out for a few minutes.

"Listen, Gen..." I said "I have someone coming to see me this evening. I will have to leave you here for 5 or 10 minutes while I deal with it. I'm warning you now so as not to appear rude. I hope you don't mind."

"Not at all..." she said with raised eyebrows "Work-related?"

"Yes" I replied "Nothing serious but unfortunately he has had to come at this late hour. It's wrong to leave you sitting here but I'll be as quick as I can."

"Don't worry!" She said with a bemused smile, pointing at the bottle of wine "I have another good friend to keep me company while you're gone."

At that very moment, my phone rang and I cursed silently as I pulled it from my pocket. The name 'Omar' was on the screen.

"Yes..." I said impatiently.

"Hi Mr Green, it's Omar. I have your items. I'm at the archway now."

"Wait there for me please..." I said before hanging up.

"Sorry, Gen..." I said as I stood up.

"Go!" She said with a smile and a gesture of her hand "I'll be here..."

I nodded and left immediately.

The crowds in the souk were winding down as I jogged through, dodging the various obstacles. I reached the archway within minutes and found Omar waiting just outside as promised. The items I had asked for lay at his feet. He had a bemused, almost quizzical look on his face.

"Is this what you requested, Mr Green?"

I took a quick look at what he had brought. The young man had done well. The ladder was the right size and the nylon rope and rake were exactly what I needed.

"Yes, that's fine..." I said handing him the car keys. "Go and put it all in the hire car, lock it, and drop the keys off at reception afterwards. Understood?"

"Yes sir, no problem..."

I reached for my wallet and handed the young man another $100 note. His eyes lit up at the sight of it.

"Well done, Omar..." I said, "I have to go back now."

By the time I made it back to the hotel and the table I was panting and had a light film of sweat on my face.

"That was quick!" said Genevieve as I sat down at the table "I hope you don't mind but I took the liberty of ordering your dinner."

"Excellent," I said.

"Is everything okay?" she asked.

"Yes, fine..." I replied "All good."

The evening progressed agreeably with the conversation and wine flowing. We dined on Harira soup with a Kefta tagine main. Genevieve was lively and talkative and the sound of her laughter was like the tinkling of the water in the fountain nearby. Once again I noticed the sultry, almost furtive look in her eyes when our gazes met.

I found myself cursing the plans I had made for the night. It was 10.00 pm when I saw her yawn and I decided to pre-empt the situation.

"You're tired, Gen," I said "Perhaps we should call it a day."

"I'm okay, actually," she said, biting her lower lip "But maybe you're right…"

We walked together through the gardens and up the stairs with her arm locked in mine. When we reached her floor she suddenly turned and pulled my face down to hers from behind my neck. Her mouth tasted of wine, her lips were soft and wet, and her skin smelled of expensive perfume. Her kiss was deep and sensual and I felt her breasts rising and falling against my chest as her breathing became heavier. Suddenly she pulled back, her eyes wide, with a shocked look on her face.

"I'm sorry, Jason." she stammered "I don't…"

"Don't be sorry." I said stepping forward, still holding her hand "I'm not…"

Once again she bit her lower lip as she looked up at me. At that moment she was both vulnerable and lovely.

"I must go…" she said breathlessly as she pulled away and turned to enter her room. She stared at me briefly with a wistful look in her eyes as she closed the door.

"Good night…" she said quietly.

I stood there for a few seconds not quite knowing what to do. Eventually, I turned and made my way up the stairs to my suite. I lay on the bed staring at the ceiling and thought through what had just happened. The moment had been nothing short of electric *Why, oh why did you make these plans tonight you idiot? Too caught up in your work as usual. Fuck!* Shaking my head and forcing the bitter disappointment from my mind, I got up and studied the grid photos from the drone flight once again.

I intended to enter the Zukman premises that very night and I needed to identify a suitable place to get in. I decided that I would leave at midnight which gave me an hour and a half to kill. Using the time wisely, I pulled out my darkest clothing and laid it on the bed. I placed my phone and wallet on the table near the laptop. I would not need either. Finally, I checked my smallest camera to see it was working properly. It was. When I was sure that I had gone through my preparations thoroughly, I stepped out onto the balcony to smoke.

It was as I was standing there that I heard Genevieve playing the violin from her room below. It was a slow, classical piece from a composer I couldn't recall. A beautiful, sombre tune which at the time sounded like an invitation. Genevieve had kept her balcony door closed but I could still hear her playing clearly and the hairs on my arms stood up at the sound of it. I shook my head once again at my mistake and made my way back into the room. It was 11.55 pm.

Time to go, Green.

Chapter Thirty-Seven: Samuel.

"I think you've made a wise choice, Samuel," said the doctor in his strong Arabic accent "You have been here far too long."

Samuel Kisimba stared at the elderly man in grim silence and eventually nodded.

"Yes, doctor," he replied in a quiet voice. "Indeed, I have been here too long. I need to see my daughter. When can I go?"

"Ah now, that may take some time. We would need to schedule the procedure and arrange everything. But it should be within the next two weeks at the most."

Samuel had made his decision in the darkest hour of the second night after the departure of his cellmate, Pierre. But this news of the delay caused him even more despondency and he dropped his head in bitter disappointment.

He had reached the end of his tether and he knew, deep down, that he had been truly broken. The abuse from Uday, the isolation and depression had got the better of him, and in the middle of the night, he had called for the guard and asked to see the doctor. He had been made to wait until the following morning but at last, he had been led by the armed men through the packed storeroom to the familiar office he had visited so many times during his recovery from the gunshot.

"Two weeks?" He asked softly, raising his eyes one again.

"Up to two weeks my friend..." said the doctor "Of course, I will try to speed it up for you."

Samuel dropped his gaze once again, and with his elbows on his legs, he brought his hands up to his eyes and covered them to stop himself from weeping. The thought of spending another day in that hell hole was just too much to imagine. But now he had been told it might be another two weeks. At that moment he wished that he had left with Pierre.

He took a deep breath and steeled himself.

"Very well..." he said without emotion "Thank you, doctor. As soon as you can arrange it I will be waiting for you."

"Don't worry, my friend..." said the doctor "I will do my best to expedite this."

Chapter Thirty-Eight: Unlawful Entry.

The souk was eerily quiet at 12.05 am that night. I had picked up the car keys from the sleepy-looking receptionist on my way out. He seemed somewhat puzzled that I was leaving the riad at that late hour but asked no questions. On my back, I carried a small bag containing the equipment I had selected. I had left my phone and wallet in my room seeing no need for either. I made my way through the dimmed corridors of the souk. Most of the shops and kiosks were boarded up with not a soul in sight until I passed a small spice trader. I noticed a small bundle wrapped up in a dirty blanket to the front of the store. As I passed, I realized it was an old man who had been left there as a night watchman. He lifted his head and watched me as I passed. His cheeks were hollow and his skin was like yellow parchment. His sunken eyes glowed in the dim yellow light as he stared at me silently.

I made it to the archway a few minutes later and crossed the now-empty street to the parking lot under the giant Argana tree. Omar had put the ladder, rope and rake in the car as I had requested and I took a moment to mentally go through my plan once again as I started the small vehicle.

I set off turning right onto the street and headed down the familiar route through the city towards the Sidi Ghanem industrial zone. The yellow street lights above the manicured streets glowed brightly and there was very little traffic at all. This changed as I left the new city and entered the outskirts of the industrial area. Here there was still a small amount of moped and truck traffic but my small vehicle was not out of place at all. Eventually, I arrived at the crossroads with the building I had flown the drone from to my right. At that moment the adrenalin started to flow with the prospect of what I was about to attempt and I felt the familiar sensation tingling in my arms and legs.

Using the aerial grid map, I had identified a spot at the boundary wall of the Zukman premises where I would scale the wall and enter. It was only metres from the small pump house I had seen earlier in the day during my visit to the vault. I knew it was roughly halfway down the length of the front of the premises and it was roughly three metres past a pillar in the wall.

I had also logged the location by the presence of a building on the opposite side of the street. There were a series of water tanks on the roof of this building and their position was such that I was sure I would see them from street level. I slowed the vehicle as I approached the service entrance of the Zukman premises.

It came as no surprise to see a motorcycle and a refrigerated truck leaving from the raised boom at the guardhouse. I knew that the abattoir operated 24 hours a day. I also knew that this section of the premises would be actively guarded, but my planned point of entry would be well past there. I scanned the wall as I drove and soon enough I saw the place where I would cross. As I had seen in the aerial photos, there was a series of building with darkened side streets opposite. I glanced upwards to my right and saw the dark silhouettes of the water tanks atop the very one I had identified.

It was roughly 20 metres past the pillar when I noticed a darkened section of the wall. The limited light would offer me a good place to scale it and get over unseen. The buildings and shop fronts on the opposite side of the street were shuttered and deserted.

My biggest worry was that there would be security guards stationed there but as yet I had not seen any. *Looking good so far, Green, looking good.* Despite the cool air, I found myself sweating lightly as I drove. I guess it was the adrenalin and the pressure of having to complete this task unseen. *You need to drive past at least twice before you do anything, Green. At least twice.* I drove on, picking up speed until I passed the main entrance to the Zukman Group. As expected, the gates were well lit and there was a man stationed in the guardhouse. I glanced in and saw the now-familiar fountain and lights of the main office block which had all been left on. Soon enough I came to the boundary of the premises and made a right up a potholed street to head around the block and drive past once again. The surface of the road was appalling and there was a pack of goats picking around an overflowing rubbish tip. The overhead lighting was poor but I could see a series of darkened streets to my right running towards the main road with the Zukman wall beyond.

Eventually, I made a right turn and came out at the spot where I had parked that very afternoon for the drone flight. Feeling impatient and keen to get going, I drove up the length of the wall slowly once again.

This time I concentrated mainly on the buildings to the right, looking for any signs of security guards or vagrants who might see me as I executed my plan. There was not a soul in sight. I followed the same route I had taken, heading past the boundary and right and around the block past the goats once again. The tension and tingling sensation in my arms was growing more pronounced. *One more time around then you go, Green. It's looking good for now.*

It took another round to convince myself and finally, I made a right turn down a filthy and darkened street opposite the pillar in the wall. I parked the vehicle behind a pile of barrels and climbed out. The night was dead quiet and the air was filled with the smell of rotten vegetables and blocked drains. I walked slowly down the darkened street until I emerged on the main road opposite the pillar in the wall. I lit a cigarette as I stood in the shadows to wait and watch. In the distance to the left at the service entrance was a steady flow of motorcycles and trucks. To my right, the main entrance was quiet. Directly in front of me, across the street, was the very spot where I intended to scale the wall. I glanced at my watch to see it had just gone 1.45 am. I took a last look around for any signs of life. There was none. *No time like the present, Green. Get it done, now.* I took a look at the electric fence on top of the wall. Four separate wires were running above the wall. They were mounted on metal risers with ceramic insulators mounted on the top of the wall every five metres. The bottom wire was 20 cm above the top of the wall. I knew then that I would only need to lift the wires by 50 cm to enable me to climb under them. Touching them would set off an alarm and almost certainly give me a hell of a shock. I walked back to the vehicle and opened the back hatch. Pulling the rake out, I measured roughly 50 cm down from the head and snapped the wooden pole on my knee. The break made a loud cracking sound and I tossed the excess wood into the nearby gutter. Suddenly there was a loud squeal from a cat. It had obviously been asleep in the gutter and I had awoken it. The break on the pole had left a few spiky splinters but I quickly snapped them off leaving a relatively flat surface. *Good, that'll work perfectly.* I took a final walk to the main road and looked around for any signs of life. There was nothing except the rumbling of a truck in the distance.

    I stared across and gauged how long it would take me to get over. *20 seconds max, Green. No more than that. It's doable. No doubt about it.* I walked back to the car and removed the rope and the step ladder. I unravelled the rope and tied the end of it to the top of the ladder. The rest I coiled around my shoulder. Finally, I looked around me then locked the car. With the ladder and rake in hand,

and the adrenalin coursing through my veins, I walked down the dark alley to the main street. I stopped a final time to look around before making my move. *Go, Green. Go now!* Without hesitating, I crossed the street and walked onto the manicured grass that surrounded the boundary wall of the Zukman premises.

I felt woefully exposed in the light so I moved as fast as I could. Arriving at the base of the wall, I quickly set up the ladder. Climbing up, I reached the level of the electric wires. Wasting no time, I lifted the rake and held it sideways against the wires. The plastic barbs slipped past them and I turned the handle in my hand bringing the broken piece down. Next, I pushed upwards. The wires were taut, but the blades of the rake kept them separated evenly, and I forced them upwards until I was able to wedge the base of the pole on top of the wall. The plan had worked. I had effectively lifted each of the wires by 50 cm without touching them or setting off the alarm system. *Good, keep going, Green, you're halfway there!* I climbed onto the top of the wall under the wires and pulled the aluminium ladder upwards. It clattered lightly against the brickwork but I held it out as I brought it up. The ladder was light and I carried it under the wires easily. Next, I lowered it down into the darkened area below. It landed on the grass silently and I climbed down onto it and pulled the rope back up behind me. Finally, I carefully lowered the rake until the electric wires were back in place where they had originally been. I climbed down silently onto the grass and crouched down in the darkness as I lowered the ladder and laid it flat. My entire body was sweating and buzzing with adrenalin and I squatted silently in the darkness as I gathered my breath. *You did it, Green. You're in!*

Chapter Thirty-Nine: Awakenings, Part 2.

Pierre Lumumba first tried to open his eyes at 2.30 am. His left eye was stuck closed with a crusty line of dried mucus, but with his right eye, he scanned the room in which he lay. The space was tiny and above him hung a single electric bulb. The glaring light from it stung his good eye. There was a single window near the base of the bed that was covered by a dirty piece of hessian scrap. Feeling confused and unable to recall the events that brought him to this place, he closed his right eye and drifted back into a troubled state of semi-consciousness.

It was his great thirst that awoke him once again some 20 minutes later. This time he moved his head and looked at the walls of the tiny room. They were filthy and had turned a grimy yellow colour with patches of paint peeling and covered with scribbled writings and torn posters. He frowned as his mind began putting the pieces together. There was the memory of the hotel and the trip to the medical facility. He remembered changing from his clothes into the medical gown and getting the first jab of sedative.

It was at that moment Pierre tried to open his mouth, but it too was stuck and his tongue was swollen to twice its usual size. *Thirsty...So thirsty.* He thought. Pierre Lumumba turned his head to the left and once again the bright light above stung his open eye. Next to the bed was a small wooden table with a 2-litre bottle of water on top of it. A wave of relief swept over him as he saw it. He tried to lift his left hand to reach for it, but his arm felt like lead and it took three attempts before he was able to grasp it. In his weakened state, the weight of the bottle was immense and as he brought it towards him, his grip slipped and the bottle fell to the floor with a thud. Pierre closed his right eye and breathed heavily. He could think of nothing but the water. The refreshing life-giving liquid would end this terrible thirst and help him regain some sort of normality.

He brought his left hand to his face and began carefully rubbing his left eye. The mucus was thick and crusty but it came away easily enough and finally, he was able to open it. At first, his vision swirled and spun but eventually he steadied his gaze by focussing on the filthy hessian curtain at the window.

There was not a sound around him and he blinked repeatedly as he concentrated on gathering his thoughts. *Where am I? How did I get here? Where is the guard? Why am I not in the hotel?* Then it dawned on him. *Why am I able to see out of my left eye? Did the surgeon not complete the operation?* These thoughts persisted until five minutes later he had gathered the strength to roll over and attempt to retrieve the water bottle that had fallen nearby.

With a supreme effort, he pushed himself over, using his right hand. It was only when he was lying sideways that he felt it. It began as a stabbing pain in his left side at first but was soon followed by a deep ache that emanated from the very core of his side and lower back. At first, the need to retrieve the water superseded this but as he leant further over, it became unbearable. With a gasp, he flopped back into the position he had woken up in on his back. A deeply disturbing feeling that something was terribly wrong filled him and he lay there trying to make sense of it all.

It was ten minutes later when he finally brought himself up into a semi-upright position on the filthy pillow. The persistent, dull pain was growing in intensity in his left side and he lifted his shirt to take a look at what was causing it. What he saw then was truly horrific. The ugly 30 cm wound ran around his midriff from his back to his stomach. Cut in a semi-elliptical shape, it had been roughly sewn up and protruding from the middle of it was a 10 cm transparent plastic drain. Dripping from this thin tube was a steady flow of clear liquid with a hazy pink tinge to it. The mattress where he had been lying was soaked with this liquid and it was already beginning to congeal and smell. Pierre Lumumba stared down at this in a mixture of disbelief and abject horror. Although his body was still heavily sedated, he began to shake and he let out out a long groan of agony and terror. At that moment he saw the water bottle lying on the floor nearby. Slowly he reached over for it until he was able to grab it. The effort of doing so was immense and he lay back on the pillow sobbing and moaning from the effort and the pain. Eventually, he managed to unscrew the top and began drinking slowly. Sip by sip, the liquid calmed his burning mouth and gave him strength. *What had happened? Had there been a mistake? Was this just some bizarre nightmare from which he would soon awaken?*

He lay there whimpering and sipping the warm liquid from the plastic bottle.

Pierre Lumumba was too afraid to open his eyes.

Chapter Forty: Secrets Underground.

I sat silently leaning against the wall in the darkness for a good ten minutes. During this time my eyes became accustomed to the gloom and I was able to see most of my immediate surroundings. The car park, the fountain, and the head office building to my right were all bathed in bright light. The vaulted building directly ahead of me was also lit up although less so than the rest. The perimeter fence around the vault and its immediate surroundings was illuminated by rows of downlights, while a series of ground positioned spotlights focussed on the building itself. To my far left, in the distance, was the familiar buzz of the band saws and the constant hum of activity in the abattoir and factory buildings.

The small pump house, which was the reason I was there, was 20 metres to my left near the boundary wall. Had I not known its location I would not have seen it in the darkness. *That's because it's designed to appear inconspicuous, Green. It's not meant to be noticed.* With my breathing calmed, and feeling confident enough to make my move, I took the bag from my back and opened it. The night vision goggles would be essential as would be the lock pick set. I removed these items and pulled the goggles onto my head so they sat on my forehead. I placed the lock pick set in my pocket and took a final look around. *All clear. Time to go, Green.* I placed the bag on my back once again and stood up keeping my back against the wall. Slowly and carefully, I made my way left, keeping my eyes on the vault building.

There were no security guards in sight but I knew full well that there would be a 24-hour presence with regular perimeter patrols. As I came up to the pump house, I recognised what I had seen from the aerial photographs. Set in the lawn, the thick, flat-topped concrete slab stood 3 feet high and was roughly 3 by 3 metres in area. To the rear of it was a set of steps that led down below the structure. This area was in complete darkness so I pulled the goggles down over my eyes to take a look.

Suddenly my surroundings were transformed into a strange monochrome green. The lights from the vault building ahead of me were almost blinding so I kept my gaze low and concentrated on the staircase.

As expected, there was a steel door with a single large padlock at the base. It appeared as it was designed to, like a simple utility station that one would find in any normal factory complex. But I knew it was much more than that. I lifted the goggles and took a final look around. At that moment I saw the figure of a man making his way around the perimeter of the vault building.

I froze where I stood and instantly my entire body began tingling with adrenalin. Fully uniformed and armed, the guard walked quietly up the boundary fence towards me. The man was whistling softly to himself as he walked. I crouched down slowly and lay flat on the grass as I watched him. *Fucking hell! Just stay still, Green. Pray he doesn't see you!* The man arrived at the front right corner of the perimeter fence and made his way around to the vault entrance. Not once did he even look in my direction. I lay there frozen as I brought my breathing under control once again. The guard let himself into the gate and went on to enter the vault building itself. *That was close, Green! Too close for comfort.* I glanced at my watch to log the time he had made his rounds. It had just gone half past the hour. Feeling confident the guard would be gone for some time, I stood up, stepped forward and made my way down the concrete steps until I arrived at the base near the door. Above me, the concrete lip of the pump house roof protruded slightly, blocking out any residual light. Once again I pulled the goggles over my eyes and looked around the space for any motion detectors in the immediate area. There were none.

Wasting no time, I pulled the lock pick set from my pocket, squatted down and set to work. The lock was a standard heavy-duty Stanley industrial model. It hung on a sturdy clasp in the middle of the left-hand side of the heavy steel door. As I worked it struck me how simple the entrance was. The irony was that just 40 metres ahead of me was one of the most secure buildings I had ever entered, while here I was so close to it, opening a simple padlock. *Remember, Green. It's supposed to be this way. Even the security guards in the vault building are likely unaware of this place. Their focus will be on the vault itself. Very few people at all likely know of this place, let alone the day to day staff. No, this is meant to be nothing more than a plumber's utility station.* It took a full 10 minutes to crack the lock but eventually, I heard the satisfying click as it opened.

Placing it on the concrete below me, I stepped silently back up the steps and poked my head above the concrete lip of the pump house to take a look around. Everything was as it had been when I had come down. *Looking good, Green. Keep going.*

Placing the goggles back on my eyes, I stepped down once again to the base and slowly pulled the steel door by its handle towards me. The top hinge squeaked quietly as if it hadn't been opened in some time. The interior was dark, musty and humid. Directly in front of me was a small room roughly the same size as the concrete roof above. To the left-hand side was a large industrial electric pump bolted into a raised section of the concrete floor with a tangle of steel pipework around it.

Beyond this, on the far wall was a large mains electricity switchboard. The pump emitted a constant low hum so I knew it was functioning. To the right-hand side of the room was an identical pump which I imagined was a spare unit in case the other developed a fault. I looked around the space searching for any alarm systems or hidden motion detectors. It came as a surprise to see none at all. The subterranean room was, by all accounts, a simple, confined concrete space housing the water pumps and electrical switchgear for the vault. Nothing else.

I stood there feeling somewhat puzzled. *You need to take a very close look at this, Green.* I turned to my left and saw the main light switch for the room. It was set into the concrete wall at shoulder level and was almost certainly for the two neon tubes that were positioned in the centre of the concrete ceiling. I lifted the goggles from my eyes and turned to close the steel door behind me. This would prevent any light from escaping the room while I searched it. With the door closed, I flicked the switch and the neon lights above immediately bathed the entire room in cold bright light. My eyes scanned the walls and the floor of the room searching for any obvious signs of a trapdoor or hidden entrance. I walked around the room studying the concrete floor, squatting down regularly to knock on the surface with my knuckles. There was a fine film of dust on the floor that indicated that there hadn't been much activity in the room for some time. This was somewhat puzzling and for the first time, doubts began to form in my mind as I made my way around the two huge pumps. Eventually, I stood up and stared down at the solid concrete floor around me.

What the fuck? How can this be? I turned around and began studying the spare pump. *Perhaps it's hidden underneath? It would make sense and it's certainly big enough to cover a trapdoor.* I studied the heavy machine and saw immediately that it too was bolted into the concrete floor. Getting down onto my hands and knees, I crawled around it looking for any sign of a trigger mechanism or lever that would allow it to be pushed aside or moved. The pump must have weighed close to a tonne and the heavy steel bolts that held it in place were well and truly immovable. *You might just have fucked up big time here, Green! There is no trapdoor or tunnel here. This is just a concrete cellar. A standard underground industrial pump house. There's nothing remotely resembling a trapdoor here. Concrete walls, floors and ceiling. That's about it. All that effort and risk for fuck all! Idiot!* Feeling defeated and angry at myself, I sat down on the electric motor of the spare pump. I was dusty, sweaty and exhausted. I had risked a lot for a hair-brained theory that had turned out to be completely false.

"What a fucking waste of time..." I whispered to myself as I wiped the sweat from my forehead.

I sat there for a good five minutes planning my exit from the pump house and the Zukman premises. At that stage, all I wanted was to get back to the hotel and go to sleep. I knew I would need to make my move immediately after the guard had completed his patrol of the vault building. I glanced at my watch and looked at the steel door as I readied myself to leave. It was at that moment that I had a thought. At the time it felt random, improbable, and comically futile. But the thought refused to go away. I turned my head and stared at the electrical switchboard on the far wall beyond the pumps. Like most electrical boards, it was filled with meters, gauges, wiring and switchgear. Mounted in the centre of the wall, it was basically a grey pressed metal box that stood proud of the concrete by roughly 25 centimetres. At 1 metre wide and roughly 1,5 metres high, it struck me as being rather oversized for its purpose. *No. You're clutching at straws here, Green.*

Preferring to avoid further disappointment, I turned my head and looked at the exit once again.

But it's certainly big enough. Surely worth a look. I stood up slowly and walked over to the switchboard. The spinning metres and flashing lights were clear indicators that it was live and working. With limited electrical knowledge I knew better than to tamper with any of the switches, so instead, I concentrated on how it had been mounted against the wall. 6 large bolts attached the board to the concrete. These would have been fixed in place using heavy-duty plastic Rawl plugs or anchors. Seeing nothing out of the ordinary, I ran my hand along the top of the box. My fingers came back dusty as expected. But it was when I ran my hand down the right-hand side of the box that I felt it. It was so small as to almost be imperceptible, but there was a 2 cm square of slightly raised metal near the wall in the centre of the box. I stepped to my right to take a look at what it was but even the light from the neons above was insufficient for me to see it clearly. I quickly removed the bag from my back and pulled out the penlight torch. Shining the thin beam of light on it revealed what it was. A small square section of the sheet metal that made up the side of the box was slightly raised and set into a slide. I applied some pressure to it with my thumb and it slid easily to the left revealing a hole that had been drilled into the metal wall of the box underneath. Barely big enough to poke a finger into, it had been ingeniously concealed and had I not run my fingers across it I would never have seen it. In the hole was a single red button. I frowned as I stared at it and my immediate thoughts and fears came in waves. *What could it be? Why has it been so cleverly hidden? If it's merely part of the regular electrics, why would someone have gone to such an effort to conceal it? What will happen if I push it?* Beads of sweat formed on my forehead as I stared at it.

My biggest fear was that pushing it would set off some kind of alarm, but after further thought, I decided this made no sense given the fact that there were no regular alarms in or around the pump house. *Concentrate on the facts, Green! You know what you saw on the aerial pictures. Nothing in this God-forsaken room indicates there is a trapdoor or tunnel entrance anywhere. You were about to leave when you stumbled on this. Push the fucking thing and see what happens!* I put the thin torch in my mouth and held it in place with my teeth. Using my left hand I wiped the sweat from my forehead and blinked as I prepared to push the button.

Well...Here goes nothing. Using my thumb I pushed the button and immediately there was a short electronic buzzing sound followed by a metallic clunk. I stared in amazement as the side of the entire switchboard came away from the wall and swung open on hidden hinges that had been placed on the left-hand side of it within the concrete of the wall.

"It's a door..." I whispered to myself "Will you look at that. It's a fucking door!"

Chapter Forty-One: Pierre Lumumba.

"Hello!" called Pierre in his croaky, weak voice "Hello! Please, someone, help me!"

It had just gone 6.00 am and the morning sun glowed through the tatty hessian curtain that covered the single window. Since wakening at 2.30 am that morning, Pierre had drunk nearly all of the water in the bottle he had found on the table near the bed.

Although he had felt the need to urinate, he had been unable to move from the bed. There was a door near the window that he imagined would be the toilet but the horrendous pain he was feeling in his side coupled with the fear of opening the roughly stitched wound on his midriff had prevented him from attempting to get up.

Thankfully he had found an empty 5-litre bottle on the floor near the bed and he had managed to relieve himself in that. The steady flow of blood-tinged lymph that dripped from the plastic drain in the centre of the massive wound had slowed somewhat but it had left the mattress sticky, wet, and smelling. Pierre Lumumba had spent the last three and a half hours in a state of deep shock and terrified confusion. At first, he had told himself that this was simply a bad dream. A side effect from the anaesthetic which would wear off if he closed his eyes and tried to sleep. But the deep, gnawing pain in his midriff coupled with the discomfort of lying in his own body fluids had ensured he had lain awake throughout. It had been in the darkest hours before the dawn that he had begun to accept the reality of his situation. He had been lied to all along. The guards and the doctors had fooled him and his desperate desire for freedom and money had cost him one of his kidneys. Added to that he had found himself abandoned in some filthy room with no aftercare or support of any kind. He had no clue as to where to he was and his meagre belongings were nowhere to be seen. The warnings from his cellmate, Samuel Kisimba, had become reality.

Crippled with pain and fear he had sobbed forlornly through the final hours before the sun had risen.

But now there were noises around him. Sounds of people talking and doors opening and closing. There were conversations in Arabic and the distant sound of a radio or television. The fact that he was not entirely alone gave him a small sense of hope. He would call someone into the room and ask for help. Perhaps the guards would come and take him to the hotel? Perhaps he would still get the money he had been promised? Maybe it had all been a mistake?

With his spirits lifted, Pierre raised his right arm and pulled the grubby pillow from under his head. He placed it against the wall near the bed and carefully shifted his body making sure not to disturb the ugly stitches on his side. The pain was excruciating and he felt like he had been eviscerated. Still, he pushed himself over until he sat in a semi-upright position against the wall. Below him, the bed was soaked with the fluid that had dripped from the plastic drain in his side. As he drew the sheet up to cover this he saw the small brown envelope that had been lying under the pillow. He reached over and picked it up with his left hand. Sweating and panting heavily from the exertion, he opened the envelope to find a blister pack of pain killers and two $100 bills. With shaking hands he popped four of the tablets from the silver foil pack and stuffed them into his mouth. He swallowed them with a single gulp of water from the plastic bottle and his head fell back against the wall. It was a full five minutes later when he brought his head forward once again and looked at the two banknotes in his left hand. Pierre Lumumba's bloodshot eyes were filled with tears of pure despair which ran down his cheeks and dripped on his chest. Once again there were the sounds of people moving around outside the door.

"Help..." he called out weakly "Please, help me!"

Chapter Forty-Two: Rat in a Drain Pipe.

The opening to the tunnel was neatly framed by 4-inch angle iron set into the concrete wall. The entrance was large enough for a fully grown man to step into if he were to stoop slightly. Beyond this was a set of concrete steps that led down to the floor of the tunnel which stretched off into the darkness in the direction of the vault building. The light from the neons in the pump house was sufficient to illuminate the steps but the tunnel beyond was in complete darkness. *This is it, Green. You were right all along! All you need now are some photographs and your job is done. Get in there!* Once again I pulled the night vision goggles over my eyes as I stepped through the entrance and made my way down the steps beyond.

The tunnel stretched straight ahead as I expected it would. Formed from solid concrete, there were neon lights spaced at intervals of every 3 metres along the roof. To my left, I saw the light switch in the wall but as a precaution, I walked along a stretch of the tunnel using only the goggles and the residual light from the pump house to see. After walking for 5 metres I could see nothing to suggest any alarm systems or motion detectors. I decided to walk back to the entrance and turn the lights on. Flicking the switch revealed exactly what I had seen through the goggles. The tunnel was simple but extremely well built. At 2 metres high and 1.5 metres wide, it was more than big enough for its intended purpose. It stretched off into the distance as a perfectly rectangular subterranean passageway. There was no debris or obstacles of any kind for as far as the eye could see. The urge to continue walking down the tunnel was overwhelming but as a precaution, I decided to check the entrance one more time. *Better to be safe, Green.* I climbed the steps and made my way back into the pump house then flicked the light switch off and pushed the heavy steel door open once again. The fresh night air was sweet compared to the humid, musty atmosphere below and I could hear the familiar sounds of the band saws and other activity emanating from the abattoir in the distance. I quietly climbed the steps until I reached ground level and poked my head over the lip of the structure. The vault building stood in illuminated silence and there was not a soul to been. *Good. Now go do this, Green. Get it done and get the fuck out of here!* Once again I padded down the steps and entered the pump house. With the light from the tunnel shining through the hole in the wall, there was no need to turn on the main lights.

Instead, I made my way through the room between the two pumps and stepped down the stairs into the tunnel.

The silence was deafening and my footsteps echoed as I made my way down its length. There was no doubting the sheer genius of its design and I marvelled at its simplicity. A brilliant piece of advanced engineering hidden so effectively while in plain sight. *Just get the pictures and get out Green. This is not a tourist attraction.* It took me just over a minute to reach the end of the tunnel and by the time I arrived, I knew I was directly under the vault building itself. My breathing was quickened with the excitement of my discovery and what I found there did not disappoint.

As I had predicted, there was another subterranean room roughly 3 by 3 metres in area. In the corner, set in the concrete roof on the far right side was the trapdoor to the vault itself. Directly underneath it was an elaborate mechanical opening system made up of an electric motor, a large oil pump, switchgear, and two powerful looking hydraulic rams. These rams were attached to a heavy steel frame and the moveable extension arms bolted into thick steel eyelets at the far side of the trapdoor itself. I knew these would have been essential to safely lower the trapdoor itself which would be enormously heavy having being built from solid reinforced concrete and tiles. The system would allow the thick concrete door to lower itself on its massive hinges and then raise itself once again, leaving no evidence of its existence above. Access to the vault above, once the trapdoor was opened, was from a sliding set of steel steps that stood to the right of the trapdoor. In my mind, I could see clearly how the whole system worked. The door would be slowly lowered on the hydraulic rams, the stairs slid into place, and all that was left was to climb up and step into the vault itself. Once the items from the vault had been removed and brought down into the tunnel, the steps would be slid away, the switch would be flicked and the door would slowly raise itself on its hinges once again. I shook my head in amazement as I stared at it.

So...As you suspected, Green. It can be none other than Zukman himself who is stealing the treasures from the world-famous Zukman Hoard. Who will police the police?

"Genius..." I whispered to myself as I stared at the elaborate machinery. "So simple yet perfectly effective."

I wasted no time removing my camera and set about taking several pictures and videos of the trapdoor system. The fatigue I had felt earlier was all but gone due to the thrill of my discovery. I glanced at my watch as I did so.

It had just gone 3.00 am. *It's getting late, Green. Get the pictures and get out of here pronto!* I planned to finish documenting the trapdoor system and then take several pictures of the hidden entrance to the tunnel behind the switchboard in the pump house.

Then all that would be left would be to make it back to the ladder, set the rake under the wires of the electric fence, get over the wall and head back to the hotel. *You'll be back by 3.45 am. The evidence you'll have from tonight combined with the aerial pictures will be enough, Green. The proof will be there and your job will be done.*

A minute later I had finished with the trap door and was making my way back through the tunnel towards the pump house. I was feeling buoyed by my success and confident I would easily make my escape over the wall. But just then I heard the clang of a steel door, the scuffle of rapid footfall and the sound of two men shouting angrily in Arabic. My heart sank as I realized the noise was coming from the pump house up ahead of me. Despite my precautions, I must have set off some hidden sensors and alerted the guards to my presence. With no weapons, I was defenceless and trapped. Trapped like a rat in a drainpipe with nowhere to run. I froze where I stood and the adrenalin coursed through my body with such force that I could hear and feel the blood pumping in my neck and temples.

"Fuck!" I whispered to myself through gritted teeth as I looked behind me back down the tunnel and considered my very limited options "Fuck!!"

Chapter Forty-Three: Pierre Lumumba.

"Please, can you help me?" said Pierre in a weak, croaky voice.

The young woman stood at the door and stared at him suspiciously. It had just gone 8.00 am and after two hours of trying, Pierre's repeated calls for assistance had finally brought her into the room. On her head, she wore the usual hijab and she eyed Pierre with distrust and a wicked glint in her dark brown eyes. Her black robes were dusty and the skin on her cheeks was pockmarked from acne. Unusually for a woman, she was chewing gum and she glanced casually around the filthy room as if she was accustomed to seeing such things.

"What do you want?" she said bluntly in perfect English.

"I need water..." said Pierre. "I need water and a cellphone. And some food. Will you help me?"

The young woman smirked knowingly as she chewed her gum.

"I will need money..."

"I have money," said Pierre as he pulled a $100 note from the envelope and showed it to her.

"Then I will help you..." she said, her eyes lighting up.

"Thank you..." said Pierre breathlessly, "thank you."

"When do you need it?" asked the woman.

"As soon as you can..." replied Pierre as he lifted his shirt to show her the grotesque scar on his side "I have nothing, and I am unable to move."

The woman stared at the ugly wound unflinchingly. Once again, it appeared as if she had seen this sort of thing before.

"Where am I?" Asked Pierre.

"You are in an apartment in Tangier..."

"My name is Pierre. What is your name?"

"My name is Salma..."

"Who brought me here, Salma?"

The woman sighed as she chewed her gum. She cast her eyes over the hessian curtain and walked over to open the window behind it.

"It smells bad in here," she said "I don't know who brought you here..."

"But..."

"I said I don't know who brought you here!" she shouted back at him loudly "Did you not hear me?"

"Okay, okay..." said Pierre holding his hands up in surrender "I'm sorry. Please, would you go and get me a price for a smartphone, 5 bottles of water, and some fruit. Maybe some crisps. I am not sure I can eat much but I'm very hungry."

The young woman crossed the room and paused at the door. She looked down at the pathetic figure of Pierre on the bed and the curls of a smile formed on her lips as she chewed the gum.

"Okay..." she said "I will be back later."

Salma turned and slammed the door behind her leaving Pierre alone once again. Alone with a small glimmer of hope in his world of fear and despair.

Chapter Forty-Four: Surrender.

I turned and glanced down the tunnel behind me as the shouting became louder and I heard the footfalls on the steps ahead of me. The urge to run was overwhelming but I knew it would be completely futile. Even if I was to return to the trap door room and activate the hydraulic rams on the trap door, the guards would be on top of me way before it would open, and even if they weren't I would emerge in the vault itself. There was simply no escape. I was well and truly trapped.

A thousand thoughts went through my mind in an instant. *They will be armed, Green. If you put up any kind of a fight, you might get shot. No, stay put, you are here doing your job. Surrender and put your hands up. Take it from there. There's fuck all you can do now.* I took the bag from my back and placed it on the concrete floor below me. Within seconds I saw the two men approaching. They were running towards me and shouting in Arabic furiously. I raised my hands slowly and stood there still as a statue as they approached. Both men carried automatic machine guns and they slowed as they saw me with my hands raised. In the dim light I could not make out their features but one of the men was tall and slim. It was only when they were within five metres that I recognised the face of Uday. His eyes lit up like burning embers as he recognized me.

"You!" he screamed "Don't you fucking move!"

I took a deep breath and raised my eyes to the roof.

"I am unarmed..." I said clearly. "My bag is on the floor in front of me."

"Shut the fuck up, you swine!" he screamed. "One move and I'll blow your fucking head off!"

I complied as he broke out into a garbled and screamed set of instructions to the other man in Arabic. Both men were panting heavily and clearly in a heightened state of agitation. The other man nodded with wide eyes and dropped the barrel of his rifle. Uday's gun was pointed straight at my face and I saw the wry grin on his face as he massaged the trigger.

It was almost as if he was willing me to make a move so he would have the pleasure of shooting me. At that moment I wondered why they were being so aggressive. Sure, I had unbundled their secret passage, but was it really worth so much? Surely this was an overreaction of some kind? I stood there resigned to my capture as the other man pulled a set of handcuffs from his belt and approached me slowly.

"Hands behind your back, swine!" Shouted Uday.

I did as I was told as the second guard passed me and shackled my wrists in the handcuffs. He squeezed them tight and I winced in pain as I listened to the clicking of the single-stranded teeth. I watched as an expression of satisfaction came over Uday's face. He shouldered his rifle and removed a handgun from his belt.

"Now I have you, Mr Green..." he said with the barrel held to my forehead "What do you think you are doing down here?"

I sighed audibly at his dramatic display of triumph.

"My job..." I said, "What do you fucking think?"

The tall man burst into a peal of hysterical laughter and large droplets of spittle landed on my face. I could smell the garlic on his breath as he brought his face to mine.

"So..." he said, his voice lowered and full of rasping hate "We have a clever swine here. We will see about your job."

"Really?" I said resignedly "Get on with it then..."

"Oh, I will..." he hissed with his mouth to my ear as he moved to my side "On your knees!"

"Is that really necessary?"

"On your fucking knees, swine!" he screamed as I felt the blow of the pistol butt on my shoulder.

The pain pulsed through my upper right side and I gritted my teeth in an effort not to show it. Slowly I lowered myself until I knelt in front of my bag. There followed a brief but tense conversation between the two men in Arabic. What I didn't see was Uday had removed his rifle from his shoulder and was holding the butt up behind my head. He brought it down with such force that I never even felt the blow.

One minute I was fully conscious and resigned to the fact that I had been caught. The next there was complete darkness as I was knocked unconscious and my body slumped forward onto the concrete floor of tunnel.

Chapter Forty Five: Pierre Lumumba.

It had just gone 11.00 am when Salma finally returned. Pierre still lay there with his back propped up against the wall on the pillow. He had been too petrified to move for fear of opening the ugly stitches on his side. In the three hours that she had been gone he had swallowed half of the pain killers he had been left with. The sight of the young woman was a huge relief to him. She was an asset that he desperately needed. At least now he would be able to feed himself, and with a phone, he could make contact with the outside world. That way he might be able to get some medical assistance and begin to try to salvage his life with what little he had left.

He had cried his tears and now his focus was on his recuperation and moving forward. The anger he had felt towards the people who had incarcerated and fooled him into this situation had subsided and now his primary focus was one of survival.

This young woman, Salma, was his only hope of pulling through and getting back on his feet. In the long three hours that she had been gone he had told himself repeatedly that he was young, strong, and fit enough to get through this. His body would heal and life would go on. Although he had no appetite, he was thirsty once again and the water she would bring would fix that. The gruesome wound in his midriff would mend and before long he would be on his feet again. The flow of sticky pink lymph that dripped from the plastic drain in the wound had slowed further and he had placed the end of it in the empty water bottle to prevent any more from seeping into the bedding and mattress. Having been unable to move, he was completely unaware of the pungent stench in the room despite the window having being opened earlier by Salma.

"I have the prices for the things you asked for" she said flatly, still chewing gum.

"Thank you, Salma..." said Pierre with visible relief. "Thank you for this help."

The young woman shrugged nonchalantly.

"The phone is $60.00, the water and food will be $15.00. If you give me $80.00 I will get it all for you..."

Pierre swallowed as he realised the true cost of this help. In his his mind he weighed up what little he had against the benefits of what he would receive. *The phone is crucial. It is your connection to the world and will be vital going forward. $60.00 is normal for a smart phone, even a cheap one. You have to have it.*

"Okay..." said Pierre "and how soon can you get it for me?"

"Immediately" she replied casually.

"Okay that is great. Would you be able to get me some paracetamol as well?"

Salma sighed and rolled her eyes at this new request.

"Yes. I can get you pain killers..."

"Thank you, Salma, thank you..."

Pierre paused as he stared at the woman. Deep down there was a niggling suspicion that she was untrustworthy. *What if she never returns?* This thought worried him but he decided he would pre empt this by the promise of more money.

"I will have more money for you if you can continue helping me..." he said.

"Sure..." she said impatiently "No problem."

With his mind made up, Pierre took the crumpled brown envelope from his pocket and removed a $100.00 bill.

He held it out, reaching forward slightly. The act of doing this caused a wave of agony to pulse through his midriff and he felt the rough stitches pull at his flesh. Immediately he lay back on the pillow and gasped.

"Please don't forget the pain killers..." he said "I am suffering here."

Salma stepped forwards and snatched the money from his outstretched hand.

"I won't" she said impatiently "I will return this afternoon..."

With that, the young woman turned and walked out of the room slamming the door behind her. Once again Pierre Lumumba was left alone. All alone but with a small glimmer of hope in the darkness of the painful and confusing new world in which he had found himself.

Chapter Forty-Six: Interrogation.

I was awoken by the shock of a bucket of icy water being thrown into my face. Until then I had been vaguely aware of being carried and manhandled but the force of the blow I had received to the back of my head had ensured I had spent most of the previous half-hour unconscious. My head was pounding with pain and my vision swirled as I opened my eyes.

"Wake up, swine!" I heard the familiar snarling voice of Uday.

Slowly it all came back to me. The tunnel, the hydraulic system beneath the trapdoor, and the memory of feeling trapped as the guards had approached. I closed my eyes once again to allow the spinning to calm and the pain to subside. My chin was resting on my chest and I took a deep breath and groaned as I raised my head.

"Haha!" shouted Uday "The pig is waking up, behold!"

I opened my eyes to see I was in a warehouse of sorts. Although the bright neons above me stung my eyes, I could see piles of scrap machinery lying around on either side. I blinked as I took in my surroundings while panting from the thumping pain in my head.

Ahead of me were a set of offices at the far side of the high roofed building while on the left above the broken machinery, a thick steel slaughter railing ran 7 feet above the concrete floor. Dangling from this was a series of large meat hooks that hung from a chain mechanism within the railing. It was clear that I was in an abandoned abattoir that had been converted into a storage area for scrap or broken meat processing machinery.

There were piles of broken refrigeration compressors and electric motors alongside damaged freezers, water towers, and cold rooms. To my right was a huge crate of copper wire and piping that was obviously destined to be sold for scrap. The familiar sound of the band saws was loud and it was only then that I realised where I was. I had been carried or dragged from the tunnel and brought to this place by Uday and his companion.

It was clear I was in a building that had originally been part of the meat processing plant but was no longer being used. I tried to lift my arms but found they had been shackled to the arms of an old fashioned steel office chair by handcuffs.

My legs wouldn't move either. They too were shackled with cuffs and I was unable to move them at all. I blinked once again and focussed on the two men who stood in front of me. Uday was leaning on the crate of copper wiring. In his teeth, he held a cigar and there was a satisfied smirk on his thin, cruel face. The other shorter man clutched the bucket which had been used to toss the water onto me. I looked at his face and immediately realized he too was a hard man. It was the face of someone whose hardships showed in the lines and creases of his features. I turned my head to the right and saw the walls were covered with shelving, full of yet more broken and scrapped machinery. My head throbbed with pain as I watched Uday take the cigar from his mouth and speak.

"Good morning, Mr Green," he said. "Nice of you to join us, it appears you slept in."

I blinked and looked him in the eye. It was as if he was trying to make light of the situation and make jokes at the same time. I frowned as I looked at him and shook my head slightly.

"What do you want from me?" I asked in a quiet voice.

"What do we want?" he repeated animatedly. "What do we want? I'll tell you what we want, Mr Green. We want to know how you found the tunnel and who you have told about it. That is what we want."

"I must say it was very well hidden," I said. "But not well enough. The game is up. It's over for you."

At that Uday broke into laughter once again. The other guard, who clearly did not understand English shrugged and laughed nervously as if he was trying to impress Uday.

"Oh I beg to differ, Mr Green..." said Uday as he walked towards me, "I think it's over for you."

The tall man placed the cigar back in his mouth as he approached.

I asked you a question, Mr Green..." he said leaning down to put his face near mine.

Once again I smelt the garlic on his breath.

"How did you find out about the tunnel? Who have you told about this?"

"Well..." I said quietly "I think that is something that you'll soon find out for yourself."

Without warning, Uday swung his right hand around and the blow connected with my left cheekbone. His fist felt like a lump of solid granite and the sheer speed and force of the punch caused my teeth to crack and my vision to change. For a few seconds, all I saw were strange swirling chequered patterns. It was both unexpected and brutal in its delivery and I knew then that I was concussed.

As my vision cleared, I felt the warm trickle of blood running down my cheek and onto my shirt. The pain was almost unbearable and I felt my head dropping once again as I drifted into unconsciousness. In the weird, semi cognizant world I found myself in, I wondered once again why there appeared to be such seemingly inappropriate force in dealing with me. Sure, I had been caught, but this treatment seemed somewhat extreme.

In the distance, I heard the two men shouting once again in Arabic. There was movement and footfalls and the sound of metal sliding on concrete. I willed myself to lift my head to look at what was happening but the darkness kept encroaching and I found I was unable to. The next minutes were a confusing blur of shouting and metallic sounds and I found a strange comfort in the darkness that enveloped me.

It was a respite from the pain in my head and it hurt to drift out of it. I have no idea how long it was, but the next thing I felt was my shirt being ripped open. I tried to lift my head but was unable. The next thing I felt was an inexplicable piercing pain in my left nipple. This was quickly followed by the same pain in my right nipple. *What the fuck is going on?* This sharp pain soon subsided as the darkness came on again but there was the same grating sound of metal scraping on concrete. Some minutes later I was once again shocked into consciousness by yet another bucket of icy water being thrown on my head. I gasped and brought my head up instantly.

The two men spun in my vision but settled soon after. Again there was the stinging pain in my nipples. I stared down at my chest to see they had been clamped between two copper alligator clips that were attached to electrical wires. *What the fuck?* Slowly I raised my head to see Uday sitting in front of me three metres away just beyond the wet floor that surrounded my chair. In his hands, he held a small grey metal box with what appeared to be a rheostat switch. The device was attached to the cables on my nipples which were in turn connected to another set of wires that ran to a power point behind the crate of copper scrap.

"I'm sure that now you will tell me what I need to know, Mr Green..." he said with a huge grin. "Are you ready?"

I watched as he turned the dial and immediately I felt the pulse of pure electricity as it powered through my torso. Instantly my entire body jerked violently as it tensed and I let out a long moan as my back arched involuntarily in the chair. The moan soon became a scream as Uday turned the dial to increase the voltage. The pain and uncontrollable vibration were so intense that the skin on my wrists and shins was broken by the force of me pulling at the cuffs. Uday held the voltage for what seemed an eternity then suddenly twisted it back down to zero again. I slumped in the chair, unable to move and teetering on the edge of reality. My body was numbed, tingling, and still shaking violently from the terrible pulses of electricity. Panting and not quite believing the situation I now found myself in, I looked up at the smiling man. He sat there grinning widely with the cigar still clamped in his teeth.

"I will ask you again, Mr Green..." he said "How did you find the tunnel, and who have you told about it?"

By then my entire body was aching, my mouth was dry, my heart was racing and I was in a dangerous state of shock. The electricity had pushed my body close to the edge and I had more than likely suffered nerve damage. I panted heavily as I stared at the smiling man. The smell of burnt flesh and singed hair rose from where the clamps were attached to my nipples.

"Go fuck yourself, you son of a whore..." I whispered through gritted teeth.

"Okay!" he said cheerfully before twisting the dial on the rheostat once again.

This time he turned up the voltage much higher and the shock and blistering pain was unfathomable. I felt the vertebrae in my back creak as my spine arched violently and I let out a tortured and continuous scream of agony as my limbs jerked violently at the cuffs.

I have no idea how long he kept the current running as I was quickly blessed once again by the gift of unconsciousness. I became aware of voices sometime later, this time three men were talking. I kept my eyes closed and listened.

"I told you not to kill him, you fucking idiot!" said the new voice.

He spoke with a wheezing, chesty sound and I knew then it was the voice of Darko Zukman.

"I'm sorry, sir..." said Uday "I was just trying to get the information you asked for."

"You may well have killed him already you fool," said Zukman. "Put him in the cells, we will deal with him later. Get rid of any trace of him having been here..."

"Yes sir..." replied Uday.

Chapter Forty-Seven: Pierre Lumumba.

It was 4.00 pm by the time Salma returned. Pierre had spent the past five hours in an ever-growing state of fear and worry. His thirst had returned and he was finally feeling hungry. *Had the woman simply vanished with his $100?* This was a real possibility, and he recalled the niggling fears he had when he handed her the money. Fears that she was was not to be trusted.

Feeling very alone during this time he had shifted his body occasionally, keeping the end of the plastic drain in the empty water bottle that he had propped up on the bed beside him. Not once did he attempt to stand for fear of opening the stitches on his side. The damp patch of lymph that had already soaked into the bedding and mattress had started to dry and crust over, and as he sat there he had begun picking at it and flicking the crystallised fragments onto the floor. His world had become one of stark solitude. There was none of the music that he loved so much. No television or anyone to make jokes or laugh with. His usual sense of optimism and lust for life was steadily abandoning him and he found his thoughts growing ever darker with each passing minute. Unable to sleep with the hollow, pulsing pain in his midriff, he had swallowed the last of the pain killers by chewing them and swallowing the bitter powder without water. At one stage he had shed tears once again as he watched the sky darkening through the hessian curtain. The thought of spending another night in that room alone filled him with dread and panic. *How could he have been so stupid? Why had he not* listened to the wise words of his friend and cellmate Samuel? Why had he been subjected to such unbelievable cruelty? Was he such a bad person? Surely not. How would he proceed if and when he was finally able to get back on his feet? The $100.00 bill he had left would not take him very far at all. He had been so close to his goal of reaching safety in Europe but he had stumbled and fallen at the very last hurdle. It was for all of these reasons that his spirits soared when he saw the door open and the young woman, Salma step inside the room.

"Thank God you are back..." he said with a smile.

Salma carried two bulging and heavy looking plastic bags in her hands. She was panting slightly as if she had just climbed a set of stairs.

"God bless you, Salma..." he said as she placed the bags on the floor near the bed.

He watched as she took two notes amounting to $15 from her small handbag and handed them to him.

"Thank you," said Pierre.

The young woman stepped back and stopped to speak at the door.

"There was a problem..." she said, still chewing gum.

"What problem?" asked Pierre, wide-eyed with alarm.

"The phone" she replied in a flat tone "The phone was stolen as I was walking back from the shops."

Pierre stared at her not quite knowing what to say.

"You mean..."

"I mean the phone was stolen!" she shouted back in annoyance.

"I was carrying it in one of the bags and a young man came past and snatched it from me. He ran away and I could not follow him."

Pierre swallowed as he realised he had just lost 30% of his money. He stared at the young woman hoping for some offer of help or even a simple show of compassion. But she stood there unmoved, and seemingly unwilling to help. *Was she lying? Had she simply stolen the money? Had his initial suspicions of the woman been right?* Tears began to fill his eyes as he realized he had been fooled once again. Kicked whilst down in the cruellest of ways.

"I see..." he said quietly as he blinked back the tears. "Will you lend me a phone? Just for half an hour so I can get onto Facebook and try to find some help?"

Salma rolled her eyes and spoke.

"No..." she said "I have done enough for you. Your water, food and painkillers are there in the bags. Goodbye."

"Salma!" shouted Pierre as she opened the door, "Salma, please!"

But there was no response, and the woman slammed the door as she left.

Chapter Forty-Eight: Incarceration.

"Here..." said the quiet voice "Drink this."

I felt my head being lifted and the blessed feeling of water being carefully poured into my mouth. It immediately had the effect of rousing me but at the time, I was not so sure I wanted to be awakened. My head was thumping with pain and my body felt like it had been through a meat grinder.

"Take some more..." said the voice. "Good, now rest."

I felt my head being lowered into some soft material and I was aware that I was lying on something that felt like hard concrete. The water woke me further and I opened my eyes. Above me was a concrete bunk and sitting to my right was a black man. He sat there studying me while clutching a tin cup of water.

"Would you like some more?" he asked.

"Yes, please," I said.

Once again the man lifted my head as he brought the lip of the mug to my lips. The water was warm but it was a much needed life-giving boost for my senses. I clenched my fists as I drank and immediately noticed my arms were severely weakened. I blinked as I looked around the room and the memories of my capture and interrogation came back to me. The savage beating and the unimaginable pain of the electrocution.

"Where am I?" I asked the man.

"You are in a private prison cell in an industrial area of Marrakesh." said the man.

The man had a kindly face but I could see from his broad shoulders that he was powerfully built.

"My name is Samuel," he said "You were brought in here by the guards a few hours ago."

I looked to my right to see the toilet, the basin, and the thick steel bars of the cell. Morning light streamed in from an unseen window above. I brought my hand up to touch my chest and immediately regretted it. I lifted my head to see my nipples were blackened and bloody.

"I washed the wounds on your chest and face while you were unconscious," said Samuel. "It will prevent infection."

"Thank you..." I said.

Feeling my strength returning, I brought my hands up to my face. My wrists were raw from the handcuffs and I immediately noticed that my hands were shaking uncontrollably. I knew that this was a direct result of the electric shocks I had been given. Despite it all, my head was surprisingly clear. It was then I heard the familiar sound of the band saws.

"We are in the Zukman premises," I said.

Samuel answered immediately.

"Yes, I think we are. Why were you brought here and how were you injured?"

I dropped my hands to my side and sighed.

"Long story..." I said. "What about you?"

There followed a protracted conversation where, after introducing myself, I learned the story of Samuel Kisimba.

He told me of his journey from the time had left the Congo up till the moment he had been separated from his daughter on the high seas six weeks previously. He told me the circumstances of the separation and how many of the migrants had fallen into this same trap.

I shook my head in disbelief as I realised the business operations of the Zukman Group were a lot more diversified than meat processing. What was being described was a well-oiled people trafficking organisation. Samuel spoke quietly and patiently as he narrated his sad tale and as he spoke I managed to sit up and lean against the concrete wall of the cell. He told me of his faith as a Christian and how he had struggled to endure his long incarceration. He told me about his cellmate, Pierre who had opted for the operation and had left only a few days beforehand. I listened quietly as my strength returned gradually. It seemed the man was grateful to have some company. Finally, he paused and stared at me with a curious look on his face.

"What about you, Jason?" he asked "How did a white Englishman end up here in a cell in Marrakesh with me?"

I went on to tell him my own story. I told him my firm in London had been hired to investigate the disappearance of gold and other priceless artefacts from the recently discovered archaeological treasure that was the Zukman Hoard. Samuel had no idea there was such a thing but he showed interest all the same. By then I trusted the man enough to tell him I had discovered exactly how it was being stolen and that I had been caught while attempting to document it. Samuel listened and shook his head in horror as I recounted my capture and subsequent torture.

"They almost killed me as well," he said "You are lucky to be alive."

"Why?" I asked, "What did they do to you?"

"They shot me on that boat..." he said, and I saw the pain of the memory in his face.

He unbuttoned his tattered cotton shirt and pulled it to one side to reveal the scar from the bullet wound.

"*He* shot me. And *he* has been torturing me mentally ever since."

"Who is this you're talking about?" I asked, "Who has been torturing you?"

Samuel took a deep breath and dropped his gaze to the floor.

"His name is Uday..." he whispered.

I watched as he looked up at me once again and I saw his eyes were swimming with tears.

"Ah, yes..." I said, nodding as the hatred rose within me. "I know this man too. He is the man who did this to me."

Samuel shook his head knowingly.

"I thought as much..." he said resignedly "But I am to leave here soon. I will be going to join my daughter in Spain."

Feeling my strength return further, I sat forward and placed my feet on the concrete floor of the cell.

"And how exactly have you arranged this?" I asked.

Samuel reached into his pocket and brought out a folded and crumpled piece of paper.

"Here..." he said, handing it to me "Read it. This is how."

Chapter Forty-Nine: Pierre Lumumba.

Pierre was desperate. After much shifting and reaching he had managed to lift one of the plastic bags that had been delivered by the woman, Salma. Thankfully she had made good on her promise to deliver the water and snacks even if she had stolen the money for the phone.

Pierre had forced himself to eat even though his appetite was non-existent. The water had been a blessing and he had drunk a full bottle as soon as he had grabbed the bag. Once again he had felt the need to urinate and had done so in the 5-litre plastic bottle that lay near his bed. One good thing was he had a full supply of paracetamol and he was swallowing two tablets every hour.

During the evening he had heard the sound of people coming and going and there was the ever-present sound of the television in the distance. At one stage he had heard what sounded like young boys laughing and playing outside. Unable to move, he wondered how high up this room that he had found himself in was. He recalled the fact that Salma had been panting and sweating slightly when she had returned with his provisions. The terrible blow of having lost the money intended for a phone was weighing heavy on his mind. *How could he have been so stupid? Why had he not trusted his instincts at the time?* The woman had looked untrustworthy and her swarthy attitude should have reinforced this. Now here he was, trapped, unable to move, completely cut off and in rapidly deteriorating health. *I need to make a plan and fast. If I stay here I will continue to be robbed and here, no one cares. No, you need to be proactive. Think, Pierre, think.* It had just gone 8.00 pm when he heard the young boys talking and laughing outside the door once again. In his mind, he thought he might have a better chance of making a friend with one of them. That was if they spoke English.

"Hello!" he called, "Can you boys hear me?"

Immediately the sound of their conversation ceased and he knew they had heard him.

"Boys..." he called out again, "Please come in. I want to talk to you."

There was a pause followed by some low whispering just outside the door.

"Don't be afraid. I am alone in here..."

At that moment he heard the door creak as it opened. Two young boys poked their heads around the door. Their expressions were open and wide-eyed and Pierre put their ages in their early teens.

"Hi guys," he said with a forced smile "How are you?"

"Fine..." said the older of the two.

"I heard you talking outside and I wanted to say hello."

The older boy looked around the room nervously and replied.

"Hello..." he said flatly.

"Would you like a packet of crisps?" Asked Pierre, taking one from the bag on the bed.

The younger of the two looked at the older and they smiled immediately.

"Yes..." said the older boy "Thank you."

"Here..." said Pierre "Take it, enjoy."

The older boy stepped forward and took the bag from Pierre. He opened it immediately and both boys began digging in.

"Do you like football?" asked Pierre.

"Yes..." said the older boy with a smile as he ate.

"Which team do you like?"

"Manchester United!" said the boys in unison.

"Ah, okay, you like Ronaldo?"

The boy's faces lit up once again and they nodded enthusiastically.

"Me too," said Pierre "I like him as well."

"What about music?" asked Pierre "do you listen to music?"

The boys nodded once again.

"Cool..." said Pierre "I was wondering if you would help me. I am not well. I gave some money to a lady earlier so she could buy me a phone and she said it was stolen. I'm not sure whether to believe her."

"What was her name?" Asked the older boy.

"Salma..." said Pierre.

The two boys nodded in knowing, then the older one spoke.

"Salma is not a good person," he said "She is a thief."

"I thought so..." said Pierre "I was wondering, does anyone you know have a smartphone? I need to get onto Facebook. I am trying to get some help from a friend."

"I have a phone..." said the older boy, pulling a battered-looking device from his pocket.

"Would you mind if I used it for a few minutes? I promise to be quick, and you can wait here while I do."

The young boy shrugged and spoke.

"No problem..." he said as he leaned over to hand it to Pierre.

Chapter Fifty: Green.

"You do realise what they are doing here?" I said as I handed the paper back to Samuel.

"What do you mean?" he said.

I shook my head in disbelief. What I had read on the piece of paper was staggering. Not only were these people trafficking people across the sea to Europe, but they were also actively involved in human organ harvesting. It was only then that I realised why there had been such a disproportionate reaction when I had been caught in the tunnel.

This was a great deal more serious I could have possibly imagined and it was clear they were protecting a lot more than the simple theft of artefacts and gold from the vault. *No, Green, these people are killers. You are lucky to be alive and be under no illusions, they intend to finish you. You need to get the fuck out of here!*

"Samuel..." I said, sitting forward "This is an organ harvesting and trafficking set-up. The money and the freedom they are promising you is a lie. They are selling corneas and kidneys to wealthy people from around the world and you are their donor. Have you any idea how much money they would sell your cornea for?"

"No..." he replied "I never gave it much thought. I just want to be free and to be with my daughter once again."

"Samuel," I said, feeling exasperated "From what you have described of your treatment here, these people are trying to break you. To break you mentally and physically."

"They have succeeded" he replied softly "*He* has succeeded."

"So that is the reason you must cancel this immediately. You are risking your life and there is a very good chance you will never get to see your daughter again. This is is probably the biggest mistake you will ever make."

The big man sighed and his sad eyes dropped to the floor.

"What choice do I have?" he asked "I am in Purgatory here."

"You do have a choice," I said "These people are not only thieves, they are killers, and no matter what that doctor told you, they don't care about you at all. I wouldn't be surprised if your friend, Pierre is dead. You said they asked you to sign a consent form?"

"Yes. They said I would have to do that before the operation..."

"Well, that is as good as signing your own death warrant."

Samuel shook his head and a look of hopeless exasperation came over his face.

It was at that moment that I heard the sound of a motorcycle over the constant buzzing of the meat saws. I stood up on slightly shaky legs and climbed up to the top bunk. Getting onto my knees I peered through the bars of the tiny window and looked down towards the end of the building. Parked there were several motorcycles and mopeds. One man was alighting from his own and I noticed immediately that he left the keys in the ignition.

"Who are these people on the motorbikes?" I asked, "Are they general staff at the abattoir?"

"Yes. They are workers from the factory" said Samuel. "They come and go all the time. 24 hours a day, non stop."

"I see. And it was Uday who brought me here earlier?"

"Yes, you were brought here by Uday and one other, I don't know his name. They threw you on the floor and I lifted you onto the bunk."

"And where are they now...?"

"They were on the night shift," said Samuel "They will probably return tonight. Uday is not always here but he comes at least three times a week. Always at night. I assume he travels to Tangier whenever there is a boat going across to Spain."

"So you think he will return tonight?" I asked.

"He may do..."

"I think he will..." I said climbing down from the top bunk once again. "Tell me about this doctor. Where do you see him? Does he come here or do you go to see him somewhere else?

"He came a few times when I was still badly injured. But now I go to see him in his office."

"Where is this office?

Samuel went on to describe the short walk he would take whenever he went to see the doctor. He described the route he would take under armed guard, turning right at the cell entrance, then left past the guard station and up to the steel door.

"What is behind this steel door?" I asked.

"It is an old factory unit, filled with junk. His office is at the far side of that building."

"And you say this place is near here, just beyond the steel doors?"

"Yes..." he replied, with a slightly puzzled look on his face.

I knew then that he was referring to the place where Uday had tortured me, and I had a good idea of the layout of the property from the aerial photographs. We were somewhere in the factory complex to the left of the vault and the head office building. The fact that I could hear the band saws and could see the factory workers arriving and leaving nearby confirmed this. I knew that we were being held near the service entrance to the property. Once again I took a seat on the bunk in front of Samuel. I looked him in the eyes and spoke.

"Listen Samuel..." I said quietly "These people are extremely dangerous. I have no doubt they intend to kill me and there is no way I am going to sit back and allow that to happen. I can guarantee that they don't have your interests at heart either. I am going to break out of here. You can come with me if you like, that choice is yours. I have a plan..."

Chapter Fifty-One: Darko Zukman.

"You almost killed him you fool!" growled Zukman from his seat in his office.

"I was only trying to..."

"You went too far!" he bellowed. "Jesus Christ! Electrocuting him, Uday! What were you thinking?"

"He was refusing to talk, sir..."

"Well, at least he is alive. When we are done here I want you to call the day shift guards and get them to check on him."

"Yes sir, I will do that."

"How the hell did he get inside the premises?"

"We found a ladder and a rake near the pump house, sir. It seems he used the rake to lift the wires on the electric fence and pulled the ladder up behind him with a rope."

Darko Zukman shook his head in dismay and stared at the clock that sat on his expansive desk. It had just gone 11.30 am.

"Now we have a serious problem..." said Zukman, his face swollen and red with fury. "We do not know what he has told his superiors. We have no idea. If he has said anything we will have a huge issue explaining that away. Fucking hell! Have you checked his phone?"

"He was not carrying a phone sir," said Uday. "He didn't even have a wallet."

"Hmm," said Zukman, wheezing as he reached for the crystal tumbler of Scotch.

"How the hell did he get here?"

"We found a car up the street, sir. We have asked but no one seems to know who it belongs to. We suspect he came alone in that vehicle. He had a set of car keys in his pocket."

"I see..." said Zukman, scowling at the taste of the neat liquor. "I want you to check if those keys are for that vehicle. If they are, you must remove it immediately."

"Yes sir," said Uday.

"There will be questions already. Why he has not appeared at his hotel. His company will soon be aware he has gone missing. This is a big fucking mess!"

"Sir..." said Uday, "If I might make a suggestion."

"Go ahead..."

"If he came alone, as we suspect he did, surely it's possible he hasn't yet told anyone. We could retrieve his belongings, his phone and computer from his hotel. That would at least tell us something. If we can get those things and we do not hear from his firm, his disappearance would surely be unexplained. As far as they would be concerned he may well have taken a trip into the desert and never returned. It may not be as bad as it seems. Surely the fact that we have him works to our advantage?"

Darko Zukman slumped in his chair. Deep lines of worry creased his wide forehead and the great folds of flesh around his lower jaw wobbled with worry and rage.

"You may be right..." he said. "The fact that we haven't heard from anyone is positive."

There was an extended period of silence as Darko Zukman drummed his pudgy fingers on the surface of the desk.

"When can you get his belongings out of the hotel?"

"Tonight, sir. Late tonight. I will ensure it is done safely and without any problems."

"And what of the woman, Professor Tremblay?"

"She will not be aware of it, sir."

"Hmm. Okay, first thing, check this bastard is still alive. Secondly, get that fucking car here and out of the way. We will talk to Mr Green again later. Either way, we will retrieve his belongings from his hotel. Then as you say, it may just happen that this Mr Green will take a trip to the desert. A long trip in his vehicle, a trip from which he will never return..."

Chapter Fifty-Two: Green.

"How often do the guards come past here?" I asked Samuel.

"Apart from bringing food at mealtimes, they might walk past twice a day. Then again at night."

"They will be coming back, and soon," I said. "I need to act as if I am seriously injured, at least unable to move. Will you work with me, Samuel?"

"Yes..." he replied "I will. What must I do?"

"If they ask you anything, anything at all about me, you simply say this man is injured. He can hardly talk and he hasn't moved since you brought him here. Can you do that?"

"Yes, of course..."

"Good," I said. "As I told you, I have a plan. I am going to get out of here. If you want, you can come with me, but I am not going to be here for long."

"I believe you, Jason," he said with an anxious look on his face.

"Just work with me and I'll keep you in the loop," I said. "But when it happens, it will be quick and violent. I'm warning you now so you don't panic. If you stay with me you have a very good chance of getting out of here. The choice is yours. I will choose my moment and tell you beforehand. Is that clear?"

Samuel's face was filled with pure terror. He took a deep breath and looked around the cell before speaking. It was as if he was experiencing the early stages of Stockholm syndrome. As if he had become comfortable in this place. But I knew different.

"What are you planning to do, Jason?" He asked quietly.

"I am going to lure the guards in here. They will be under the impression that I am either dead or dying. I need you to back me up on this. They will ask you if I have moved or eaten or drunk any water. I need you to tell them I have not. I am going to wait until nightfall if they don't come for me before then. I will ask you to raise the alarm, shout and scream and tell them you think I'm dead. I need you to put on a show for me. I want at least one of them inside here and near me. I will take it from there. For now, if they come past, I will lie on the bunk and if they ask you anything, you tell them I haven't moved. Can you do that, Samuel?"

"Yes, Jason," he said, "I can do that."

"Good..." I said as I lay down on the bunk "Now we have a plan. It's better than sitting here waiting to die..."

I brought my hands up in front of my face once again. Although it had subsided somewhat, they were still shaking and my head was pounding. I took a deep breath and exhaled slowly as I stared at the concrete bunk above me. *Pray this works, Green. Pray your plan works.*

Chapter Fifty-Three: Pierre Lumumba.

Pierre woke at 6.00 am. He had spent most of the night sitting upright, eating and drinking occasionally, and staring at the walls of the filthy room. At one stage he had managed to stand up and walk to the tiny bathroom to relieve himself. The toilet was a hovel and the bowl was stained, chipped and broken, but at least there was running water. But as he was lowering himself onto the bed once again he had fallen and pulled the stitches in his side. He saw with horror when he had examined them that two of them nearest to his front had loosened. This sent him into a panic and he had spent most of the night awake.

In the end, he had resolved to ask the older of the two young boys he had befriended, Farouk, to call a doctor the following morning. His worry was what the doctor's visit would cost. After all, he had exactly $115 to his name. The boy had been kind enough to lend him his phone and he used the opportunity to log in to his Facebook account and send out some calls for help. The problem was, however, that he had very few friends he could call on. He had sent a friend request and a message to his former cellmate, Samuel. In this message, he had told him how sorry he was that he hadn't listened to his advice. He told him how he had been fooled and described the appalling situation he had found himself in. But in his mind, he knew he would probably never hear from Samuel again. That kind, strong man who had tried to help him. The man who had pleaded with him to refuse the offer of the operation. The fake operation that had taken his kidney and ruined his life.

Pierre Lumumba had shed more tears during the night when he was at his lowest point. At the time his world was lonely and hopeless and he feared he might die there in that room. Finally, at 3.30 am, he had carefully shifted his body so he could lie down and he had fallen into a restless and troubled sleep.

But the rising sun that shone through the window behind the hessian curtain lifted his spirits. It was a new day and perhaps there would be new possibilities. Slowly and carefully he propped himself up and shifted himself into the sitting position.

It was only then that he became aware of the burning sensation in his wound. This was emanating from the area where he had pulled some stitches when he had stood up.

Slowly, he lifted his shirt and what he saw filled him with horror. The area of exposed flesh under the pulled stitches was swollen and inflamed. Seeping from the loose stitches was thick yellow pus. Pierre Lumumba's crude wound had become infected.

Chapter Fifty-Four: Breakout, Part One.

Uday appeared as Samuel had predicted, at just after 6.00 pm. During the day the guards had checked in on me three times. Good to his word, Samuel had simply told them that I was awake and breathing but was unresponsive and in an extreme state of lethargy. He told them he thought I might be concussed, which I was.

This seemed to satisfy them and I lay there on the bunk staring at them blankly when they came. They stood beyond the bars of the cell and I used the opportunity to study their attire and their weapons. All the guards carried the usual automatic rifles which were slung on their shoulders. Added to this they carried sidearms in holsters on their belts; pistols that looked like old Italian Beretta 92 models.

The lunch had been delivered at exactly 1.00 pm and two servings had been passed to Samuel through the gap in the bars in the cell door. I forced myself to eat a little but my appetite was poor and I was far too preoccupied with my escape plans to be bothered to eat. Samuel had finished his food and had told the guard who collected the chrome trays that served as plates that I had not eaten at all.

During the hours when we were alone, I had climbed up onto the top bunk and watched the comings and goings of the factory workers on their mopeds and motorcycles. Samuel had explained that it was easy to know when the guards were approaching by the sound of their boots on the polished concrete floor. In my mind, I had built up a mental picture of where we were within the factory complex and soon enough I had a concrete plan of action. It was risky, even foolhardy, but I knew I had little choice and if I failed I would be killed anyway. The tentacles of the Zukman Group were long and far-reaching and I knew far too much for them to allow me to simply walk away from this.

The one single thing that was in my favour was the fact that they had no idea if I had told anyone about the tunnel. This was the only reason I was still alive. I knew there would be more questioning and possibly more torture, and that was something I was not going to allow to happen.

I recalled the rasping voice of Darko Zukman as he had admonished Uday for his heavy-handedness in interrogating me. I had been barely conscious at the time but his ominous words rang in my brain.

'We will deal with him later...' he had said.

Uday arrived with his usual brash and obnoxious bravado. He was accompanied by the same guard who was with him when they had apprehended me in the tunnel. He beat the bars of the cell with a wooden truncheon and barked his question at Samuel.

"Good evening, Mr Baboon!" he shouted with a wide grin. "How is our guest doing?"

"He is seriously injured..." said Samuel quietly. "He has not drunk or eaten anything but he is breathing and is sometimes awake."

"Aha!" said Uday with a grin "This is good. We will need him awake later."

Uday mumbled some quiet words in Arabic to the other guard who nodded and smiled.

"See you later, Mr Baboon!" shouted Uday as he walked off down the corridor towards the guardhouse.

When the footsteps had faded and the silence returned, I spoke.

"I see he is being his usual self..."

"Yes," said Samuel from the bunk above me "His hatred of me runs deep..."

"He is trying to break you, Samuel," I said "He won't stop until you leave. Or until I deal with him..."

There was an extended period of silence before Samuel spoke again.

"Whatever happens later, Jason," he said, "I will come with you."

"Good man," I said as I wrangled with my own fears. "One way or another, this will end tonight."

I spent the next two hours in quiet contemplation as I lay on the bunk. There was only the occasional exchange with Samuel, who I imagined was dreading what might happen. I had decided to act by 9.00 pm at the latest if the guards had not come for me by then. If they did come before that time, I would do so anyway.

As far as they were concerned I was no longer a threat and would be easy to manage. The stage was set and now all that was left was to wait. It was at exactly 9.05 pm when I decided it was time.

"Samuel..." I said "The time has come. Remember everything I said. Stand at the cell door and make as much noise as you can. I need you to sound like you are in a panic. They will come and they will be flustered and upset by this. Pay no attention to them. Keep making noise until they come in to check on me. When they come in I want you to stand near the sink and make sure you are out of the way. Are you ready?"

There was a long pause during which I wondered if the big man had lost his nerve. I saw his legs swing over the side of the upper bunk where he lay and it came as a relief to hear his words when he finally spoke.

"I'm ready..." he said.

"Good man," I said as I watched him jump down to the floor. "Do it now, and make it convincing."

Samuel Kisimba walked up to the thick iron bars of the cell.

In his hand, he clutched one of the tin drinking mugs. He turned briefly and I saw his eyes were wide with fear. I nodded at him, urging him to go ahead and he turned and started.

"Guards!" he screamed. "Guards! This man is dead! Help!"

As he shouted he began beating and rattling the tin cup against the iron bars of the cell. Suddenly the relative quiet of the cell block was transformed into a cacophony of wailing chaos. As instructed, Samuel continued his performance and his pleas grew louder with every second that passed. Adrenalin filled my body as I heard the angry response from the guards down the corridor. My arms and legs were like coiled springs and events began to appear in slow motion as the savage and primal instincts of the caged animal took over. Samuel Kisimba never relented in his protest, bashing and rattling the tin cup again and again and screaming with ever-growing intensity.

His performance was convincing and I heard the panicked sound of shouting and heavy boots running on polished concrete as the guards made their way down the corridor. I lay, as I had done before, on the bottom bunk but with my right arm hanging limply over the side of it. My head hung to the right staring with a blank expression at the cell entrance. The two guards arrived quickly and I immediately saw that it was Uday and the other man who had visited us earlier. Uday was furious and red in the face. He joined in with Samuel and began beating the bars of the cell with his wooden truncheon as the other man fumbled with the keys.

"Silence, you bastard!" he screamed at Samuel from behind the bars "Silence!"

Everything was going according to plan. *So far so good, Green. Wait for it.* It took a full 20 seconds for the second guard to finally open the cell door. The scene was as I had intended it to be. Loud, chaotic and confusing.

I watched as Uday pulled the rifle from his shoulder and held it level as his colleague swung the door inwards. The man stepped forward and at that moment I saw Samuel step back near the sink as instructed. Uday barked an order to his colleague as he walked into the cell.

Although it was in Arabic I knew he was telling the man to check my vital signs. The man stooped over as he approached where I lay motionless on the lower bunk. It was as his head was coming down towards my own that I struck. My left hand shot up and I grabbed him by his shirt near his collar. I pulled him downwards with such force that his face smashed into the concrete ledge of the upper bunk with the sound of a watermelon being crushed with a baseball bat.

At the same time, my right hand reached up and quickly removed the pistol from the holster on his belt. It took a split second to lift the weapon and fire it into the soft skin beneath the man's jaw. The top of his head exploded and the roof of the cell was instantly plastered with a mixture of pink brain matter, chips of white skull bone and clumps of black hair. I swung my legs from the bunk and, still holding the dead man's twitching body, I stood up and took aim at Uday who stood stunned at the cell door. As expected, he began firing his weapon immediately The bullets thumped into the dead guard's body one after another and I felt the force of them pushing me back as the deafening barrage continued. My first shot ricocheted from one of the thick iron bars and chips of plaster and dust flew from the wall to my right.

It was then that Uday, seeing I was armed, dived to his left and rolled on the floor to avoid my next shot which thudded into the concrete wall behind where he had stood. I dropped the dead man and lunged forward, gripping the open door of the cell as I went. It was as I poked my head around the front of the cell that another spray of bullets burst from the muzzle of the machine gun. Uday had known I was coming and although he was still on the floor, he had lifted his weapon in anticipation of it. I ducked back to safety and stood rigid as I waited for the bullets to stop. At that moment I saw Samuel standing where I had told him to retreat. His entire body was vibrating with terror as he made the sign of the cross on his forehead and chest.

Without wasting time, I pushed the pistol behind my belt at my back and reached down to retrieve the machine gun from the dead guard who lay motionless in the centre of the cell. Now fully armed, and with the advantage of having what I assumed would be a full magazine of bullets, I made my way back to the cell entrance and prepared to confront Uday.

The cell was filled with acrid smoke and plaster dust and my ears were ringing from the muzzle blasts in the confined space. With the machine gun at hip level, I turned and stepped into the corridor. It came as a surprise to see Uday standing near the guardhouse not 20 metres from where I stood. His forehead was furrowed with lines of rage and his eyes glowed like raging fires.

"Die you fucking pig!" he screamed as he pulled the trigger once again.

But in his seething rage, he had made a fatal error. His magazine was empty and the weapon clicked uselessly as he pulled the trigger again and again.

The machine gun I held spat out a stream of burning lead as he threw his weapon to the floor and sprinted away out of sight up another corridor to the left. Unsure whether I had hit him or not, I made my way quickly towards the guard station, gun raised and ready to shoot. As I approached the corner I heard the clanging of metal on metal and I knew he was making his way through the steel doors Samuel had described. *He's going for cover, Green. He knows you have the machine gun and all he has is his pistol. You have the advantage. Go get him!* I rounded the corner to see the sliding door was half open and I recognised the scrap filled factory unit beyond as the same place in which I had been held and tortured.

Keeping to the left of the corridor out of range from fire from within, I made my way up the darkened corridor towards the door. I knew from memory that the room was filled to the brim with all manner of broken, trashed machinery and scrap metal. This would offer him plenty of cover and give him a distinct advantage. *Fuck!* But I was holding the machine gun and all he had was his pistol. This was an advantage I was happy to live with.

With the barrel of the gun raised, I stepped up to the door and poked my head around it. Almost instantly I saw the muzzle blast from the pistol coming from behind a pile of cold room panels that were propped up on one of the roof pillars. I pulled back instantly and stood with my back to the steel door.

Two rounds pounded into the door directly behind my head with unbelievable volume and I closed my eyes as I stood there panting heavily. I knew the cold room panels we made from thin sheet metal with light insulation inside. There was a very good chance the rounds from the machine gun would pierce them and it was an opportunity I was willing to take with the limited bullets in the magazine.

Choosing my moment, I spun around and sprayed the panels with a burst of fire, working from right to left. As soon as I was done I stepped back behind the door and waited for any sound that would indicate he had been hit. It came as a surprise to hear yet another round clang into the door behind me just above my left ear. I had found myself in a deadly standoff and every second wasted was a threat to my escape. *He only has the pistol, Green. None of the guards wore belts with extra ammunition. He'll be lucky if he has more than two rounds left in that thing.* I glanced to my right to see there was a large red fire extinguisher hanging on the wall near the door. I lifted it from its hook and swung it around the door. It clattered on the concrete noisily and I heard the single gunshot at the same time. The decoy had worked and I smiled silently when I heard the clicking of the empty gun and the furious shout of frustration from within the factory unit. Buoyed by the knowledge that I now had the upper hand, I turned and stood in the open doorway, gun held at the ready. Uday leapt like a feral cat from behind the panels and rolled across the floor into safety behind a huge pile of empty freon canisters. I knew from the speed at which he had moved where he would likely be and I emptied the last of the magazine in that direction. Suddenly the pile of steel canisters collapsed in a hissing mess of clattering steel and trapped gas. Stepping forward, I pulled the trigger once again but the magazine and chamber were empty.

Still walking, I threw the rifle to the floor, pulled the pistol from my belt and held it in front of me.

"Come out to play you piece of shit!" I shouted as I walked.

At that moment Uday sprang up from his hiding place. In his right hand, he held one of the empty freon canisters. He hurled it at me with savage force and I had to quickly swing my body sideways to avoid being hit in the face.

The move was a split second too late and the base of the canister connected with my left shoulder sending a lightning rod of pain down my side. Once again, Uday leapt to the right with the speed and agility of a leopard. At the same time, I pulled the trigger on the pistol but the shot missed his head by inches. He landed and crouched behind the wooden crate of copper scrap I had seen the last time I was there. Blind rage filled my brain as I walked towards the crate. I aimed and pulled the trigger once again but the magazine was empty and the quiet click was a sign that things were about to change.

The fight was about to take on a very personal element. Knowing my weapon was useless now, Uday stood up from behind the crate. In his hand, he held a thick length of copper pipe. His thin, hawkish face was fixed in a wide grin and his eyes were pools of fire.

"Now it's just you and me..." he whispered.

I glanced to my right looking for anything I could use as a weapon and saw the pipe wrench on the middle level of the wooden shelving. Reaching over, I grabbed it by its handle and tested its weight by swinging it.

"Let's do it..." I said quietly as I walked towards him.

Uday roared like an animal as he jumped over the crate of copper waste and ran towards me. His approach was fast and unchecked and I knew then that he was prepared to die. This was the most dangerous and unpredictable enemy anyone could face. With his mouth contorted in a snarl, he swung the heavy copper pipe at my head. Knowing the blow was coming, I countered it with a swing of the pipe wrench. The two heavy pieces of metal connected with a loud clang and the force of it sent a bolt of pain up my wrist and forearm.

I swung my body to the right and watched as the copper pipe

was sent flying out of his grip. The force of his swing had unbalanced him and his forward motion carried him past me where he tumbled and rolled head over heels on the smooth concrete floor.

Wasting no time, I turned around and lunged for him hoping to get to him while he was still down. I reached him as he was still on the floor and had just spun his body around to face me. I brought the pipe wrench down towards his head with all of my might but in the last split second, he dodged it by inches. The jagged edges of the twice hardened alloy steel jaws smashed into the concrete inches from his right ear and for the first time, I saw fear in his eyes. But the blow I had delivered had put me at a disadvantage and he used this opportunity to land a powerful sidewinder punch between my right cheekbone and ear. The blow was savage and it felt like I had been struck in the head with a solid lump of steel. My vision began to fade as the pipe wrench fell from my hand and I fought to keep my eyes open.

Seeing his opportunity, Uday landed another blow which sent me falling to the floor face first. In some distant vestige of my conscious mind, I heard my own voice. *Well, you did your best, Green. You did your best.* Reality for me became distorted as Uday got to his knees and spun me over so I lay on my back. He straddled my midriff with his legs and brought his powerful, bony fingers down onto my neck. I blinked as he began to strangle me and I heard the words he spoke through his clenched, grinning teeth.

"Now, you die..." he said.

The man's fingers were like a vice and I felt my eyes bulging as his grip tightened on my neck with unimaginable force. He held me there snarling like an animal and as he squeezed my vision began to fade once again. But it was at that moment that my right hand found the handle of the fallen pipe wrench. With what was left of my strength I swung it up blindly toward his face. Uday never saw it coming and the side of it connected with his lower left jaw. Almost immediately, his grip on my neck loosened and I felt the blood whooshing into my head once again. The blow had broken his jaw and smashed several of his teeth and he sat there stunned and unable to move. A slow trickle of blood ran from his mouth and pooled in the hollow of my neck. Feeling my strength returning, I brought my right knee up into his groin as hard as I could. The man let out a strangely muffled grunt and his eyes widened as his testicles were crushed.

With my head clearing, I knew this was far from over and I needed to act fast. Using my arms, I pushed myself up into a sitting position with the man still straddling my legs. I pulled myself clear and stood up feeling dizzy and disoriented. Reaching down, I lifted the man by his shirt. Still dazed from the blow, he used his own legs to straighten himself. It was as if he had lost his senses and was actually helping me.

Without thinking, I lifted him once again by his shirt and ran forward. I intended to finish the job by throwing him down and slamming his head into the concrete floor. But it was after I had only taken five steps that his body inexplicably stopped moving and I lost my grip on him and fell forward onto the floor once again. Feeling confused and expecting yet another attack, I spun around and looked up.

The large meat hook, which had been hanging from the slaughter rail had entered his body near his spine between his fourth and fifth ribs. With his feet and arms twitching uncontrollably, Uday hung there suspended 30 cm from the floor with his back to me. I stood up slowly and walked around him. His jaw hung open and his face was contorted in agony but his eyes followed my own as I came around. I stood there for a few seconds as I gathered my breath. It was only then that I became aware of a movement behind me. I swung around expecting to see another guard but it was Samuel Kisimba who was standing alone at the door. He had seen what had just happened and he stood there with an impassive look on his face.

"Samuel..." I said between breaths "We need to get the fuck out here now. Let's go!"

But Samuel's eyes were fixed on the face of Uday who hung twitching from the meat hook. Slowly and purposefully, he walked towards where I stood.

"Samuel!" I shouted as he approached.

But the big man kept walking and he brought his left hand up briefly to silence me. I watched as he walked up to Uday, his face only inches away, and looked him in the eyes. There was a brief moment of recognition in the face of the dying man and I saw it clearly in his face.

"Yes..." said Samuel quietly "It is me, the baboon."

Samuel Kisimba placed his hands on the shoulders of Uday in a brotherly gesture. Suddenly he pulled down with all his might and I heard the ribs cracking as he did so. Uday coughed once and his eyes rolled back as a cascade of frothy pink blood fell from his sagging jaw. Samuel turned around slowly and looked at me.

"Now, we can go..." he said.

Chapter Fifty-Five: Pierre Lumumba.

"I need a doctor, Farouk..." said Pierre, "Can you help me?"

The boy had arrived, as promised, to check up on him. Pierre lifted his shirt slowly and the young boy's eyes widened at what he saw. Pierre's wound was swollen, inflamed, and suppurating profusely. The plastic drain had fallen out and the room was filled with the sickly sweet smell of corruption. Farouk retched and brought his hand to his mouth before he spoke.

"I will go now and find one..." he said.

"Thank you..." said Pierre. "You are my only hope."

The time had just gone 2.00 pm and Pierre Lumumba had a fever. His appetite had all but disappeared and he was starting to fall into a state of malaise. On the odd occasion he had been able to sleep, his dreams had been frightening and panicked. He had drunk a lot of water and had once again resorted to relieving himself in the plastic 5-litre bottle instead of attempting to stand. His rapidly deteriorating condition had cemented his resolve to seek medical help and the cost of it was no longer a concern. All he could think about were the calls for help he had sent out on Facebook, his only hope.

"Before you go..." said Pierre "Could I check my Facebook on your phone? I'm hoping for some good news."

"Sure..." said the young boy as he dug in his pocket.

Pierre took the device and wasted no time logging into his account. Farouk walked over to the window and pulled the hessian curtain to one side to allow more air to enter the tiny room. A cool breeze blew in but it was little comfort to Pierre whose brow was damp with sweat.

The phone he held was his only connection to the world and he knew that if he was to receive any help at all, it would be there. With a glimmer of expectant hope, Pierre opened his messages page. But what he found there sent his spirits plummeting. Of the four messages he had sent out to friends and family, no one had replied. He stared at the small screen and sighed heavily.

"Are there any messages?" asked Farouk.

"No..." said Pierre as he forced a smile. "Not yet, my friend. Maybe there will be later though. I think, for now, if you could call a doctor. I'm in a bad way."

Pierre groaned as he handed the phone back to the boy.

Farouk smiled and nodded as he took the device. In the short time he had known Pierre he had become fond of him and he was genuinely concerned for his well being. Even at his tender age, he could see that his new friend's health was worsening.

"I will go now and bring a doctor..." he said.

Chapter Fifty-Six: Breakout, Part Two.

Samuel and I ran back through the steel door and into the darkened corridor beyond. It was as we passed the guard station that I saw the spare magazine lying on the desk near some empty coffee mugs. I pulled the weapon from my belt, removed the spent magazine, and replaced it with the new fully loaded one. Although events had happened very quickly, I was under no illusions that we would almost certainly run into more resistance as we made our way out.

"We need to move fast Samuel," I said, "Stay with me."

Making our way past the corridor to the cell block we arrived at yet another set of doors on our left.

"This is the exit..." said Samuel "I remember it well."

The double doors were locked and there was an electronic keypad near the centre. I knew there was no other way to open them other than brute force.

"Stand back..." I said as I pulled the pistol from my belt.

The shot was deafening in the confined space but the lock was instantly blown open and I kicked at the door immediately after. It swung open with a metallic clang revealing a clear night sky peppered with stars above. Unfortunately, this set off an alarm and a series of industrial sirens began screeching all around us. *Fuck!* I ran down the steps into the cool night air and made a quick right turn at the corner of the building. I knew from the layout of the cell block that the motorcycles I had seen coming and going were parked not 50 metres from where we were. I planned to get there and leave the Zukman premises on one of them. With Samuel right behind me, we sprinted through the darkness and almost ran into a tall, razor wire topped fence between two buildings.

This was an obstacle I had been unable to see from the tiny window in the cell and it was the only thing standing between us and the motorcycles that were parked under a floodlight only 20 metres ahead. There was a small pedestrian gate in the fence secured with a single padlock. Once again, I pulled the weapon from my belt and destroyed it with one shot.

Samuel and I raced towards the parking area to the motorcycle I wanted. The Suzuki SF 250 road bike I had seen from the cell was still parked there with the key in the ignition. It was by far the fastest of the lot and I imagined it must have belonged to a supervisor or junior manager. I grabbed the handlebars, flicked the kickstand with my foot, and reversed it from where it was parked in amongst the other smaller bikes and mopeds. At that moment a group of five armed guards ran out from the side of a nearby factory unit. Seemingly confused by the chaos and the screeching alarms, they ran towards us shouting furiously in Arabic. Wasting no time, I swung my right leg over the seat, turned the key in the ignition, and kick-started the machine into life.

"Jump on behind me, Samuel!" I shouted, "And hold on tight!"

At that moment, one of the guards pulled a sidearm and sank onto one knee to take a shot at us. Before he could even raise his weapon, I emptied two rounds from my pistol in his direction. Although none of the bullets hit their target, the sudden and unexpected burst of gunfire sent the guards diving for cover in all directions and bought us a precious few seconds to make good our escape. Samuel climbed onto the back of the motorcycle and I felt his entire body shaking as he placed his arms around my waist. I revved the motor and shouted back at him.

"You ready?!"

"Yes, Jason!" he shouted over the roar of the engine.

The powerful motorcycle jumped forward with surprising speed and the front tyre left the ground briefly as I sped off in the direction of the service entrance.

Crouched down over the handlebars, I heard two shots ring out behind us as I made a left turn at the far end of the tarmac.

I took the corner at speed and immediately saw the bright lights and boom gates of the service exit up ahead. *You're almost there, Green!* The back tyre of the motorcycle crunched on the sandy tarmac as I skidded to a halt near the glass-clad guardhouse at the centre of the exit. With both booms down, the guard inside was wide-eyed with panic as he saw us.

"Open it now!" I shouted as I revved the bike.

Instead of doing as he was told, the young guard reached for the telephone on the switchboard in front of him. I pulled the pistol from my belt and shot a hole through the glass just inches above his head. The man screamed in terror and immediately pressed the button that opened the boom in front of us. Glancing behind us as I waited, I saw three motorcycles racing up the tarmac towards us in hot pursuit. One of the riders took a shot as I pulled away from the guardhouse and I heard the ricochet on the steel pipe of the boom above us. I pulled out into the bright lights of the street beyond and made a right turn heading towards the city. There was still a fair amount of truck and moped traffic but the motorcycle was fast and powerful and before long we were moving at over 100 km per hour. Samuel clung on to me for dear life as I wove in and out of the traffic and powered around the corners. It was some five minutes later when we had left the Sidi Ghanem industrial zone and were entering the city that I pulled over to see if we had escaped our pursuers. Although two of the riders had been outpaced, the other one was racing up behind me.

"Fuck!" I shouted as I pulled away "Hold on, Samuel!"

Speeding along the only route I knew, I soon entered the clean and orderly streets of the city. Here the street lighting was good and traffic less congested. But the rider behind me was relentless and as much as I tried, I could do nothing to lose him. As we were approaching the wall of the ancient city that I shot through a red light and almost killed us both.

The beige coloured sedan screeched to a halt, almost causing a pileup, and I only missed it by inches having swerved and I very nearly lost control of the bike.

It was by sheer luck that our forward motion kept us upright and I was able to steady the machine once again. When I had recovered from the shock, I turned briefly to see the rider behind us was not only holding his pace but had gained on us. It was clear that his machine was equal in speed and power and he was an extremely skilled rider.

I knew then that it would be difficult, if not impossible to shake him off and that I would need to act fast. Accelerating and weaving in between yet more vehicles, I made my way along the street that ran parallel with the medina wall. Up ahead was the car park with the Argana tree on the left and the archway that was the entrance to the souk on the right. *You'll lose him in there, Green. It's late and there won't be much traffic either.* With my mind made up, I skidded to a halt at the archway and rode the bike inside. Up ahead the darkened, covered alleyways of the souk loomed and I gunned the engine as I raced inside. Even at that late hour, there was still a fair amount of pedestrian traffic. This was mainly the owners of the various stalls packing up and shutting down their shops for the night. Men and women yelled and leapt out of our path as we tore down the dark corridors. Both Samuel and I had to duck the many hanging trinkets and other displayed goods that hung in our way. The deafening sound of the engine served as a warning to those in our path that we were coming and most did their best to jump out of our way. At the end of one long straight, I braked and slid to a halt on the flagstone floor. Glancing back, I saw the rider was still pursuing us although he was being pelted with fruit and other objects by the outraged stall owners. The sound of revving engines and screaming filled the air as the atmosphere deteriorated into chaos. Directly ahead of me was a juice stall with a long table that had been neatly stacked with thousands of oranges. I gunned the engine once again and as I passed it I kicked the far leg of the table out. This sent both the oranges and the juicing machinery tumbling and crashing into the alleyway. The owner held his arms up in disbelief and wailed as we passed and I knew this would slow our pursuer down. Moving ahead at a slower pace, I took a right near a coffee shop and stopped to look back.

The rider had slipped and fallen on the fruit and a throng of shopkeepers were busy assaulting him where he lay on the floor. With the attention of the crowd off us for the moment, I moved ahead slowly for a further 40 metres then pulled off to the side.

"We must leave the bike here and go on foot now!" I said to Samuel.

We both climbed off the bike and I flicked the kickstand down before hurriedly making off down a darkened alleyway. The shouting and chaos behind us had caught the attention of the majority of people in the souk and many were making their way back to see what was happening. This allowed Samuel and me to move ahead unnoticed and we did so as quickly as possible. It was five minutes later that we emerged into the vast Jemaa el-Fnaa square. The air was cool and the twinkling of the stars above gave the square a serene atmosphere.

Even at that late hour, there were still hundreds of tourists and street entertainers mingling around. My head was pounding, my body was aching, and my heart was racing. But we were free. We had escaped and we were free. *You need to find a hotel now, Green. Your faces must not be seen anywhere.* I knew full well that heading back to my own hotel would be the equivalent of signing my own death warrant. The many alleyways of the souk were filled with guest houses and hotels so I turned left and we made our way across the square towards another entrance at the far side. Once again, we entered the darkened maze of the souk but this time without being chased. Fully aware of my dishevelled and battered appearance, I stopped near a trinket shop and straightened my hair in a mirror. The face that stared back at me was haunted and pale. *Better than dead.*

"Are you okay, Samuel?" I asked as we made our way further into the souk.

"I think so..." he replied.

"We will rest soon. Don't worry..."

After some five minutes of walking, I saw the faded sign for 'Footprints Backpackers Lodge' on the wall to my left.

The sign hung above a dirty looking wooden door that had been painted blue sometime in the distant past. I turned the old brass handle and the door swung open. The tiny reception area was decorated in a bohemian style with bean bags, wall hangings and posters of sixties rock bands. I closed the door behind us and Samuel and I stood there waiting for someone to appear. I glanced at him briefly and saw that he was still shaking and his eyes were wide with shock.

"Just relax, Samuel..." I said quietly "We are safe now."

I looked around to see a small staircase at the far side of a communal lounge beyond the reception but there was not a soul in sight. Stepping up to the cluttered reception desk, I rang the bell and immediately heard shuffling from the room beyond. A door opened and a short man with blonde dreadlocks and spectacles stepped out in a cloud of pungent-smelling hashish smoke.

"Hey..." he said, clearly taken aback by our appearance.

"I'm sorry to arrive out of the blue at this late hour..." I said, "We were robbed earlier in the souk and we're looking for a room for the night."

"Okay..." said the man, frowning as he blinked his bloodshot eyes "Are you injured?"

"We'll be fine..." I said "Our luggage will be delivered later. We just need a room for now."

The conversation continued for another five minutes and by the end of it, I had secured a top floor twin room with WIFI and a telephone. The man led us up the stairs past the communal dormitories to our room. It was threadbare and musty smelling but there were two beds and an old lounge suite with a coffee table to the centre.

"This will be perfect," I said with a forced smile.

The young man stopped at the door and turned to look at the two of us once again.

"You're sure you'll be okay?" he asked.

"We will be fine, thank you again," I said. "One more thing.

Could you please get me the phone number for the Riad Sahari hotel? I need to make an urgent call..."

Chapter Fifty-Seven: Pierre.

It was 4.00 pm by the time young Farouk returned with the doctor. The boy had found him at a nearby clinic and after much begging, the doctor had finally agreed to accompany him to the block of flats where Pierre had found himself. A Moroccan in his late twenties, the doctor walked into the tiny room and immediately frowned at the sickly sweet smell of corruption that filled the air. Pierre was in a delirious sleep at the time but awoke as soon as the door opened. He breathed a sigh of relief upon seeing the young man in his white doctor's coat.

"Good afternoon..." said the doctor "Your young friend came to my surgery and refused to leave until I came here with him."

"Thank you for coming..." said Pierre in a croaky voice "I am not well at all."

The doctor walked over to the window and pulled out the single wooden chair that sat beneath it. He placed it near the bed where Pierre lay, sat down, and spoke.

"Now then..." he said, "Let's take a look at this wound of yours."

Pierre gingerly lifted his shirt to expose the ugly, suppurating laceration and the doctor winced visibly. He placed his spectacles on his nose and sat forward to take a closer look.

"Yes. I see..." he muttered as he sat back.

The doctor pulled a digital thermometer from the top pocket of his coat and held it against Pierre's neck. He frowned once again as he saw the result.

"Your wound is badly infected, sir..." he said "You are running a fever and you need to be in a hospital."

Pierre went on to relate his story to the young man. He told him everything from the time he had been incarcerated in Marrakesh up to the present.

The doctor sat there nodding with a knowing look on his face. All the while, young Farouk stood by patiently. Pierre went on to explain that he had been left with very little money and the doctor confirmed that this would be insufficient for a state hospital let alone a private clinic. Pierre's hopeful expression dropped as he heard this news.

"Look..." said the doctor "I can prescribe some antibiotics and ointments for now, but you will *have* to seek proper medical care, and soon. This cannot be treated here."

A look of relief came over Pierre's face and he nodded vigorously.

"Thank you, doctor..." said Pierre "I am hoping to get some help soon. In the meantime, I will ask Farouk to get the items I need."

The doctor nodded and pulled a pen and notepad from his top pocket. He scrawled a prescription onto the paper and handed it to the waiting boy.

"Make sure he follows the instructions exactly..." he said "This is very important."

Farouk nodded and smiled at Pierre.

"Now..." said the doctor as he stood up "I must leave. I will come back tomorrow at the same time to check up on you."

"Thank you once again, doctor..." said Pierre.

Chapter Fifty-Eight: Plans.

"Omar," I said into the receiver "I didn't expect you to be at the hotel."

I glanced at my watch to see it had just gone 11.00 pm.

"Mr Green!" he said, sounding relieved. "We have been worried about you. Professor Tremblay has been asking all day. Are you alright?"

"I'm fine," I said. "Listen to me, Omar. I have some very important work for you. Are you able to help?"

"Certainly sir" he replied confidently.

"Good..." I said "Firstly, has anyone been to the hotel asking after me? Anyone at all?"

"No sir. Not to my knowledge."

"And no one has been into my room?"

"No sir..." he replied, sounding puzzled.

I breathed a sigh of relief and continued.

"Listen to me, Omar," I said "I need you to go to my room and gather up all of my belongings. My phone, my computer, my bags, everything. Can you do that?"

"Yes sir. I am here with the night receptionist. He is resting in the back room. I can get the spare key for your room."

"Good..." I said "Now listen carefully. There will very likely be some people coming there soon. They will be looking for me and asking questions. My belongings must be removed before then. I will need you to bring them to me. I am not far from the hotel. Will you be able to do that? I will make it more than worth your while."

"Yes, sir, I can do that. There is very little going on here and we are expecting no arrivals."

"Well..." I said "As I told you, there will be some people coming there soon. I need you to go *now*. Get everything, throw it all into my bags and get to me at Footprints Backpackers Lodge. Have you heard of it?"

"I know exactly where that place is, sir..."

"Good," I said "You must do it now. Waste no time at all. I will be waiting for you here. Be careful..."

"Don't worry, sir?" he said confidently. "I will go up to your room right away and will leave immediately. I will be with you in the next 30 minutes."

"Speak to no one, Omar. Tell no one about this. As far as you know, you have no idea where I am. Understood?"

"I understand, sir, I will see you shortly..."

I spent the next 30 minutes pacing the room while Samuel sat on the bed. He appeared calmer than he had been but I could see the strain on his face. It was clear he was unaccustomed to such violence and the past two hours had traumatised him deeply. I made two cups of coffee and handed one to him. Both our hands were shaking slightly.

"Try to relax, Samuel," I said. "As I told you earlier, we are safe now. We will take this one step at a time from now."

"Thank you, Jason," he said, looking up at me as he took the mug. "I trust you..."

It was not long after that I heard footsteps on the stairs beyond the door. For a moment my body tensed up in preparation for a confrontation.

There was the distinct possibility that Omar had been intercepted by Zukman's men and they had forced him to lead them to us. It came as a great relief to see the dreadlocked receptionist and Omar step into the room alone.

"This man had brought you luggage." Said the bleary-eyed manager.

"Thank you..." I said firmly "We will be fine for now."

The man left with a puzzled expression on his face and as soon as he had gone I spoke.

"Did anyone come to the hotel while you were getting my bags, Omar?"

"No, sir..." he replied with a worried look on his face.

"And no one followed you here?"

"Not at all. The souk was very quiet, I walked here without incident."

"Good," I said pointing to the corner of the room "You can put the bags on the bed."

I walked over after he had done so and immediately opened my bag. I pulled out my computer and phone and tossed the drone to one side. As I did so, I saw Omar's eyes light up. Seeing no need for the device in my immediate future, I decided to give it to the young man.

"Here..." I said, holding it up to him "You can have this for your trouble."

The young man's eyes lit up and a huge grin formed on his face.

"Oh, wow!" he said as he took it "Are you sure, Mr Green? I can have the drone?"

"Yes..." I replied "Take it but stick around. I will be needing you to do some more work for me."

"No problem at all, Mr Green!" said the beaming young man.

I rummaged further in my bag until I found the carton of cigarettes. I pulled out a packet and wasted no time lighting up. The smoke was calming and it served to focus my mind.

I looked at the two men in my room. *How the fuck did you get yourself into this mess, Green? And what a total fucking mess! Jesus!*

"Right, gentleman..." I said. "We all need to talk. Let's sit down at the table and discuss, shall we?"

There followed a long and in-depth conversation between the three of us. During this time I smoked profusely and made sure not to mention the reason for my disappearance to Omar. Samuel sat, silent and stoic the whole time but I noticed his eyes were constantly on my phone. Omar, clearly overjoyed at becoming a new drone owner, sat listening attentively and nodding as I spoke. Finally, I sat back in my seat and lit another cigarette.

"So..." I said to Omar "I will need another vehicle. I need to get to Tangier. My friend here, Samuel, is going to Spain. He has been separated from his daughter and will be joining her there. The vehicle will have to come from another car hire company as the last one is gone."

"I can easily arrange that, sir," said Omar. "We have several car hire firms we use. Say the word and I will have it delivered."

"It cannot be delivered anywhere near the Riad Sahari," I said.

I can have it delivered to the far side of the main square. I can have it there by 9.00 am tomorrow. And I will take you to meet the vehicle."

"Good," I said "We're making progress..."

I sat back and looked at Samuel. His wide forehead was lined with worry.

"Um, Mr Green," said Omar "You mentioned that Samuel needs to get to Spain..."

"Yes, that's right..."

"Well..." said Omar, "My uncle is based in Tangier. He runs a small business there. An export business shall we say. He makes the trip in his boat to Spain three times a week."

There was a moment's silence as I took this new information in. I stared at Omar who sat with a half-smile on his face. I realised then what he was talking about.

"This business of your uncle's..." I said, "Would it involve the smuggling of hashish to Spain?"

Omar raised his eyebrows and replied.

"Yes, sir. That is correct..."

"And you think he might be open to the idea of carrying a couple of passengers on one of these nights?" I asked.

"I'm sure he would open to that, sir." he replied "For a small fee, of course."

I watched as Samuel's eyes darted from Omar to me. The sadness had all but disappeared from his face and for the first time, I saw hope in his eyes.

"This would obviously require an introduction from yourself," I said. "Is this something you might be able to arrange?"

"I am due to take the next three days off, sir," said Omar. "We porters work in 3-day shifts. If you are going to Tangier, I could accompany you and I would be more than happy to introduce you to my uncle. It would be my pleasure."

I sat back and thought about the offer. My original intention was to simply get Samuel safely to Tangier. To leave him with some money and be done with it. But this new development was unexpected, and for some reason, I felt a duty of care towards Samuel. The man had been mentally tortured and broken during his incarceration and I knew full well how desperate he was to be reunited with his daughter. I looked up to see both men were staring at me expectantly. I took a deep breath, stood up, and spoke.

"Let me think about this..." I said.

I walked to the window and lit another cigarette. Staring out at the Jemaa el-Ffnaa square in the distance, I took a deep draw of smoke and contemplated my next move. *You are safe now, Green. You have all your belongings including the aerial photographs. You have everything you need to blow this whole shit show right out of the water. You need to get out of Marrakesh immediately. Stay here any longer than needed and you might just end up dead. There are some very powerful people here who would dearly love for you to disappear. You have trusted young Omar and he has not let you down yet. This offer of carriage to Spain sounds legit, especially as it seems to be a family business. It will cost a bit but you will be helping both Samuel and yourself in the process. There is no reason you shouldn't go ahead with this plan and leave tomorrow morning.* I scratched my chin as I tried to think of any negatives, but there were none. I turned and walked back to the table.

"Right..." I said as I sat down "I will go with your plan, Omar. You arrange the new vehicle, make sure it is there at 9.00 am tomorrow. You come here at 8.30 am with your bags and the three of us will drive to Tangier. How far is it from here?"

"It is six hours drive, sir..."

"That's fine," I said as I looked across the table. "Are you in agreement, Samuel?"

The big man nodded silently.

"Good," I said "Then it's settled. Do not breathe a word of what we have discussed to *anyone*."

"No, sir. I am not even going back to the Riad Sahari. I am officially off duty for the next three days. Do not worry. Even if someone comes asking questions. No one knows I brought your bags here. You can trust me."

"I hope so..." I said. "As usual, I will make it worth your while."

The young man smiled as he stood up to leave. He held out his hand and I took it in my own. I looked into his eyes as we shook and I knew I could trust him.

"See you tomorrow at 8.30 sharp," he said as he closed the door.

I turned to see Samuel staring blankly at the table. He appeared deep in thought and the lines of worry were on his face yet again.

"Are you okay, Samuel?" I asked.

"Yes, Jason..." he said "I am fine. I was hoping to get online to see if my daughter's guardian has made contact."

"Go ahead," I said pointing to my phone. "Help yourself..."

I walked to the window to smoke as Samuel busied himself with my phone. Outside the huge square was silent and deserted. My mind was still racing with the unbelievable events of the last 24 hours. *You came very close to death there, Green. Don't slip up at the last hurdle. The situation is very dangerous and will continue to be.* The air was still and tendrils of smoke drifted from the window out into the night. But it was at that moment that I heard the quiet sobbing from behind me. I spun around and walked towards where Samuel sat.

"What is it, Samuel?" I asked "Is there bad news? Is it your daughter?"

The big man looked up at me and I saw his eyes were filled with tears. But they were not tears of sadness. They were tears of joy.

"No, Jason. It's not bad news..." he said with a smile "My daughter is well. She is with her guardian, waiting for me across the sea in Tarifa."

Chapter Fifty-Nine: Tangier.

The sun was making its way down the sky as we entered the port city of Tangier. Omar had made good on his promises and the three of us had made our way across the square to meet the car hire representative that morning at 9.00 am. With Omar's help, we made it through the city and headed north up the A7 motorway through the desert until we reached the coastal town of Casablanca. There we stopped for some food and I took Samuel into a mall to get him some clothes. I had also purchased some pain killers and antiseptic ointment for my wounds.

It was a relief to have left the city of Marrakesh although I knew that we were still far from safe. The fact that we had escaped knowing what we both knew about the operations of the Zukman group would have sent shock waves through those in charge. The implications of their secrets becoming public knowledge would be terrifying and unimaginable for them, and I knew that they would have feelers out everywhere searching for us. This would include all seaports and airports as well. We were effectively moving targets in a foreign country but I was grateful for the assistance of young Omar who was still oblivious to the true reasons for our flight.

The young man sat in the back of the Toyota sedan eating crisps and listening to music on his headphones. Samuel, who sat in the passenger seat next to me, was spending a lot of time on my phone exchanging messages with his daughter and her guardian. It was pleasing to see the relief and joy the simple communication had brought him, but in the back of my mind, I feared for us both. This was far from over and I was more than aware that there would be more danger ahead.

Although I had slept like the dead, my persistent headache meant I was swallowing pills every two hours to stay on top of things and the worrying shaking in my hands was still there. The trail of absolute destruction I had left at the Zukman premises would have long and far-reaching consequences and I hung onto the hope that we would not end up being a casualty of them. At the coastal city of Rabat, I had stopped to fill the vehicle with petrol. I had also used the opportunity to book three rooms at a hotel I had found online.

It was situated near the port and was popular with budget tourists. During the brief conversations with the two other men in the vehicle, I had stressed how critically important it was that we stay together at all times and keep our heads down. I warned them that no one was to venture out at all. Not even to the restaurant. We would take our meals in the safety of our rooms and only move out when I said so.

Both men were in full agreement and seemed happy to go along with my plans. Omar had set up the meeting with his uncle. The man was due to visit us that evening at 8.00 pm at our hotel where I would negotiate the terms of our passage to Spain. With so much riding on our safe escape from Morocco, I found it hard to concentrate on my own plans afterwards. There would be much to do that would require a good deal of preparation. One thing was for sure though. The entire Zukman organisation would be brought down in spectacular fashion. The extent of their criminality was staggering, and the pain and suffering they had caused would not go unpunished. But my focus was on the present and getting myself and Samuel safely across to Spain.

I pulled over at a lay by and activated my Google maps to guide us through the city to our hotel. It turned out to be a high rise budget resort near the port. There was also an underground parking lot which suited me well. We checked in without any issues and made our way up to our rooms where I immediately called a meeting. It had just gone 6.45 pm when we all sat down in my room to discuss our plans. I asked Omar to call his uncle to confirm our meeting was on. This was confirmed and he gave his uncle the address and room number before hanging up. I ordered dinner from room service and only when it arrived did I realize how hungry I was. I had not eaten properly in some time and the food helped to settle my nerves and strengthen my resolve.

Although my phone had been ringing constantly, I had put it onto silent mode and had not answered any calls, some of which were from unknown local numbers. There was little doubt that whoever was trying to reach me did not have my best interests at heart. The calls would have to wait until I was safe across the water in Spain. *To hell with the rest of them.* After the meal, I stood on the balcony in the cool sea breeze and looked out at the dark vista of the ocean.

Six floors below, the bright lights of the city of Tangier twinkled and the vehicles hooted as they passed. As I lit a cigarette, Samuel walked outside to join me. We stood in silence for a good few minutes until he spoke.

"I wanted to thank you, Jason..." he said "My daughter is just over that ocean. And it is because of you that we will soon be reunited."

Leaning on the balcony railing, I took a deep breath as I thought about his misguided enthusiasm and confidence in me.

"Samuel..." I said, "This is not over yet. Please understand that. We are still in grave danger."

He turned and looked out at the ocean once again.

"All will be well..." he said quietly "All will be well."

I watched his face as he spoke and somehow I knew the words had some kind of special significance for him.

Omar's uncle arrived dead on time. A swarthy, bearded man with keen eyes and a bush of untidy black hair, he spoke no English and seemed initially suspicious of us. It was only after Omar had greeted him, offered him tea, and introduced us all that he set out to explain our needs. It was clear Omar did a good job as I saw the man softening visibly as he listened. He nodded in understanding as Omar spoke and Samuel looked on nervously. It was some 10 minutes of conversation later that Omar turned to me and smiled.

"My uncle is prepared to take you both..." he said. "He told me that he has done this a few times in the past, but explained that his current business is more profitable and safer for him."

"Well..." I said, "Please ask him how much he will charge and when we can leave."

It turned out this had already been discussed as Omar answered immediately.

"He is due to make a trip tomorrow night. He said he will charge $1000 each. If you agree to his fee, he will collect you here at 11.00 pm. The boat will leave at 1.00 am and will meet a Spanish fishing boat 10 miles west of Tarifa. From there, his shipment will be offloaded and you will travel on the Spanish boat to the coast."

I looked at the man and he nodded at me confidently. Something deep down told me I could trust him.

After all, he was not a regular people smuggler and his nephew had helped me a lot already. $2000.00 was a small price to pay for our safe passage and I made my decision immediately.

"Tell him I agree to his terms," I said "The payment will be made in the equivalent Moroccan dirhams."

There followed a brief conversation between the two men after which both of them smiled. Omar turned to me once again and spoke.

"It is done, Mr Green. My uncle said he will be happy to take you across the water."

A wave of relief washed over me and for the first time, I saw the possibility of an end to the perilous situation we had found ourselves in.

"Good," I said. "Please thank him for me. We will meet here tomorrow, as arranged, at 11.00 pm."

We all stood and Omar's uncle smiled once again. He thrust his hairy hand out and bowed curtly as I shook it.

"Shukran..." he said before walking out of the room.

The three of us sat alone for another 10 minutes discussing our plans for the following day. I told them I would venture out to a cash machine that night and again the next morning to withdraw money. I stressed the need for them both to stay in their rooms and told them I would make sure they did. There were no objections.

"Well gentlemen," I said "I'm exhausted. I am going down to get some cash and then I will be coming straight back to sleep. I suggest you both go to your rooms and get some rest as well."

Omar agreed and left immediately, but Samuel stayed on to have a word.

"Sorry, Jason..." he said "Would you mind if I use your phone again? I would like to say goodnight to my daughter, and tell her guardian of our plans."

"Sure..." I said "You can sit here while I go downstairs. I'll be back soon."

"I'll be waiting for you here..." he said as I handed him the phone.

I took the lift down to the reception and asked where the nearest cash machine was. It turned out there was one 50 metres up the street. As I walked up the pavement under the bright lights of the Tangier waterfront, I felt that things were finally coming together. *Let's hope it stays that way, Green. Let's hope.*

I withdrew the equivalent of $2000 in dirhams then made my way back to the hotel and up to my room. But it was as I walked in that I saw Samuel sitting on the chair clutching my phone. Once again his face was a picture of worry.

"What is it, Samuel?" I said, "What's the problem?"

The big man looked up at me and spoke quietly.

"I have just received a message from my former cellmate, Pierre. He is here in Tangier. He has lost a kidney and is in a very bad way. He says he fears he might die. He is begging for help."

Chapter Sixty: Complications.

"Samuel..." I said angrily, "You do realise that if we try to help him we are putting ourselves in danger. This could be a trap. The Zukman people may well be watching him. We would be exposing ourselves at the worst possible time."

"I know..." he replied, staring down at the phone on the table, "But he helped me through the darkest of times when I was in that cell. He's so young and he has no one."

I shook my head and walked out onto the balcony to smoke. Below me, the traffic had slowed and the night air was cool and smelt of salt. I lit a cigarette and stared out into the night. *This is a fuck up you really don't need right now, Green. Out of the frying pan and into the fucking fire! Jesus.* But as I smoked, I thought about it and decided that with the vehicle, we would be at least be mobile. *If anything, you could drive past and check the location out. If anything looks wrong there is no need to stop. You simply drive off and get the fuck out of there.* This new issue had brought my headache back, and that combined with the overall stress of the situation was a reminder that I was physically exhausted and this was affecting my thinking. *Tell him we will see what we can do in the morning, Green. It's best to be 100% honest. He understands the danger that is clear. He will understand if we are unable to do anything. His daughter is his main priority over and above this poor young man who is more than likely not going to make it anyway.* I crushed the cigarette out in the ashtray and walked back into the room. Samuel sat as he had been with a frown on his forehead.

"Tell him to send his location..." I said, "Tell him we will do our best to help him."

Samuel nodded and immediately picked up the phone to type the message.

"Warn him that we may not be able to do so..." I said.

Once done, he handed the phone back and I read the message he had typed. Satisfied that it was good, I spoke.

"Well, Samuel," I said, "I think you had better go and get some rest. We will see if we have a reply from your friend in the morning. I'm not promising anything, but we will see what we can do. Okay?"

The big man nodded as he stood.

"You're right, Jason. Thank you," he said. "I will go now and try to sleep. See you in the morning."

Samuel closed the door behind him and I immediately headed for a shower then applied antiseptic ointment to my injuries. My entire body was aching so I swallowed another two painkillers and lay on the bed thinking about this new development. *You need to rest, Green. See what gives in the morning and take it from there. Your brain will be clearer and you can make a decision then. If you can help, so be it. If not, then that's it. You lie low until it's time to move, and do nothing else.* At that moment my vision began to swim with fatigue. My eyelids felt heavy and it was a relief to close them. I immediately fell into a deep dreamless sleep.

I awoke at 6.00 am sharp and blinked as it all came back to me. Lifting my hands I was pleased to note that the shaking had subsided although it was not fully gone. I stood up slowly and walked over to the kettle to make coffee. I felt a lot better and the headache was gone. My wounds were healing well and for the first time in days, I felt almost human.

Walking barefoot and carrying my coffee, I went to check on Samuel and Omar in the adjacent rooms. Samuel was awake and sitting in bed with the television on. I told him to come through to my room to discuss what we would do about his friend. As he went through, I poked my head into Omar's room. The young man was fast asleep but he heard me as I entered.

"Is everything alright, Mr Green?" he asked.

"Everything is fine..." I said, "Relax, I'll call you later."

I walked back into my room to find Samuel sitting on the couch.

"I think you should check to see if there are any messages from your friend, Pierre," I said, handing him my phone. "See if he has sent a location."

Samuel busied himself as I made him a cup of coffee. As I handed it to him, he looked up and spoke.

"Yes..." he said "He has responded. He has sent a location and an address with a room number. I can read you the message of you like?"

"Let me read it..." I said as I took a seat.

Although the text was typed in broken English, the main part of the message was clear.

'Samuel, my brother. I cannot tell you how relieved I am to hear from you. I wish I had listened to you all along. I made the biggest mistake of my life by making the choices I did. I am now very sick and unable to move. There has been a doctor who has visited and prescribed medication but he is not happy with my situation at all.

He has said I need to be hospitalised urgently but unfortunately, I cannot afford this. I have no idea how you managed to get out, but it is wonderful that you are now free. I am sorry to burden you, my brother, but my situation is getting worse by the hour. Any help would be much appreciated. You are my only hope. God bless you. Pierre.'

I tapped on the location pin above the message and waited for Google maps to find the best route. It turned out he was in an inner-city slum area but it was only a 20-minute drive from our hotel. I handed the phone back to Samuel, took a deep breath and sat back.

"Send him a reply," I said "Tell him we will be in that area at around 11.00 am this morning. Tell him we will see what we can do to assist him. Warn him that it may not be possible for us to see him, and if we fail to, he should send the phone number of the doctor who has been attending to him. There is no need to explain any more than that."

Samuel busied himself with the message as I got up to pour another cup of coffee. I took it out onto the balcony and lit my first cigarette of the day. The morning was cool and bright as I stared out onto the flat blue expanse of the Mediterranean Sea. *Pray this doesn't end in trouble, Green. Fucking hell. That is the last thing you need now.*

Chapter Sixty-One: Mercy Mission.

The sun glinted off the bonnet of the Toyota sedan and I pulled my sunglasses from my pocket to shield the glare from my eyes. It had just gone 10.45 am and we had been driving a good 40 minutes through the heavy traffic of the downtown slum area we had found ourselves in. Here the streets were littered and the traffic unruly. All around were shabby looking apartment blocks with peeling paint and laundry hanging from the balconies. The place looked as if it had a layer of desert sand coating it and the dust blew in clouds behind the vehicles as they moved through the crowded streets. Piles of vegetable waste lay festering the alleyways and there were throngs of pedestrian traffic moving on the side walks.

Samuel Kisimba sat in the passenger seat next to me while Omar sat in the back seemingly undaunted by the surroundings. Samuel and I had told him nothing of the purpose of our visit to this place but I had insisted that he accompany us so I could make sure he didn't venture out from his room unaccompanied. The Google maps app on my phone had led us through the maze of streets and was now telling me that we were 400 metres from our destination. Beneath my shirt, tucked into my belt, was the pistol I had liberated from the cell block at the Zukman premises. There were three rounds left in it and I was more than prepared to use them should I need to. I glanced over at Samuel who sat with an anxious look on his face. He had been silent since leaving the safety of the hotel and I knew that he had taken heed of my warnings. Perhaps now he was seeing that we were indeed putting ourselves in danger by exposing ourselves. Still, he was determined to help his friend and was prepared to risk our progress so far to do so.

"I need to find a parking spot somewhere here..." I muttered.

"Pull up near that shop, Mr Green..." said Omar, pointing ahead "Parking is free and I will stay in the vehicle to look after it. Everything will be fine."

I did as suggested and parked near a general store with trays of fly-covered raw meat on trestle tables outside it.

The place was bustling with people and no one seemed to give us a second look as we parked.

"Right, Omar, " I said turning in my seat "We will be back soon. See you shortly"

Samuel and I climbed out of the vehicle and once more I secured the gun under my shirt. We made our way down the pavement steadily making our way through the sea of humanity. I pulled my phone from my pocket and looked at the screen. We were now near the building and I heard the electronic voice announce our arrival. With my nerves on edge, I scanned the crowds in front of us looking for anyone who might seem out of place. Someone who was watching and waiting for any unexpected arrivals. Most of the people seemed to be busy getting on with their daily business and nothing seemed out of the ordinary. *It might just be okay, Green. Perhaps they have taken what they wanted from the poor man and have simply abandoned him. You might be in luck.* But it was as we were crossing the street in front of the building that I saw something that raised my heckles and sent my arms and legs tingling with adrenalin. The man stood on the opposite side of the street-facing building. For some reason, he stood out from the rest of the crowd in that he wore clothes that were slightly smarter than the rest. His beard was trimmed short and he wore Rayban aviator sunglasses. He was a stockily built man in his early forties and I saw his wide jaws pulsing as he chewed his gum. *You might be getting a bit paranoid here, Green. Could be nothing.* But I knew better than to ignore my instincts and I watched him from behind my sunglasses as we crossed the street. There was something about him that I couldn't quite put my finger on but I felt he was there for a reason. He was watching the building.

"This is it..." I said to Samuel as we climbed the pavement "The entrance is up ahead. 4th-floor room number 8."

Samuel nodded as we walked out of the blazing sunlight into the gloom of the building's foyer. We crossed the cracked tiles and walked towards the stairwell which was at the far side of the room.

Acutely aware of the man who had been watching, I kept an eye on the reflection of the entrance behind me in the corner of the inside of my sunglasses. I had prayed that I was simply being paranoid and that we would be able to proceed as planned, but my fears were realised when I saw the man enter the foyer behind us. Saying nothing to Samuel, we began walking up the stairs. Out of the corner of my eye, I saw him lurking in the gloom beyond the entrance as we turned to climb the next set of steps.

Fuck! Fucking hell, Green! You knew this was a mistake. Why the hell did you agree to this? Saying nothing, we climbed the steps until we reached the 4th floor. There we took a right turn and walked down the gloomy corridor until we reached door number 8. I paused and raised my hand to listen for approaching footsteps but all I could hear was the sound of a television blaring away in a nearby room.

"This is it..." I said as I knocked on the door and pushed it open.

The smell hit me like a ton of bricks. It was the unforgettable stench of rotting flesh that sticks in the back of your throat and nostrils, and I could hear the flies buzzing from within. I watched as

Samuel winced at the same as we entered. To the right lay Pierre Lumumba. A skinny young man with skin as black as coal, his forehead was covered in tiny drops of fevered sweat and his eyes were yellowed and glazed over. This changed as we walked in and he smiled immediately.

"Samuel, my brother..." he said with a croaky voice.

I pulled the sunglasses from my face and raised my eyes at both men.

"Shhh..." I said with my forefinger to my lips.

Quietly, I grabbed Samuel by his right arm and brought him across so he stood near the bed. The young man on the bed stared up with a confused look on his face, and I felt Samuel begin to shake with fear. Bringing the gun out from behind me, I held it up near my face and stood with my back to the wall near the door.

"Shhh," I said once again.

It was not long before I heard the footsteps on the tiles outside. The man had failed to shake the dust from his shoes and the tiny granules crunched on the surface as he approached. With my entire body tingling, I waited as I watched the wide-eyed men in the room. The door swung open without warning and I saw the pistol before I saw the man.

Before he had time to turn his body, I smashed the gun out of his hand using my own and it clattered noisily to the floor. The man let out a yelp of surprise and pain as the bones in his wrist were crushed. I swung my left arm out and grabbed him by his shirt beneath his collar. I rammed the barrel of my pistol onto his forehead. It broke the skin immediately and served to stun the man further. He had not suspected that I had seen him and the element of surprise had served me well.

"You make a sound, and I'll blow your fucking brains out..." I said.

The man whimpered and I watched his bulbous eyes fill with terror. Pulling the man roughly into the room, I forced him to take a seat on a wooden chair that sat beneath the single window.

With the weapon still held to his head, I brought my face down towards his and hissed at him through gritted teeth.

"Who is with you?" I said.

"I am alone..." he replied with a shaky voice.

"Don't fucking move!"

I stood up and looked at the two other men in the room. Pierre lay on his filthy bed, clearly very ill and unable to respond. He appeared somewhat confused but I put this down to his fevered and sickly state.

"There is no way we can take this man anywhere, Samuel," I said "He cannot travel across the sea like this."

Samuel nodded and blinked as he looked down at Pierre.

Pierre slowly lifted his shirt to reveal a gaping, septic wound that cut around his side like a burst watermelon.

"Look at what they did to me..." said Pierre with tears in his yellowed eyes. "I should have listened to you, Samuel. You were right all along."

"Samuel..." I said "We don't have time for this. We need to go now. We can arrange to get this man out of here and into some proper medical care. We have the address and number of the doctor who has been attending to him. We will go there now and arrange for him to be picked up."

"But what about..." said Samuel, pointing at the seated man near the window.

"Don't worry about him..." I replied.

Without wasting time, I ripped the hessian curtain from the window. I handed it to Samuel and pulled the Swiss army knife from my pocket.

"Cut it into thick strips..." I said, "I will need five of them, and be quick!"

Samuel busied himself with the task while I gripped the man by the collar and pulled him to his feet.

"Move!" I said, motioning towards the bathroom door with my eyes "And take the chair with you..."

The man complied immediately and I kept the gun to his head as he carried the chair through. I told him to place the chair in the centre of the shower cubicle and sit down.

By the time he had done so, Samuel had finished cutting the strips of hessian. I called him into the room and told him to bind the man's arms and legs to the chair. He did so quickly and efficiently, and by the time he had finished, the hessian was wound around each limb multiple times and knotted fast. I could see that the bindings were tight enough to cut the blood flow to the man's extremities and it was clear that there was no way he would be able to remove them without assistance. Samuel had done a good job.

"Get me some more to gag him," I said, "Some to put into his mouth and another strip to tie around his head."

This job took less than a minute to complete and by the time we were done I was confident that we had immobilised him completely. The man's bulbous eyes watched me as I stepped out of the room and took a look out of the window down to the street.

"We dodged a bullet there, Samuel," I said "We need to go, now."

I picked up the gun that I had knocked from the man's hand as he had walked in. As I placed it under my belt, I spoke to Pierre.

"We will go to your doctor now," I said. "You can expect to be picked up and taken to a clinic sometime today. I can do no more than that, but you will be a lot better off with some decent medical care. Samuel will stay in touch with you. Once you have recovered fully, he will give you a number to call. The person you speak to will arrange for you to travel to Spain. This is a man who is known to us. You now have a fighting chance. Good luck."

Samuel squatted down on his haunches and took Pierre by his hand.

"I will pray for you, my brother..." he said "I will stay in touch."

"Thank you, Samuel..." said Pierre "Thank you both..."

Chapter Sixty-Two: Fisherman's Blues.

The night was cool and a steady wind blew in from the Mediterranean sea as Samuel Kisimba and I sat on the wooden bench in the open shack at the port in the city of Tangier. I glanced at my watch to see it had just passed midnight. Even at this late hour, there was still a fair amount of activity at the docks, with fishing boats mooring and offloading their catches under the bright spotlights along the piers. There was the sound of laughter and banter from the fishermen who had returned from their journeys and the breeze whistled in the rigging of the hundreds of boats that were moored all around us. The air was filled with the smell of fish and everything we touched seemed to have a layer of salt on it. Omar's uncle had collected us on time at 11.00 pm and we had taken the short drive to the port in the back of a panel van. It was clear that the man knew the security staff at the gates as they had spent a good 5 minutes cracking jokes and showing each other pornographic videos on their phones. Samuel and I sat silently in the back of the vehicle behind a pile of foul-smelling plastic crates and the guards never bothered to look inside.

We had left the block of flats in the slum where we had visited Pierre and had travelled to the nearby surgery where I had met the young doctor who had been attending to him. My visit came as a surprise and the young man was relieved that Pierre would finally be taken to a nearby private clinic where he could be cared for properly. It seemed that he had seen similar cases in the past which had almost always ended badly for the victims. Not wanting to discuss too much, I had used my credit card to pay for an ambulance to ferry Pierre to the facility plus full board and medical care for the next two weeks. The fees for the clinic were the equivalent of $40 per day and I was more than happy to shell out given the sorry state the man was in. I watched as the doctor called the clinic to send the ambulance immediately and was then issued a receipt for my payment.

"You have saved this man's life, sir. Thank you" said the doctor. "I will visit him personally later this afternoon at the clinic and once a day thereafter. He will be well cared for."

"Tell him we will send him some money soon..." I said, "He knows what to do once he recovers."

The drive back to the hotel had taken over an hour in the lunchtime traffic and it was a relief to finally park the vehicle in the underground car park and head up to our rooms. I ventured out later that afternoon to withdraw some more money from the nearby cash machine and returned immediately to my room where a meeting was held.

Omar had been paid a generous gratuity for his assistance and he agreed to drive the hire car back to Marrakesh the following day. The young man had been a lifesaver and had asked very little of us. For that I was grateful.

The final test would be our journey across the ocean that night which we were soon to embark on. Although Omar's uncle spoke no English, his instructions were clear. Once the crates had been offloaded, we were to wait in the shack until it was time to leave. During the 40 minutes we had been sitting there, I had seen the flashing lights of the port authority cruiser on two occasions as it passed. I had no idea if the real cargo of hashish had already been loaded, but by the look of the boat we were about to board, it appeared it was indeed a genuine fishing vessel. My bags had been loaded onto the boat at the same time as the crates by the crew who appeared relaxed as they got on with their various jobs. My nerves were frayed and strained to breaking point and it came as some relief to see the casual attitude of the crew.

Samuel sat beside me nervously staring out into the port. He drummed his fingers constantly on his knees and I knew that this moment was one of the most important of his life. Everything he had lived for up until then was riding on the success of what we were about to attempt. I understood his fears completely and although I wanted to reassure him, I knew better. If the events of the previous few days were anything to go by, I could expect the expected and would be surprised by nothing. It was 12.55 when Omar's uncle approached us from the dockside. Wearing a green high visibility jacket, he smiled as he tapped his watch and gestured for us to follow him to the waiting boat.

Samuel and I stood up and walked down the pier to the small gangway. Once aboard we were ushered down into the galley where one of the crew presented us with mugs of hot sweet tea. The wooden body of the old vessel shuddered as the ancient diesel engine coughed and spluttered into life and before long I felt the vessel moving forward as it left the pier. I glanced at Samuel and saw him making the sign of the cross and whispering a prayer as the engine revved and the vessel picked up speed.

It was some five minutes later when it seemed we had left the port, that I heard the squeal of a siren and heard the footsteps of the crew member above coming to warn us of the visit by the port authority. The man who had given us the tea stood up and walked to the far side of the galley. He climbed down onto his knees and pulled aside a section of filthy blue matting from the floor. Then he lifted a section of flooring and casually motioned for us to climb down into the bowels of the vessel. Samuel and I descended into a dank, dark space no bigger than a cupboard. The boards and matting were replaced and we crouched there in the darkness as the engine idled and the boat rocked on the swells. *Jesus, Green. If you get rumbled now you'd better put your fucking hands up and ask them to kill you now.* The next ten minutes were spent in trepidation that we would be discovered, but to my surprise, I heard the engine rev and felt the old boat lurch forward once again.

"I think they're gone..." I whispered to Samuel.

I was proved right when the hatch above us was lifted once again and we were invited to climb back out into the galley once again. Omar's uncle appeared from the deck above and lit up a cigarette as he sat down. I took the opportunity to do the same and stared at the man as I did so. He smiled and gave me the thumbs-up signal as he sat back on the tattered bench.

"Two hours..." he said in a strong Arabic accent as he pointed north "Two hours to Spain."

I nodded and gave him the thumbs-up sign in return as the galley man brought us two fresh mugs of tea.

It must have been an hour later when the exhaustion and the constant motion of the boat caused me to nod off where I sat. I was awoken with a start some later by the thunderous sound of footfalls on the deck above and a change in the tone of the engine as it slowed.

Omar's uncle appeared at the hatch above and called to us to come up on deck. The boat was swaying heavily from side to side and Samuel and I had to grip the railings on either side of the stairwell as we climbed up. We were greeted by a spray of saltwater and the panicked shouting of the crew. The night was black and the soaked deck glistened like gold under the yellow overhead lights. I looked over the port side of the vessel to see a large semi-rigid inflatable boat had pulled up alongside us. The swells rocked both vessels as the three crew members from the inflatable tied a series of ropes to the gunwale of the fishing boat. Wasting no time, the crew from our boat began lifting hefty rectangular blocks of hashish from the hold. The blocks were tightly wrapped in thick black plastic and I put the weight of each at roughly 30 kilograms each. Omar's uncle stood near the wheel, gripping a handhold as he watched the steady flow of cargo as it was offloaded onto the next boat. I counted 20 blocks that would make a shipment of over half a tonne of product. The entire operation took less than ten minutes and it was at that point that Omar's uncle tossed my bags to the crew of the next boat and then approached me.

"You go Spain now..." he said in broken English.

I pulled the wad of cash from my pocket and handed it to the man. He took it without counting it and spoke.

"Shukran..." he said as he led us to the port side of the deck.

Samuel and I swung our legs over the gunwale and jumped down onto the cluttered wooden deck of the semi-rigid vessel. At that moment, a rogue wave crashed over the side, soaking us both. The three crew members busied themselves untying the boats as they shouted cheerfully to the crew of the fishing vessel.

Finally, the ropes were freed and the powerful engine of the smaller boat roared into life. The three men sat down and gripped the rope that ran around the inflatable gunwale as the driver pushed the throttle forward. I closed my eyes from the stinging spray as the boat pounded northwards through the swells. The bone-jarring journey was cold and uncomfortable and on more than one occasion I spluttered and coughed as I breathed in random sprays of salt water.

Twenty minutes later I heard the engine slow and opened my

eyes to see several blurry lights on the horizon. I turned to look at Samuel who had seen the same thing. I realised then that it was the first time I had seen him smile. The driver continued towards the shoreline until eventually, I heard the hiss of waves around the boat and the sound of sand crunching under it. With the engine lifted and still idling, one of the men stood up and spoke.

"Bienvenido a españa," he said as he tossed my bags onto the beach.

Samuel and I stood up and climbed out of the boat. The water surged around our shins as we walked towards the sand.

"Gracias..." I called back as the boat was pushed back into the waves.

Before I knew it, the engine was lowered and it sped off into the night. My vision began to clear as I lifted my bags and walked up the gentle slope of the beach. It appeared we had been dropped on a deserted section of shoreline but I could see lights in the distance to my right. I dropped my bags near a line of vegetation and turned to look for Samuel. At first, I couldn't see him in the darkness but then I noticed his figure crouching some ten metres behind me. I walked back to find him kneeling on the beach, his entire body was trembling. He had scooped up a pile of sand and was holding it with both hands in front of him.

"What are you doing, Samuel?" I asked, feeling puzzled.

In the limited light, the big man lifted his face and once again, I saw tears in his eyes.

"This is Spain, Jason." he said, his voice quavering with emotion "We've made it..."

Chapter Sixty-Three: Amsterdam, One Week Later.

The pale April sun shone down onto the tree-lined canal that ran between the grand old houses in the well-heeled suburb of Nieuwmarkt in the Dutch city of Amsterdam. Far from the hordes of tourists seeking out the notorious fleshpots and bars of the red light district, this was a peaceful and pleasant neighbourhood where the wealthy residents of the city lived.

I had arrived on a flight from Seville in Spain the previous evening and had checked into a boutique hotel a mere ten minutes walk from the residence of Mr Darko Zukman. The old fashioned pastry shop I sat in was directly opposite the grand old four-storey building that was his base in The Netherlands. The young waitress had just delivered a steaming cup of coffee and a croissant and I thanked her before she made her way back to her counter.

The time had just gone 11.45 am and I noted with satisfaction the healing of the wound on my wrist below my watch. I had spent the previous five nights in a hotel in the coastal city of Tarifa where Samuel Kisimba and I had been dropped after the crossing into Spain from Morocco. I had used the time to rest and recover from the appalling ordeal we had endured at the hands of the man I had come to visit. Apart from sending a single email to my firm in London, I had remained under the radar and kept my phone off for most of the time. It had taken several days, but I had finally compiled a detailed report that would expose the methods used to remove the priceless treasures from the vault at the Zukman premises in Marrakesh. I had also completed a separate report detailing the sophisticated network of people smuggling and human organ harvesting that was their secondary business. This included maps of the detention centre and cells within the factory complex and a written testimonial from Samuel Kisimba himself. There would also be more evidence in the form of testimonials and photographs from the doctor who had attended to Pierre Lumumba.

As I had expected, Zukman had panicked after the trail of destruction I had left in my wake and he had fled to Serbia the following day. I had followed his journey from there to Amsterdam by simply making a few enquiries on the phone.

A man of such wealth and prominence in the world of business was easy to follow and I knew his crimes would be difficult, if not impossible to conceal. I had taken my time to create a completely watertight report that would bring him and his business crashing down in spectacular fashion.

I had researched the unbelievably cruel phenomenon of human trafficking and had confirmed that trafficking and associated practices such as slavery, sexual exploitation, and child and forced labour were themselves basic violations of human rights and as such were punishable by international laws. It just so happened that The Netherlands was the perfect place to report such crimes and in that country, there would be serious repercussions for those responsible. I planned to personally confront Zukman and deliver him to the nearby police station to be held and subsequently charged. I had managed to purchase a powerful electric stun gun in Tarifa and had also acquired several heavy-duty cable ties which I would use if necessary. I did not doubt that there would be bodyguards beyond the walls of his home. I knew the man would be spooked, and given the fact that I had managed to escape, he was more than likely living in a state of perpetual fear.

Samuel Kisimba had been reunited with his daughter and her guardian on the afternoon of our arrival in Spain. The meeting had been emotional but joyous and had taken place after both of us had cleaned ourselves up and rested in the hotel room we had checked into upon arrival. The young girl's guardian, a woman by the name of Elizabeth Nkulu, had taken a job at an olive canning factory nearby and had secured a small but decent two bedroomed apartment. On our way to the reunion, I had stopped the taxi at a cash machine and had withdrawn an amount of money to loan to Samuel to get him started in his new life. The big man had accepted this humbly but only on the strict condition that it was to be repaid as soon as he had found work. I had said my farewell to my unlikely new friend and had returned to the hotel where I had slept for 24 hours straight.

It was as I was sipping the coffee that I saw the large panel van arrive at the home of Darko Zukman across the canal. It parked near the front door and a crew of young men alighted from the cab. I frowned as I watched them staring up at the facade of the narrow old building.

It was clear they were there to make a delivery of something large. I knew from previous visits that the old 17th-century homes that lined the canals of Amsterdam were extremely narrow. This was a legacy of the exorbitant taxes that were levied on building owners in the past. The larger the facade of the house, the more taxes one would have to pay. It was as a result of these buildings being so narrow that many of these houses still had the roof-mounted hooks that homeowners and merchants would use to hoist goods from the barges into their attics. I watched as one of the men rang the doorbell and saw him enter the house after being let in by a tall, broad-shouldered man. *That's a bodyguard for sure, Green. No doubt about that.*

Leaving a tip on the table, I nodded my thanks to the waitress and stepped out into the cold bright morning. The young man I had seen entering the house appeared at the top floor windows and opened them to shout down at his workmates below. I lit a cigarette and leant against the wall as I watched proceedings. It was ten minutes later that I saw the forklift trundling down the opposite side of the canal. It was clear that it was to be used to remove whatever was in the truck prior to it being hoisted up to the top floor of the building. Deciding I needed to take a closer look at what was going on, I took a walk up the street and crossed the ornate bridge that spanned the canal. By the time I arrived at the far side, the rear of the truck had been opened and the forklift driver was positioning his vehicle behind what appeared to be a giant wooden crate. Around this box was a series of thick canvas straps attached to a central hook. I watched as one of the young men retrieved a coiled length of heavy nylon rope and a pulley which he carried to the door before ringing the bell. I waited until the man had entered before walking towards the truck to take a closer look. There appeared to be some confusion between the men at the window above and his workmates below. Phone calls were being made and there were shouted exchanges between the men. The man near the rear of the truck pocketed his phone and stood staring upwards with his hands on his hips as I approached. He glanced at me briefly before I spoke.

"What is it?" I said pointing at the huge box in the back of the van.

"It's a Steinway grand piano..." said the man in a Dutch accent "It cost $150000.00 and the genius who ordered it didn't bother to measure the windows up there properly. We have to wait for carpenters and a rigging crew to come now to remove the frames."

"Hmm..." I said, "Sounds like a tricky job."

The young man shook his head ruefully and looked upwards.

"Ya..." he said "It's gonna be a long day."

"Good luck..." I said as I walked off past the truck.

I knew of Zukman's love of music from my visit to his offices in Marrakesh. I recalled the marble bust of Beethoven and remembered him saying how he admired the work of the great composer. It struck me that given recent events, it seemed an unusual time to order a massively expensive musical instrument. I could only assume that it had been purchased some time back and its delivery at the time was purely coincidental.

I arrived at the bridge further down the canal and crossed to the opposite side where I could watch proceedings from a safe distance. Entering the pastry shop once again, I took a seat near the window and ordered another cup of coffee from the waitress. I spent the next three hours reading newspapers and browsing the internet on my laptop as I watched the events across the road. It was 2.30 pm when the carpenters and rigging crew arrived and made their way up to remove the massive black window frames from the top floor of the old building. The frustration of all involved was evident as I could see the men arguing and shaking their heads at the delay this was causing. Eventually, after much fuss and painstaking work, the huge antique window frames were prised free from the walls and carefully lowered down on the pulley to the street below. By the time the huge crate was removed from the van by the forklift, the daylight was starting to fade.

The men wasted no time hooking it up to the pulley above and went upstairs as they prepared to lift the giant 600 kg instrument to the top floor. I watched as a series of steel barriers were placed on the pavement around the immediate area to prevent any members of the public from getting too close as it was lifted. The operation was tricky and not without danger. Slowly and painfully, the huge crate was lifted until it was level with the top floor windows. Next, the rigging crew attached their ropes to the straps on the crate and began the delicate process of pulling it into the grand old house. By the time the crate was safely inside, the sun had set completely and the street lights along both sides of the canal had been illuminated. I watched as the men from the delivery service and the rigging crew congregated below near the van for a meeting. They spoke for a good ten minutes until an agreement was made and a large square of folded canvas was removed from the back of the van. *What the hell is going on here?* I stepped outside the pastry shop and lit a cigarette as I watched. The men unfolded the canvas and draped it over the window frames which were propped up against the wall. They secured it in place by leaning some pallets against it, then one of the men knocked on the front door. The tall, broad-shouldered man I had seen open it earlier came out and engaged in a conversation with the men. Once again, there appeared to be some disagreement between the men with a number of them pointing up at the gaping hole in the top of the building and shaking their heads.

Finally, after another ten minutes of discussion, the barriers were removed from the front of the van and both it and the forklift trundled off into the night. The remaining men from the rigging crew rearranged the barriers around the canvas-covered widow frames, obviously to prevent them from being tampered with by members of the public. Finally, they too moved off, leaving the building with its grand piano delivered but with the windows yet to be replaced. I nodded to myself as I realised what had happened. The delay caused by the men having to remove the window frames had resulted in them having to wait until the next day to be replaced. This was clearly what the argument had been about. I had no idea but it was surely something to do with local safety regulations for contractors working after hours. I glanced at my watch to see it had just gone 6.00 pm. Feeling cold and hungry, I decided to take the short walk back to my hotel for a shower and some dinner.

I would then wait till much later before heading back to visit Mr Darko Zukman. I wanted my arrival to be a surprise and I had already decided that it would be best to wait until after 9.00 pm to do that. I pulled my jacket tightly around my frame and took the short walk up the street to the bridge. But it was as I was halfway across the bridge that I saw her. At first, I could not believe my eyes but there was no mistaking her tall frame, her long blonde hair and her quick, confident gait. She was making her way down the street on the corner in front of me and I stopped in my tracks as I watched her take a right turn and walk up to the front door of the Zukman house. The woman was none other than Professor Genevieve Tremblay.

"What the fuck?" I whispered slowly to myself.

Chapter Sixty Four: Darko Zukman.

The sight of her sent shock waves through my body and I froze where I stood in the darkness. She rang the doorbell and I watched as the door was opened by the big man I had seen earlier. Needing time to think, I walked back to the far side of the canal and lit a cigarette as I watched the front of the house. *What the fuck could she be doing here? Surely she's not involved with Zukman? There's no fucking way.* Then it struck me. *The music. They are both classical music aficionados. But even then. What on earth would she be doing here when her job is on the dig site back in Morocco?* I stood there shivering in the cold as I smoked and a thousand jumbled thoughts raced through my mind. *There is nothing you can do, Green. You have to wait and find out. Even if it takes all night you need to get to her and find out the answers. Jesus Christ!* I considered walking back to the pastry shop but it appeared that it was closing down for the night. Instead, I kept warm by walking up and down the length of the street while I watched the front of the grand old house on the opposite side of the canal.

Although I had made my plans for Zukman, this was a development that could change everything. Feeling confused and stressed, I decided to cross the bridge once again and wait in the darkness near the corner where I had first seen her arriving. At least that way, if she was to leave, I would be able to intercept her and find out what the hell was going on. The very thought that she would be involved with Zukman sent shivers down my spine. *Had she been deliberately planted to escort me all along? Had she been secretly watching me while trying to seduce me at the same time? Had the whole thing been planned?* I stood there in the darkness under an oak tree stamping my feet and rubbing my hands to keep the chill out. I would stay there the whole night if need be. But it turned out that that would not be necessary. It was exactly one hour later when I saw the front door of Zukman's house open and I watched Genevieve walk out and make her way towards me back to the street where she had arrived from. Even from that distance, it was clear she was upset about something. Breathing heavily, I waited until she had turned the corner and was making her way up the gentle slope before I began following her. It was some three minutes later that I saw the illuminated sign for the Italian restaurant that was directly in her path.

I decided that I would stop her there and then. Stepping up my pace, I gained on her until I could hear the clicks of her boots on the pavement in front of me. There were several pedestrians on the same street but they were preoccupied with getting to their destinations. I arrived at her left side just before arriving at the widows of the restaurant and I gripped her gently but firmly by her left arm.

"Hello, Genevieve..." I said quietly.

She turned to face me in an instant state of shock and surprise.

"Jason!" she said, her eyes wide with alarm "What are..."

"Come with me please..." I said, guiding her towards the restaurant door.

She made no attempt to struggle as I pushed the door open and stepped inside. We were greeted by a young Italian man in a black and white waiter's uniform.

"Table for two?" he asked with a smile.

"Yes, please..." I said.

With Genevieve in stunned silence, we walked to a table near the window at the far left of the restaurant.

"Will this table be alright?" asked the man.

"Perfect..." I replied.

The young man pulled the seat out for Genevieve as I sat opposite and stared her in the eyes.

"Some drinks to start?" asked the waiter, clearly picking up on the tension of the moment.

"A few minutes please..." I said raising my left hand.

The young man nodded politely and made a hasty retreat.

"You had better start talking, Gen..." I said quietly.

There followed a strained and tearful half-hour conversation during which Genevieve admitted to having being paid a fee by Zukman to host me in Morocco. It turned out that he had been a long time patron to the orchestra she had played in back in France and their association had started there. She explained that she had been encouraged by Zukman himself to join the team at Oakland Archaeology at the time of the discovery in the Atlas Mountains. When I pressed her for the reason she was in Amsterdam, she explained that she had been asked to take a week's urgent leave to visit him. She admitted that she had suspected that it must have something to do with my sudden disappearance and she confirmed this was the reason as she related the conversation she had just had with Zukman. It was clear she was confused and extremely upset by the whole thing, and I could see that she was now in a state of genuine fear. I pressed her hard to relate every detail of what had been said in the house and she explained tearfully that it was all to do with me.

"He kept asking me if I had heard from you, Jason," she said. "He was angry and irritable, and I was afraid. I still am! What is going on?"

Finally satisfied her reason for being there was legitimate, I moved to reassure and warned her to leave the city as soon as possible.

"Genevieve..." I said leaning forward in my seat "There is going to be a whole lot of trouble happening here very soon. Darko Zukman is about to be arrested and put away for a very long time. If I were you, I would put as much distance between here and yourself immediately. You have no idea what these people have done. What Zukman has been doing. This is a criminal organisation on a massive scale. From what you've told me, and I sincerely hope I'm right, you are an innocent pawn in all of this. Do yourself a favour. Leave the city now and get back to work as if nothing happened."

"Am I in danger?" she asked in a shaky voice "Are you in danger, Jason? What happened back there in Marrakesh? Where did you disappear to?"

I reached forward with both of my hands to hold hers, and she saw the injuries on my wrists as I did so. She drew a sharp intake of breath as she saw them.

"Go, Genevieve..." I said "There's no time to explain. Go now, and don't look back."

I watched as she dabbed her eyes with a napkin and prepared to leave. Walking out of the restaurant, I accompanied her up the street to a taxi rank. I opened the rear door of the front cab but she stalled and embraced me. Her entire body was shaking as she whispered in my ear.

"I'm so sorry, Jason..." she said.

"Do not phone anyone..." I said. "Speak to no one about this.

You never saw me tonight. Is that clear?"

Without a word, she nodded and I saw her face was pale with fear.

"Goodbye, Gen..." I said as she climbed into the cab.

It was 15 minutes later that I arrived in my room at the nearby hotel. The events of the last two hours had shocked me to the core but I knew in my heart that she was being truthful about her reasons for being there. I sat down at the dressing table and stared at my face in the mirror. In front of me on the table was the equipment I had laid out earlier that I would use when I made my visit to Zukman later that night. There was a sheet of hotel stationery, a bunch of zip ties, and the electronic stun gun. *There's no way she will warn him, Green. That was real fear in her face. She's afraid and she has no idea what is going on. Her reaction at seeing the injuries on your wrists confirmed that. The plan must go ahead without fail.* I spent the next hour and a half pacing my room and occasionally leaning out of the window to smoke.

Once again my nerves were frayed but I was determined and wholly committed.

Zukman would be stopped and I would ensure he would be spending the first of many nights in a jail cell.

Five minutes later I arrived at the bridge opposite his house. There was a light drizzle falling onto the deserted streets and the air had a biting chill. I stopped halfway across the bridge as I had done earlier and smoked a final cigarette as I watched the house.

All of the lights were on except those on the top floor where the piano had been delivered. The canvas-covered window frames were still propped up behind the steel barriers against the wall on the ground floor. I had no idea how many goons Zukman had behind those walls but my sudden arrival at that late hour would give me the advantage of surprise. In my right pocket was the stun gun while in my top pocket was the folded sheet of hotel stationery. I flicked the cigarette butt into the canal and took a deep breath.

"Well..." I said quietly to myself, "Better get on with it then."

The walk to the front door took less than three minutes. I made my way up the stone steps and rang the doorbell immediately. In less than 30 seconds I heard movement behind the door and instantly my entire body coiled up with tension. I pulled the sheet of hotel stationery from my pocket and waited. The door opened and I felt a rush of warm air hit me from the inside. Standing in the doorway was the same tall man with broad shoulders I had seen earlier. Square-headed with a closely cropped blonde brush cut, he stood there frowning and blinking the sleep from his eyes before he spoke.

"Wie ben jig?" he said in an angry voice. 'Who are you?'

"I'm sorry to bother you at this late hour..." I said, holding out the piece of paper in my left hand for him to read.

The man scowled and lowered his head to read the scribbled writing on the paper.

At that moment, I pulled the stun gun from my right pocket and plunged the two electrodes into the flesh on the left-hand side of his neck. The machine crackled noisily as it delivered a series of short, high voltage pulses that peaked at 50,000 volts. This resulted in him immediately losing voluntary control of the muscles in his entire body and he made an unusual grunting sound as he fell towards me. The man's dead weight was unexpectedly heavy and I strained as I forced him back, where he fell with a heavy thud onto the carpeted floor beyond. Wasting no time, I closed the door behind me, replaced the stun gun and removed the cable ties from my pocket. Starting with his ankles, I pulled the heavy-duty cable tie until it could tighten no further. Next, I flipped the man over onto his front and pulled his arms behind his back. I repeated the process with a cable tie on his wrists. I had no idea how many more goons I would have to confront before I found Zukman so I worked as quickly and as quietly as I could. Finally, I pulled the man's ankles up behind him and bound another two cable ties between his wrists and ankles. The man was now effectively hog tied and would be completely immobilised when he regained consciousness.

With the job done, I looked around at my surroundings from where I was squatting next to the man. As expected, with such a narrow old house, there was a single corridor with a set of stairs to the far end. The fittings were expensive and in keeping with the neighbourhood. Set into the wall on the left was a series of three doors. With no idea of the layout of the house, I would need to make a slow and silent inspection of each room. But at that moment the man below gave out a long, low groan. *Fuck!*

I pulled the stun gun from my pocket and gave him another three-second jolt to his thick neck. The electrodes crackled loudly and the man's body vibrated as the electricity pounded through his body. I stood up slowly and prepared to venture further into the house. But it was then that I heard the familiar, wheezing voice that had haunted my dreams ever since I had left Morocco.

"Thomas!" said Zukman from one of the rooms nearby, "Thomas! Where are you? Thomas!"

I stepped forward silently and opened the door on my immediate left. Peering into the room, I immediately saw it was decorated with all manner of antique splendour and finery. But the room was empty although there was an empty coffee mug on the fine, burr walnut centre table. It was clear that this was where the now sleeping bodyguard had been stationed.

"Thomas!" came Zukman's voice once again "What is going on, Thomas?"

I moved forward slowly and opened the second door on my left. It was then that I saw him. He wore nothing but a wide silken nightgown that spread over his massive squat frame from his shoulders down to just above his pudgy ankles. On his feet, he wore a pair of blood-red velvet slippers with an embroidered crest on the front of each. The great folds of flesh that cascaded from his thick head to his shoulders were exposed and they wobbled as the wide knife wound that was his mouth opened in an expression of abject terror. Darko Zukman stood in front of the doors of a custom made elevator. It was clear he had just stepped out of it as the gold plated double doors were still open behind him. His porcine eyes opened like bulbs as he saw my face and he let out an unexpectedly high pitched wail of terror. I immediately pulled the stun gun from my pocket and started walking towards him but the room was cluttered and filled with all manner of antique furniture and artefacts. I watched as the fat man backed away into the open elevator with surprising speed.

"Thomas!" he screamed, once again in that high pitched voice.

"He can't help you now!" I shouted as I kicked a Georgian armchair over in an effort to reach him.

Ahead of me was a huge table that was covered with silver platters and crystal decanters. I sent it crashing to the floor as I made my final lunge towards the man. But it was too late. He had made it back into the elevator and the doors closed a split second before I reached them.

"Zukman!" I screamed as I pounded my right fist into the gold plated doors.

But it was too late. The lift had gone up and I had no idea which floor he had chosen. *Fuck!* I ran back through the room and made a left at the corridor where Thomas lay unconscious. My feet pounded on the stairwell as I bounded up to the second floor. By then my anger was cold and mechanical and I wasted no time opening any doors. The finely panelled wood cracked and splintered loudly as I kicked each door in as I searched for him.

"Zukman! You stinking bag of pus!" I shouted, "Where are you?"

But he was nowhere to be found and once again I returned to the staircase. *He could be anywhere, Green. You have to check each room on every floor. He could be calling for help. You have to hurry!* I was panting heavily and a film of sweat had formed on my face by the time I reached the third floor. I repeated the same process, kicking in each door and rampaging through every room. Still, he was nowhere to be seen. Finally, I made my way up the last set of stairs to the 4th floor of the old building. I arrived expecting to see yet another corridor with three doors but there was only darkness. Panting heavily, I stopped and blinked as I tried to force my eyes to see through the gloom. It was then that I heard the feeble and pitiful whimpering.

The man was hiding somewhere in the darkness but I could not see where. As I caught my breath, I fumbled on the wall to my right to locate a light switch. The air was bitingly cold and it was only then that my eyes adjusted to the darkness and I saw the yellow glow of the trees that lined the canal through the open window frames at the far side of the massive room. Suddenly my fingers found a light switch and I flicked it downwards immediately. I found myself standing at the far side of a massive library. The entire 4th floor of the building had been converted into one long room and the walls were filled from floor to ceiling with thousands of leather-bound books on oak shelves. Although the room was sparsely furnished, there were several occasional chairs and couches placed at various positions in the space.

But standing in pride of place was the huge wooden crate I had seen hoisted up from the street earlier in the day. Darko Zukman had been in the process of creating a private reading and music room, and the grand piano was to be the centrepiece. This was further evidenced by the various marble busts of famous composers that stood on ornate wooden plinths around the room.

"Zukman!" I shouted between breaths "It's over now! Come quietly and I won't hurt you."

Suddenly I saw the grotesque looking man stand up. He had been hiding behind the wooden crate that housed the piano. His wide mouth was split in a gaping grimace of fear and he wheezed loudly as he shuffled his enormous frame towards the opening on the far side of the wall where the window had been removed.

Fearing he would jump out through this, I ran towards him across the polished wooden floors. He turned to look at me a final time as he neared the window opening and let out another pathetic wail of terror. But it was at that moment that Darko Zukman lost one of his velvet slippers and in the process tripped and fell forward through the gaping hole where the window frame had been.

"Zukman!" I screamed as I sprinted towards him.

Hanging from the roof-mounted hook above the window was the pulley and the coiled blue nylon rope the riggers had used to hoist the piano. Darko Zukman's head travelled through one of the loops in the rope as he lost his footing. The rope tightened around the vast expanse of flesh that was his neck as he fell, and it only broke his downward trajectory after he had travelled a full six metres. I watched in horror as the rope vibrated under his weight as his fall was abruptly halted below.

In the process of falling, the upper part of his silken night robe had been caught up in the rough threads of the rope. The top part of it had bunched around his neck exposing his naked lower body.

The force of the fall had snapped his neck instantly, and a full half metre of his lower intestine had passed through his anus and hung swinging from his pale, exposed buttocks. The stinking brown contents of the intestine lay splattered and steaming on the flagstones below. I stared down in horror at the hideous sight below me. There was no doubt.

Darko Zukman was well and truly dead.

Chapter Sixty-Five: London. Two Months Later.

The warm midday sunshine shone down on the crowded streets of the Islington Angel in North London. I was feeling hungry and was heading to one of my favourite pubs for a beer and a spot of lunch. Having taken a day off work, I had just returned from one of the local malls where I had purchased a new drone to replace the one I had given to the young porter, Omar, in Marrakesh. I had, of course, claimed the cost of it in my expenses report as I had done with the many other payments I had made while on that ill-fated assignment. Carrying the new machine in the white retailer's bag, I entered the cool atmosphere of the Royal Oak pub. The interior was dark and I removed my sunglasses as I entered. After buying a chilled pint of Lowenbrau, I made my way to the dining booths and took a seat in one that had a view of the street beyond the windows. The beer was refreshingly bitter and it burned my throat pleasantly as it went down.

A great deal had happened since my return from Amsterdam. I had left the house of Darko Zukman in a hurry and had returned to my hotel immediately. I had flown back to London the following afternoon after posting a copy of my report to the chief of police in The Netherlands.

Upon returning to London, I had emailed the same reports to the Moroccan police service, the Policia Nacional in Spain, the Metropolitan Police in London, and the UK branch of Interpol.

Added to that, I had forwarded these reports to all the major news networks and had included the Discovery and National Geographic television networks who were still on-site documenting the archaeological dig of The Zukman Hoard in the high Atlas Mountains of Morocco.

As expected, it did not take long for the story to make international news, and the subsequent uproar it caused kept it in the headlines for over a week.

Upon the news breaking, the Moroccan ministry of antiquities had taken over stewardship of The Zukman Hoard, and it had been removed to a secure government warehouse under the glaring scrutiny of most of the major international news channels. The custodianship of the Zukman Group of companies was in the hands of top lawyers and negotiations were underway to have its shares transferred to its employees in a settled buyout. This was partly due to the national embarrassment that had been caused to the Moroccan government by the many crimes of Zukman that had been globally exposed. Throughout it all, I had managed to keep my head down and had avoided any uncomfortable questions from my head office and other authorities. I counted myself lucky for this and was more than happy to get back to my normal routines.

I had heard from my friend, Samuel Kisimba, a month after my return. He had sent me half the money I had loaned him and had told me about his new job in the olive canning factory in Tarifa. He had once again thanked me for helping him to escape and reunite with his daughter. He had also gone on to tell me that the young man, Pierre Lumumba, had recovered fully and that he too had successfully crossed into Spain. He was currently employed as a waiter in a popular tourist restaurant in Barcelona where he had earned the team member of the month title. Pierre had also joined a local hip hop group that were playing weekly gigs in the city.

Samuel's message had ended with the phrase I had heard him use on the balcony at the hotel in Tangier. 'All will be well' he had said. I felt certain this phrase held some special meaning for him.

It was as I was staring out of the window and taking another draw of the beer that I was approached by a young waiter.

"Good afternoon, sir..." he said with a smile "Would you like to see a menu or perhaps I can tell you about our specials today?"

"Sure..." I replied as I placed the glass on the table "What's on special today?"

"Well, we have our very popular steak and kidney pie with mash and gravy, or there is the hake and chips with tartare sauce..."

I dropped my gaze to my beer as I thought about the choices for a second. But my mind was already made up. I looked up at the young man and spoke.

"I think I'll go with the fish..." I said, "Thank you."

The End

Dear Reader.

I'm guessing if you're seeing this you will have finished this book. If so, I really hope you enjoyed it! There are another four Jason Green titles before this one so be sure to check them out if you haven't already. Why not come and say hi on my Facebook page? You can find it right here:

https://www.facebook.com/gordonwallisauthor

I love hearing from readers and I'm happy to answer any questions. You'll also get to know of any new releases in future. If you have a spare minute, please take the time to leave a review for my books on Amazon and Goodreads. I can't tell you how much they help me reach new readers.

Thanks again and rest assured,

Jason Green will return...

Printed in Dunstable, United Kingdom